The door opened, ad: to her to sit back. Abse prowl over to the sofa, si in her movements. Runni listened to his client.

"I'm looking for an ancient religious artifact originating in Neolithic times. Athens should be your first stop."

There was an odd note, something he couldn't put his finger on. Greece. He hadn't been there before. He glanced at Ellora who looked as though she were listening with every fiber of her being.

"No problem. What is it?"

"A chalice, possibly Roman Catholic. It needs to be returned to its rightful owner. You know the budget."

No budget. Spend what is needed.

"Understood. What information can you give me?" He nodded at Ellora and watched as she pulled an iPad from her bag.

"It is made of metal and has engravings of three spirals and eagles on the outside with a cross in the center of the bowl."

He knew better than to ask for any images, knowing Constantin didn't put anything on paper. All business was conducted over the phone, and then only very briefly.

"Do you know when it was last seen?"

"No. You know all I know. Keep in touch."

A click preceded the dial tone.

Dear Pat
Happy Birthday ♡
Hope you love
the books,
Cait xxx

Pride, A Dance of Flames

by

Cait O'Sullivan

A Dance of Flames, Book 1

Pride, A Dance of Flames

Cover Art by *Debbie Taylor*

The Wild Rose Press, Inc.
PO Box 708
Adams Basin, NY 14410-0708
Visit us at www.thewildrosepress.com

Publishing History
First Edition, 2022
Trade Paperback ISBN 978-1-5092-3627-5
Digital ISBN 978-1-5092-3628-2

A Dance of Flames, Book 1
Published in the United States of America

Dedication

As ever, big thanks to my wonderful editor, Lill Farrell. I do love working with you.

To my wonderful husband—thank you for the patience and the time you spent with Ellora and Lee making sure they worked together well. Having you read it whilst I was beside you was a bit nerve-wracking but seeing you invest in the story and enjoy it made me so glad.

And to Julia Astapova—you superstar friend. Thank you so very much for all the time and effort you spent searching for mistakes and inconsistencies, for the advice and the sounding board you provided—time after time. My faith in Lee and Ellora has increased manifold because of your contributions.

Finally to the wonderful and ever-inspiring way of life that is shamanism. My life is all the more richer and unexpected because of its underlying presence and support. I hope I've reflected clearly and correctly some principles and practices, and if not, I apologize sincerely.

Chapter One

Ellora jerked upright and banged her head on the
bonnet of her racing green MG. Cursing loudly, she
wiped her oil-stained hands on the rag she kept on the
side before rubbing the tender part of her crown.

Only then did she see fit to turn to the man who
had startled her. Tall and imposing, the amused light in
his eyes only irritated her further.

"Yes, and you are?" She turned the rag over and
over in her hands.

"Lee North."

Vague recollections rang of seeing his name
somewhere. She rubbed her forehead exasperatedly.
Nope, nothing there. He was returning her gaze with an
air of expectation. Holy hell. What had she forgotten?

"You caught me unawares. Ellora Radley."
Reluctant to shake his hand, she shoved hers deep into
the pockets of her navy overalls, keeping them hidden
as she blindly tried to get the grease out from under her
nails.

A gleam of frustration crossed his glance, and he
stretched an arm to expose his Breitling watch.

"My assistant made an appointment with you for
this morning. I understand there has been a
miscommunication somewhere, but I would nonetheless
appreciate you fulfilling our meeting. Is that possible?"

"Clearly. Um..." She racked her brain, finding

nothing whatsoever of use in there. No excuses or reasons not to give him some time. Besides, of course, for the voice that screamed *danger*.

"I don't invite just anyone into my home, though."

Eyes sharpening, he reached into his inside pocket and pulled out his wallet. Opening and quickly flicking through it, he maneuvered a couple of cards out and handed them over. A driver's license confirmed that this rather delicious-looking man was indeed Lee North. The other card was his business card, citing his profession as antiquarian. She yawned inwardly. North Antiquaries though. Wasn't that...?

He cleared his throat. "Your assistant has my details and can corroborate who I am. Call her." Quickly pulling out his smart phone, he clicked on something and showed her the screen as the phone connected through to Ruthie.

"No that's fine, I believe you." She had abandoned all hope that her brain mist would clear. No such luck. "Just give me a moment. My car broke down unexpectedly and I had to just...um, fix it." *Unhelpful.* It was abundantly clear the old, battered MG hadn't gone anywhere recently—she was just in the process of replacing the engine.

Freeing the support bar, she lowered the bonnet, wincing as it slid into place with a screech. With a bit of luck, he knew nothing about cars and engines, but after catching the slightest of raised eyebrows, she somehow doubted Lady Luck was keeping her company today.

"Please, come inside." She gestured to her bungalow perched at the top of her driveway. Politely he stood back, and she marched over to her glossy red front door, thinking furiously as she did. Surely he was a client, but she never messed up her appointments, nor did she ever have clients at home. What had happened? Following an incident where her phone had fallen from her pocket and into the guts of the car, taking forever to free it, she always left it inside the house—valuing the time free from its demands. Now, however, she could do with it. Swinging the door open, she stood back and allowed him to enter her house.

"After you, please." He gestured inside at the same time as standing back, something of which she was glad. His presence—a high energy—reached to her, something she did not want to get caught up in it. An image of a hurtling comet came to her, and she brutally shoved it aside.

She nodded in Mr. North's direction and stepped into her own home, leading the way to the small office at the back of the kitchen. On the way through, she switched the coffee machine on, grabbing her glowing mobile phone. She showed him down the two steps into the back office.

"Would you like a coffee, please?" Please? If she could use some time away from his disturbing presence, there was no need to, like, *beg* him.

"Lovely, please. Black, no sugar."

Was he laughing? A quick glance neither confirmed nor denied her suspicions as a blank gaze was rapidly smoothed into place. But his irritation at her not being prepared seemed to have fled as he settled into the easy armchair she kept in front of her basic wooden desk, eyeing up her small office with its no frills. Nothing graced either the walls or the desk to indicate a life of any kind.

Scattered around were old car magazines, and these not artfully, for the time she spent here was either checking out the latest parts for her beloved cars or working. And as researching wasn't exactly the glossiest of careers, there weren't many eye-grabbing documents lying around. The only nod to a life was the tattered old wood scene she had since she was a child, nailed up haphazardly on the wall beside the door to the kitchen.

She backed out, muttering something about coffee and escaped, pressing her fingers to her frontal lobe. *First, clothes—get out of the overalls.* She fled to her bedroom, discarding overalls as she went. Moving as fast as her mind was whirling, she quickly threw on some clothes and raced back down.

Back in the kitchen, she whipped out her phone, cursing inaudibly as she saw four missed calls from her office, complete with message-left icons glowing. *Deep joy.* Yesterday, she had booked Thursday off in order to work on the MG, as she had finished one high-pressure job and needed an escape. Scrubbing her fingers through her ponytailed hair, she gently gave her scalp a massage whilst bracing herself to listen to the increasingly panicked tones of her PA, Ruthie.

"Your 9 a.m. has arrived, Ellora." "Ellora, where are you?" "Ellora, I've messed up. My Wi-Fi was down this morning, so I took a booking for you, only realizing too late that you weren't in. But please call me—I don't know what to do." In lowered tones, "There's a man here adamant to see you and he's not taking no for an answer. And I don't know but he's a bit, ooh, disturbing. Call me."

These three messages came in hot and quick on

each other's heels, but there was a four-minute delay until the next, with Ruthie's voice nearly breaking on the phone. "Ellora, he's got your address—I had to leave my desk. When I got back, he wasn't around, but my phone with your number and contact details on the screen was still alight. I'm sorry and call me. As soon as you get this. Otherwise, I'll send security over."

Disconnecting, she stood by the counter, tapping her lip with the phone. This man was certainly used to taking what he wanted. A low throat clearing alerted her to the fact he was now lounging in the doorway. Taking a deep breath, she swung to face him, crooking one arm on her hip.

"Excuse me, but who are you?"

"Do you not know?" His gaze looked nothing but amused as he returned her stare.

"No, I bloody well don't. Lee North or something." Sometimes she took refuge in her English accent inherited from her London Mum, and articulated the words with a clear, precise, cut-glass accent. Her dad used to also tease her mum sometimes, trying to copy her words, but his tongue couldn't quite get the words out without sounding woolly. Without fail, her mother would laugh, and her father often used it when treading on dangerous territory. Her heart panged.

He smiled crookedly, but it wasn't enough to mask the determination in his gaze.

"I run North Antiquaries. I had set this day aside for appointing myself a new researcher, and this I intend to do. You are the fifth person I'll have seen. I made an appointment this morning, and I admit, someone must have made a mistake, but that's not my problem." He gestured in a way that indicated "as are you."

"You thought you could just *purloin* my address from my PA and rock on over here?"

He raised an eyebrow and a wry smile pulled at his lips. "I guess you could call it purloin, Ms. Radley."

Damned if this man was going to laugh at her. She held his gaze. "Is this the way you normally do business?"

He looked down at the ground briefly and smiled wryly. "No, I normally don't purloin addresses from unsuspecting PAs, although you might think about re-hiring. I apologize."

The eyes that met hers now were clear. She nodded, unthinkingly.

Deep breaths, girl. Don't be getting all rattled.

"I'm sorry you've wasted your time. I'm not looking for a new job."

He straightened and all amusement fled his gaze.

"Would you hear me out? Maybe that coffee might help." Did that quirk of his lips suggest he was flirting?

She turned back to the coffee machine, pressing buttons rather blindly and welcoming the answering hum. *Deep breaths.* Taking her favorite mugs out, she filled them before handing one to him.

"Let's go into the office." It gave her a degree of professionalism, and she needed something with which to cloak herself.

She settled in her chair, propping her forearms on the desk, coffee cupped. After a pause, he leaned against the bookshelf on the right wall to her desk.

"Being an antiquarian, I require a researcher for my services." He held up his coffee cup and gave a brief nod to her before taking a sip.

To the point.

"Antiquarian, aren't you supposed to be all, oh I don't know, dusty? Shouldn't you be wearing a tweed jacket with leather elbows and have incorrigible curls?"

She should be quiet—she really should. But this was a problem of hers, allowing words out before any kind of brain censorship took place. Sometimes she gabbled when she was nervous, and looking at the man lounging in her increasingly small office was making her nervous. Very nervous. Hot on its heels came annoyance.

Dusty and a tweed jacket, she could handle. Heck, curls even she could put up with. But not this tigerlike man, watching her with eyes that could only be described as whiskey colored. She tried not to trace the shape of his cheekbones and firmly held his gaze, hoping she wasn't looking like a mad woman, staring at him.

Nope, if she were on a show trying to guess what he did, such a dusty profession would not enter her head. *A model maybe, for designer watches, staring moodily at the camera...*

He waited, watching as she slowly heated as the range of emotions flooded her with adrenaline. She blew a stray lock of hair back from her face in the hope a long low breath might calm her. Time to regroup.

An antiquarian, he would be looking for someone to track down artifacts. Easy. But did she want a new job? Hers was fine as it was. Working in the large world-renowned museum in the city had been a great job when she started three years ago. Had it become slightly boring now? What matter if it had? She didn't crave excitement—quite the opposite in fact. Routine—

7

the key to a peaceful life.

Or was it? Did routine kill any kind of peace because there was no room for anything new, boundless, exciting? Could peace be felt if nothing different or new happened, forcing a change of thought and a reassessment? Does peace mutate to boredom?

"Don't judge a book by the cover—perhaps I am all dusty and just forgot to don my tweed today."

He was rewarded with a small smile.

Lee allowed his gaze to wander over the small study. Thin-paneled plywood lined the walls, a crooked wooden landscape placed behind a well-worn chair, and beyond that, nothing to suggest personality. Although, the well-thumbed magazines, *Hemming Classic Car*, made a refreshing change from the glossies. Carefully expressionless, the office spoke volumes. The twenty-seven-inch monitor on the corner of the desk was blank, as was the legal pad neatly situated in the center, with a fountain pen—capped of course—by the side. A round coaster completed the non-inspiring look.

But the woman herself, now that was a different matter. Long, black hair was scooped back into a messy ponytail. Her three-quarter-length sleeved polo top clung to her curves, emphasizing her neat figure whilst her soft jersey, high-waist, flared trousers made the casual look something more indefinable.

He liked her. And he wanted her to like him—something rather foreign to him. From what he had gathered about Ellora Radley, he wanted her on his team. She sat herself with a small sigh, and picking up her red pen, clicked it and wrote the date in bold letters on the top of the pad along with his name.

"Let's just say I'm in the market for a new job.

Where would that put us today?"

Large, solemn gray eyes under her fringe gazed steadily back.

"How about we start with your experience of working with antiquarians?" He allowed his lips to curve. He did enjoy what he did—not least because it was not the most common of careers.

She tilted her head, and he felt the seriousness of her gaze.

"I started out in research seven years ago. My first client was the Royal Society of Antiquaries in London. I stayed with them for four years but then came back to Chicago." She stopped abruptly.

Impressive. No wonder the reputation his PA, Jonathon, had uncovered had been exemplary. The Royal Society of Antiquaries was the biggest archaeological research library in the UK, itself one of the largest holders of ancient artifacts. This day had started strange and was becoming progressively more so.

"Why did you return?"

"Because of a job."

These words she delivered flatly and moved on swiftly to her work experience. *What had happened? Failed love affair?* He settled into the stiff leather chair in front of her desk and listened as she went through her duties and responsibilities. She was well respected, this much he understood from her carriage.

Yet while watching her, he noted not once throughout her dialogue did her expression diverge from serious. There was no lightening up, perhaps due to being in an interview. Although he doubted she bowed under pressure.

Aware of her coming to a stop, he realized one thing and one thing only. Only she would do.

"Great. Welcome to North Antiquaries."

A surprised laugh burst from her, but the corresponding look was anything but amused.

"How do you know I want to work for you?"

"Fair point. I'll run through our credentials. NA is one of the top employers here in Chicago. The company is top of the Crain's Chicago Business best companies for employees for the third year running. My offices at the Loop are well maintained, and it is a great building to work in. I value my employees and invest heavily in them. I have only twenty-seven members of staff, but the beauty of keeping it small is we are all on first name terms and often we feel like a family, albeit a large and unwieldy one. What else can I say?" He spread his hands out. "The staff have an extra two vacation days annually, and I pay above the average."

She didn't move a muscle as she listened to him. "Sounds all right. Tell me what the role entails."

He blew out an exasperated breath, not used to having to sell his company. "Generally, my team is more than capable of tracking what is requisitioned. But sometimes an odd and interesting item request comes into the building—and this is where I need an experienced researcher. Some artifacts take weeks or months to track down. I travel and most times would require you to come with me, or you may uncover something that requires following up outside of the internet."

At her quirked eyebrow, he continued. "Maybe about four times a year, my clients need me to journey to far-flung places to find ancient artifacts. I won't lie to you. The trips sometimes take a couple of weeks and it is always useful to have an experienced researcher with me."

Was it his imagination or was there a spark of interest in those cool eyes? She glanced away and picked up her black biro, scrawling something over those yellow pages. Stopping, she fixed him anew with her gray eyes. She was impossible to read.

"Why are you recruiting now?"

"My current researcher is moving with her family to Florida. She has been with me since NA's inception, and I am sorry to see her go. She leaves in two weeks' time. It has all been sudden."

"Would you want me to work exclusively for you?"

She was asking the right questions. "Yes. For which I would pay $125,000 annually. Plus all expenses on trips, needless to say. Although you can buy your own postcards." To give her credit, she didn't bat an eyelid. Knowing the average pay for a worker of her experience would be less than half his amount, he was impressed.

Yet something within him laughed—it wasn't as if she looked like the type of woman who was interested in money. "You could buy yourself a new sports car, save you having to do up an old one."

There—definite reaction. Askance, her gray eyes narrowed on his face, one eyebrow raised.

He smiled, making a conciliatory gesture with his hands. Yet she gave nothing back. Did he really want someone this cold on his team? He ran through his office team and wondered whether she'd fit in. His team was a good one, handpicked personally, and their disparate characters enhanced the atmosphere and got the job done fast. His gut instinct was rarely wrong. But he had gone over and above now and was damned if he was going to beg.

Standing up, he winced as the chair scratched on the linoleum. He took the one step required to get to the door, turning for a last aside before he left. "I'll leave you in peace, Ms. Radley. I'll give you twenty-four hours to make up your mind. Thank you for your time, and the coffee." He sketched a bow and left.

Flicking out his keys, he unlocked his Audi and settled himself into its quiet interior. Damn. He resisted the urge to punch his steering wheel. He had never come across someone so casual about his company. He was proud of it, having built up the small business his dad had started years ago. Discovering a love of all things ancient at an early age had certainly set him apart from his contemporaries, but this love had focused him throughout university life. And now here he was, the man that *most* folk wanted to work for. He ruffled his hair.

He needed a shake-up, and he picked up his phone to call his club. "Matt, hi, are there any courts free?" He listened. "Great, I'm on my way." Nothing like a game of squash to run the edge off.

Chapter Two

Ellora stared at the door North had just exited, sure she saw flurries in the air. Releasing a long breath, she stood, not wanting to be in the relentlessly small room. She paced through the kitchen and on to the living room to gaze out the French doors at Potawatomi Woods. Would her beloved trees provide the answer today?

Fond of walking, she had a trail through the ancient woods and would listen to the winds and the murmurs of the trees. As a general rule, she would arrive home with clarity of thought, whether because of the exercise, the surroundings or both, who knew. Yet today, she didn't even know the question.

For a start, she did not know what to make of Lee North. A part—the small feminine side she hadn't managed to entirely quash—had enjoyed watching him in her house. Another and far bigger part towered in her mind telling her he was trouble and she the fool if she went for it. She didn't want to think too hard, for who knew what she'd hear if she allowed her brain to tunnel through these thoughts.

Marching back to her PC, she woke it up, mulling the conversation over. She plugged his name into the search engine, watching avidly as the results appeared. For a man as successful as he was, there were remarkably few personal stories about him. One of the few successes in his field, a determined bachelor, and a man who appeared to keep very much to himself judging by the few reports available.

Only one significant other, which apparently had fizzled out after four years. Any photos, though, showed one beautiful girl or another on his arm. Yet if she asked her mother what she thought, the answer would surely be "Looks like a fine upstanding man, hot to boot."

She glanced at the clock—her attention for the MG was shot. Needing instead the dry nature of her best friend, she dashed off a text before grabbing her keys by the door and exiting sharply. Hopefully Flicka was free. She reversed at speed down her driveway and took off into town, ignoring the little pulls from her stomach. No, she was going to say no. Definitely. Five minutes later, she pulled into the parking lot, which backed onto their favorite coffee shop, Lazy Days—an apt name, as often was the time she and Flicka sat there for hours.

Not thirty seconds after she entered the shop did the door fly open with the wind and leaves outside, and Flicka stepped in—all tall, rangy six foot of her, long red hair back up in a ponytail. She did envy her her height, which Flicka always rejoined with envying Ellora's neat, strong figure.

Smiling in relief at the sight of her best friend, she waved from the queue and pointed to the sofa in the window. An age-old routine existed between the pair and Flicka strode to the table, divesting herself of her jacket before crossing her long jean-clad legs insouciantly and sitting back.

When her Americano orders came through, Ellora hugged her best friend hard on the sofa. They had known each other for the past eighteen years, becoming joined at the hip a mere week after meeting at school. They'd laugh, saying they were clearly soul mates, as they each knew what the other was thinking.

Sometimes they'd dream nearly the same dream, telling each other the next day, knowing the other had dreamt similar. And the times when she felt too buffeted by life, she would crawl under Flicka's shelter and stay there, safe and secure, until she felt strong enough to head back out on her own into the world.

"Hey, what's up?" Flicka pulled back to look her in the face. "You seem, oh I don't know, unraveled?"

She spluttered a laugh. Trust Flicka to find the best word to describe her. She felt pretty much unraveled. She sat up and pulled her coffee close, pushing Flicka's over. Chewing her bottom lip, she glanced at Flicka.

"I've had a kinda odd morning."

"Go on…"

"I had the day booked off to work on Bertie, but my new PA booked in an appointment. This man wasn't the type to let something little like a day off mess his diary up."

She glanced at her coffee, absentmindedly admiring the color. Today was a good coffee day.

"I didn't know anything of this. I was outside, my phone was inside, my head was on valve connections, not work. It was going great. But the next thing I know, I was banging my head against the bonnet because this, not sure how to describe it, presence was behind me. Him."

Flicka didn't take her eyes from her.

Aware of the portentous sound of it, she remedied, "From the office—not that I knew that at the time. There was just this strange man looking rather intensely at me. The funny thing is there was something about him…anyway, I digress. After a couple of stuttering minutes and embarrassing blushes, I find out that the reason he's come out to my house is to interview me for the role of researcher."

Flicka frowned slightly. "I didn't know you were looking for a new job."

"No, nor did I. Thinking back on it though, I sporadically check new jobs in the area—just to keep current with the market. One had caught my eye, and I had registered with the recruitment agent. But it was only a passing fancy. I guess he must use the same recruitment team."

"But even so, wouldn't they have contacted you first?"

"You'd imagine so. But who knows how the world operates in the land of the rich? Perhaps he makes his own rules."

"He head-hunted you."

Ellora smothered a laugh. "I know I'm good, but not *that* good."

Flicka's eyes narrowed over her coffee cup. "Who was it?"

"Lee North, North Antiquaries."

Flicka spluttered and placed her cup on the table, eyes widening. "You're joking. Lee North came looking for you? And you said what…tell me you said yes, Lorrie, please. I mean, even I know of him." Flicka sculpted carvings from fallen wood out of the forest behind Ellora's house—only she didn't call it sculpting, she called it freeing the images. She reached out and picked up her hand. "Please lady. For me."

"Um…"

"You didn't. Oh my god. You didn't bite his hand off. Ellora Radley, what am I going to do with you?" Flicka dropped her hand, rolling her eyes to heaven as she did. She slumped against the back of the sofa to gaze out the window as the wind picked up the rust, orange, and dark brown leaves and flung them against the window, along with a tide of water.

"Well, why would I have said yes?"

Flicka treated her to a scathing look before sitting upright. Determination squared her face. "Let's take a quick look at your life, shall we, Ms. Fond of Looking a Gift Horse in the Mouth."

She held up a hand, forefinger out. "One. You are twenty-eight, smart as all get-out, and sexy as hell. Two. You are living in the same house in the same town as you have lived *all your life.* Three. You're on your own."

Her fierce look softened and she reached over and squeezed her knee, mouthing a silent sorry as she did before carrying on. "Four. You are in a dead-end job. Five. You tinker about with cars because you have nothing else in your life. If it weren't for me, Harry, and the kids, you wouldn't have a social life at all."

"Hang on, Flicka."

Her friend stopped with a of don't-you-be-stopping-me-I'm-in-the-flow look.

"Anthony and Juliet, I socialize with them."

"Your boss and his wife? I've been out with you, remember, kid? All you three ever talk about is dusty manuscripts and ancient devils. Exciting? Not so much." She held up her second hand. "Six, and probably the most important, don't you remember sitting up in the oak tree in your garden, making all

17

these glorious plans for life? I wanted a shop, husband and kids, I got 'em. But you? Ellora Radley? You wanted the world, you couldn't wait to travel and see it, you just couldn't wait to grab life by the balls and live it. Remember?"

She stared over Flicka's shoulder at the blustery day. She did remember and could see vividly her younger self. But it was hard to witness the glorious teen she had been. Certain she knew it all, mad hair flying as she ran from place to place. She didn't walk— heck, she didn't have the time to walk. Time was for the living, not the watching. Her mother used to say laughingly, "Slow down Lorrie, you'll trip yourself up coming back from where you're going."

Flicka squeezed her hand. "Sorry, was I too harsh?"

She swallowed the lump in her throat. "Well if you were, you are the only person I'd let get away with it."

After a concerned glance, Flicka carried on. "You were, are, so brave, Lorrie. Remember that. The one who took off to London without a backward glance. The one who put her backpack on her back to explore Europe with nothing more than ten pounds in her back pocket."

Dammit. Sometimes she hated knowing someone who knew her so well. The reminders of the past were too painful to look at.

"What, Lorrie? What're you thinking?"

She didn't want to answer. The thoughts coming in thick and strong were too raw to divulge, even to her best friend. She had been full of hope and glory, looking to each day with an air of excitement. Now look at her—jaded before her time. If she carried on like this, what would she be like on her death bed? What regrets would she have to take to her grave?

There was once upon a time when she refused to regret anything, secure in the belief that life was there to be explored and experienced, raw and painful though that might be. Ha, what little had she known. But now, rather than regretting what she had done, would she regret that which she hadn't done? Her head hurt. Damn Lee North for putting her through such a quandary.

Flicka sipped her coffee and nodded decisively. "Listen to what Rachel said this morning before school. When we were getting ready, she looked outside and saw the sunrise and she said, 'I love the sky when it's skin colored.' Nice, hey? And a good way of describing it."

Rachel was Flicka's oldest child, nine years old. She had another girl, seven-year-old Anastasia, a thinker with large brown eyes that thoughtfully viewed the world, with Harry her husband who worshipped the ground all his girls walked on. She was rightfully proud of her family.

Knowing Ellora needed distraction, she chatted on about her children and her latest artwork.

She allowed Flicka's voice to wash over her, comforting as it was, only bringing herself back to the here and now when she became aware Flicka asked her something. "This weekend? Not sure. Maybe I'll head over to Lake Michigan or go out for a hike."

"Come and join us tomorrow night if you like. We're going to have a barbecue out on the deck. Mad I know, but it'll probably be the last barbecue of the year. The neighbors are coming over, and we may have fireworks in honor of your Guy Fawkes night."

"Sounds great." Ellora's mother being English, they had always celebrated the English holidays. It did sound great too, as she was sure by the time tomorrow night came along, she'd be bored to tears of her own brain's machinations. She knew herself well enough to know what was coming up, and the ensuing time on her own could prove to be counterproductive.

She felt Flicka's concerned gaze and forced tears back, pretending her eyes were a sponge to soak back the water. Now was not the time to get sentimental.

"Listen, Lorrie, I'm sorry if I've opened a can of worms."

She sat upright and consciously expelled a long breath of air—along with her old life? "No, you didn't. Well, perhaps you did and I needed it. I needed to be reminded of who I was, before, you know. That's what best friends are for, right? Waking you up when you need it." She reached over and rubbed her friend's knee, smiling crookedly.

Flicka didn't smile back. "I do worry about you though, all on your own in your parents' house. It's got to be tough, no matter how much you brush it aside. And you know I wish for you what I have for myself, someone who loves you exactly for the fabulous you. Because you, lady, of all people, deserve nothing less than the best."

Ellora hugged her. "I know, I know. Yet that would be someone who might not come home one night. I'll be fine. I'd prefer to be alone than be lonely waiting for the sound of his key in the door."

"I understand. But there's nothing to say that you'd ever be lonely in a relationship—I know you loved Charlie, but he was a shit and not representative of all

20

A word about the author…

Cait O'Sullivan has a deep love of words, music, and magic, having had the good fortune to grow up in Ireland. The wanderlust in her blood sent her out to travel the world. Then, reluctant to give up on following her dreams, Cait gained a degree in English and Creative Writing. Now, residing in the English Midlands, it is her thoughts and memories that journey far and wide in order to create her stories.

http://caitosullivan.blogspot.co.uk/

men."

"Mmm." Ellora refused to be drawn on this—she knew the way the conversation would go, inevitably ending with Flicka trying to set her up with any one of unsuitable single men she knew. She allowed the pause to deepen until Flicka sighed.

"So, North Antiquaries?"

"Oh, I don't know. No. Yes. Maybe." Yet the thought filled her with a feeling of launching herself out of a nice safe *comfortable* plane into so-thin-it-was-nearly-non-existent air. A vague shadowy fear blanketed her senses very briefly, making her feel slightly suffocated. No. It wasn't possible. Yet.

You'd have a parachute!

As quickly as it had appeared, the voice subsided. Over the past five years, she had trained herself out of hearing the voices, no small thanks to her wonderful therapist.

"Are you okay?"

"I'm fine thanks. I know you have school pick-up so let's head away."

The two girls bustled about getting themselves ready to leave. As they walked out into the parking lot, she turned to her best friend. "I don't think I can do it, Flick."

Flicka's face softened and she put her arm around her. "Ah okay, Lorrie. I understand. I'll see you tomorrow about five."

Ellora gave her a grateful squeeze. "Sure. Let me know if I can bring anything."

****

At approximately 11.55am, Ellora sat in the plush waiting room comprising part of North's suite on the

21

top floor of the towering skyscraper. Unable to relax, she stood and walked the length of the windows, gazing sightlessly at Chicago's skyline, tugging at her hemline. She had been a fool to wear a new dress, but after parting company with Flicka yesterday, she hadn't wanted to go home. Instead, she found herself in the busy shopping mall, surrounded by bustling people shopping early for Christmas. *Christmas. Another one on her own.*

So, when a dress in the window unlike any she had owned before caught her eye, she went ahead and bought it without trying it on. After a night of tossing and turning, her devil-may-care attitude hadn't departed and when she had put it on this morning, even the most negative part of her did not see why she should not wear it.

The high neck and bare sleeves showed off her arms, something she often thought were her best feature, and gently emphasized her—in her opinion, too small—breasts, before hugging her waist and flaring out over her hips. Her knee-high black suede boots with a wedge gave her a nice wiggle and sent the dark teal silk flaring around her thighs. Why had she eschewed her normal, plain, and classic style in favor of this? Did she want North to look at her and see a woman? Really?

Right now, what she wouldn't give to be in the comfort of trousers and a top. Nice and simple. No statement whatsoever. Plus, she had been foolish enough to braid her hair back off her face, leaving nothing to hide behind. What was she trying to do? Sabotage this meeting? She refused to believe that the photos she had seen yesterday had influenced her style today.

She heard a quiet door *shush* open and turned from her contemplation of Chicago's skyline. The smoky glass door to North's private office framed the man himself. The air was sucked from her lungs and she walked over on legs suddenly rendered weak.

"Ms. Radley. Please come in."

All rationale fled as he opened his arms to her, and swallowing drily— *heck she was going to accept his job, perhaps he hugged all his employees*—she stepped into the circle just as the realization hit that he was only holding one hand out for her to shake at the same time as gesturing into his office. *Too late*. Awkwardly, she placed one hand on his shoulder whilst trying to recover by grasping his other hand to shake. Furious at herself for allowing such an impasse to happen, she struggled not to be overwhelmed. A quick look at his chiseled features made it clear he found it nothing but amusing. Did she feel worse or better?

"Would you like anything to drink? Water, coffee, tea?"

"Water, please." Anything more to say would be too much for her grown-too-small mouth. Taking a deep breath, she turned to look at his office. Encompassing the entire floor, the wall of glass in the west provided a perfect view of Lake Michigan. The water reached to the horizon, and as ever, she marveled at the fact that it was a lake and not an ocean kissing the next continent. She walked over and breathed the view, inwardly scrabbling around for composure, forcing herself to maintain silence until the red mist of awkwardness passed.

"Please sit." His words were accompanied by a

tinkle of ice against glass, and she walked back to him at the coffee table and sat on the low cream sofa opposite. Careful to keep her knees together, she picked up her tumbler and took a sip, appreciating the cool clearness slipping down her parched throat. She gave a gentle cough and took another sip, grateful for the returning clarity.

"Mr. North—"

He held a hand up. "Please, call me Lee. Let's not stand on ceremony, especially after your greeting." His tone was impossibly dry, his face impossibly blank, yet he must be enjoying what he was doing. But the water refreshed her, and she lifted her chin and nodded.

"Lee it is then. And please, call me Ellora."

He smiled briefly, giving Ellora a quick glimpse of his face in repose. It was a nice face, open and honest, and she wondered what changes a big smile would bring.

"You have a wonderful office."

He raised an eyebrow. "Thank you. I like it." His eyes were keen as he watched her carefully, then sat back, stretching his arm over the back of the sofa opposite her, releasing her.

"I was taken by surprise yesterday. I apologize, both for my abruptness and for the fact that the appointment messed up your day. My PA actually offered to resign."

"Did you take her resignation?"

She snorted in surprise, inwardly thanking her lucky stars that she hadn't just been taking a sip of water, then colored.

"Of course not, would you have done?"

"My PA wouldn't have made such a mistake.

Perhaps I wouldn't have taken his resignation, but then again, perhaps I wouldn't have hired him in the first place."

She bit her tongue to stop herself from saying, "But I didn't hire her," as it sounded a bit too much like she was justifying herself. "She was terribly apologetic." Enough said. The grand clock behind North's shoulders crept towards 1230. Was her job offer about to go up in smoke? She cleared her throat.

"Can I ask how you found me?"

At the look of mild exasperation that crossed his face, she amended her words. "I mean, not my house, but me, professionally?"

"I have a team of head-hunters. They tracked you down."

Her stomach twisted with excitement. So, she had been head hunted. If only she could tell her parents or share this news with someone other than Flicka. At the thought, she straightened her spine. No need for that. She had herself, that was enough.

"Well, thank you. I'm flattered and would very much like to take you up on your job offer." She went as to sit back, but something in his face kept her back straight.

Whiskey-colored eyes deepened to amber as he watched her. "I have to say, Ellora, I am surprised. After our conversation yesterday, I had the impression that you were happy where you were. What changed?"

She nodded slowly, *fair enough*. "The package you offered is very good, and upon thinking over it overnight, I decided I'd be a fool to say no."

He tilted his head as he appraised her, and she tried not to fidget. "I didn't think you would be swayed by

25

the money."

Hour-like seconds passed as she returned his gaze. She didn't want to tell him what she had decided in the early hours of the morning—to break free from the constricted life she had built. A girl cannot live on work, cars, and a very good friend alone. Could she trust this man? Possibly, but not just yet. She sat back and cast through her mind, wondering how to water down what had eventually swayed her. *Anything less than honesty was not good enough for this relationship.*

"It's just me in this life. Nothing or nobody relies on me, nor I on anyone else. If I can't throw caution to the wind, who can?" Too late, she realized she had revealed more of herself than planned. "I want to travel. More, I mean." This latter, she had blurted out in an attempt to cover her mistake. *Quiet.* The voice was coming back. But this advice she gladly followed.

Fortunately, North took the gambit. "Have you traveled much?"

"Just to Europe. When I worked in England, I used it as a base to explore parts of Europe—namely, France, Switzerland, Spain, Prague, Istanbul. Not forgetting Ireland, of course."

"Why of course?"

"It's only a hop, skip, and a jump from the UK. I spent many long weekends there, exploring and following family roots."

He nodded. "Interesting place, Ireland. Deeply steeped in mystery and intrigue from an early age. I like it. My research assistant didn't come with me when I went—and that was a mistake, one I'm keen not to make again. What did you do in Prague?"

"Just the usual—seeing the astronomical clock,

crossing Charles Bridge, and up to the castle. I only had a weekend there but loved it and would appreciate returning."

He placed his cup on the glass table. "Did you see it change on the hour?"

She smiled lightly, "I did. I had no clue what to expect, as I only joined the crowd to see what they were watching, and had to laugh when the twelve apostles paraded past the windows above the clock, looking out. I loved it and wished they had miniatures to buy as souvenirs."

Her nerves were untwisting. He watched her with a steady gaze not many got away with. But it wasn't uncomfortable. Something within her, which hadn't been heard in a long time, told her it was safe to return the look.

"Prague is a wonderful city. I look forward to returning." He allowed the pause to lengthen, then sat straight, steepling his fingers.

"I'm happy to hear you will accept the role." He stood and crossed to his desk, picking up a folder. Flicking through it, he nodded and brought it back to her. "Your terms and conditions and contract of employment, along with the nondisclosure agreement, which all employees are required to sign."

It had taken his solicitors a while, but the contract had everything sewn up. North Antiquaries were set strange tasks, and silence from his employees was mandatory. "I just need a signature at the end of the first page, then once you have read through it all, two more on the last page."

She took it, feeling her mouth slightly open and snapped it shut. He had known she was going to accept.

Opening the folder revealed it, all in glorious black and white. Ellora Margaret Radley, the newest researcher for the renowned antiques hunter, Lee North. She scanned the first page, then glanced once more at her soon-to-be boss. He watched her, but with his eyes overshadowed, she knew not what to think. Only that her stomach was turning cartwheels. With a deep breath, she scanned the document as thoroughly as was possible in her state of mind and signed the duplicate page, handing the copy to North.

There, the die was cast. She didn't know whether to feel exhilarated, apprehensive, or just plain nostalgic already for her safe life left behind. Gathering the documents, she placed them in her bag to read thoroughly when he wasn't around and conflicting her rationale.

"Thank you, and welcome. How long is your notice period at the museum?"

"Three months."

He nodded, pursing his lips. "I wonder can we get you out of that?"

"Oh no, I don't think—"

"Let's see."

A low chime sounded somewhere in the office. She startled, she had been so sure there was only herself and North in the world. She needed to focus now her life was changing before her very eyes. Her stomach twirled once more, and she wished she had put food in this morning, but she didn't feel anything else would fit in along with the butterflies and rollercoasters.

"May I use your restroom please?"

"Of course. Just through the door behind you and on your left." His tones slipped over her skin. *Breathe. Walk. You'll be fine.*

Chapter Three

Although he tried not to, Lee watched the sway of her hips as she walked to the bathroom. Underneath her dress was a curvy, fit figure. Unbidden, an image of her in khakis and a tee shirt, hair in a ponytail, slight sheen of sweat on her upper lips, blowing back hair as she turned to look with him with excitement on her face. He blinked. Almost as though it was a memory not a…not a what? Wish, dream? Hope? Forbearer of things to come?

Another chime, and with an effort, he brought himself back to the present and clapped his hands to make the connection with his PA outside.

"Jonathon."

"Mr. Constantin is on the line, Lee. He says it's urgent."

He nodded. It always was with Johannes Constantin, one of his more affluent clients. Twice in the past year, Lee had been abroad hunting some artifact or another for him. An interesting person, the items he required were almost always things Lee had never heard of, which is where the role of researcher was integral.

His previous researcher, Felicity, had been stumped a few times but managed to drag up some information. Last time, he was out in Ireland tracking a cross, and it had proved nearly as damned elusive as his client. He shivered. The cross had escaped him, although he had laid hands on it. But money was no problem for Constantin.

"I'll take it. Will you check Ms. Radley's current employment and see whether we can have her working here sooner than her notice allows?"

"Sure, Lee. I know a few people over at the museum." The ensuing tone ensured disconnection.

Rising from the sofa, he wandered over to the windows, awaiting the call. The brusque tones of Constantin soon filled the room. Always to the point, normally something he admired, there was nonetheless something about this man he didn't like.

"North, I need your services."

"What can I do for you?"

The door opened, admitting Ellora, and he gestured to her to sit back. Absentmindedly, he watched her prowl over to the sofa, sitting with grace and economy in her movements. Running a hand through his hair, he listened to his client.

"I'm looking for an ancient religious artifact used in Neolithic times. Athens should be your first stop."

There was an odd note, something he couldn't put his finger on. Greece. He hadn't been there yet. He glanced at Ellora who looked as though she were listening with every fiber of her being.

"No problem. What is it?"

"A chalice, Roman Catholic. It needs to be returned to its rightful owner. You know the budget."

No budget. Spend what is needed.

"Understood. What information can you give me?" He nodded at Ellora and watched in approval as she pulled an iPad from her bag.

"It is made of metal and has engravings of three spirals and eagles on the outside, with a cross in the center of the bowl.

He knew better than to ask for any images, knowing Constantin didn't put anything on paper. All business was conducted over the phone, and then only very briefly.

"Do you know when it was last seen?"

"No. You know all I know. Keep in touch."

A click preceded the dial tone.

He glanced at Ellora who sat on the sofa, poised, ready to take direction. "You have an up-to-date passport, I assume?"

She nodded, eyes narrowing.

Clapping once, the ensuing low chime brought Jonathon through his door, iPad in hand.

"Jonathon, meet Ellora Radley, our new researcher. Ellora, this is Jonathon, my PA."

She rose to shake his hand and both smiled before Jonathon turned his attention to North.

"Ellora, how soon can you be ready to leave?"

She frowned and shook her head a little. "Really? I mean, um, day after tomorrow?" Wariness widened her eyes, and he saw shadows scudding through them.

"I need better than that, I'm afraid."

"Tomorrow?"

He maintained silence, waiting for the penny to drop.

"You've got to be kidding me. There's no way I can be ready by today. It's, like, 1:00 pm already! Plus, I still work at the museum." Her gray eyes were black with panic, and she looked to Jonathon for support, of which there was none, and back to him.

"I don't think getting you out of your notice period will be a problem."

He heard her gasp. "But what if I don't want to?" Awareness filled her face, and she had the grace to look shame faced and turned to the windows.

"What times are the flights?"

Jonathon nodded to himself as he ticked something on his iPad. "7:35pm from O'Hare International, arriving 4:05pm the next day. Nice flight."

"Great—do it."

At her "but" he swung back to her. "Problem?"

"Um, no of course not."

He nodded at Jonathon, who, impeccable PA as he was, left the office. Lee walked to the windows beside Ellora.

"Can you do it?"

There was a pause. Where once determination had sat on her face, now was hesitation. Dammit. She swallowed deeply and chewed on her bottom lip. Had his gut instinct, the one that said this girl wasn't afraid of life, that she was a go-getter, led him astray for once?

She was looking more like a flake at the moment.

Her mind was whirling, emotions crossing her face faster than he could clock them. Casting her eyes from side to side, he knew she was weighing up her options. Finally, a big sigh.

"As I'm still an employee of the National History Museum, I can check out their files there? See if there's anything suitable?"

He smiled in relief. "Certainly, but it would be a waste of your time. The items I'm sent to uncover are below the radar, never having been catalogued or acknowledged anywhere. I don't see the chalice would be anything different."

"Where would you suggest I try?"

He glanced at the screen with his diary in the background.

"For now, you need to go and get your passport. We fly in six and a half hours. How did you get here?"

"My car."

"Okay. Leave your keys with Jonathon. He'll get a car to take you home. Give your passport to your driver, who will come back for you at 5 p.m. to take you to O'Hare International. I'll see you there."

The sideways glance she shot him was loaded with nerves.

Baby steps, North.

"If you need anything, you can buy it there. We're not going to Timbuktu. You don't have any pets or children. You said it yourself, you wanted to travel. So here I'm offering you Athens, maybe Istanbul on the side. If there's something you have to do, let Jonathon or your driver know, and they will sort it out."

A thousand expressions crossed her face, it was obvious she just didn't know what to think. "How long will we be going for?"

"I don't know. Pack enough for a few days. And in future, you might do as I do and keep a bag ready to go."

"What about my job?"

Oh details and delays. He clapped his hands once and Jonathon appeared in the doorway.

"Any news on the museum?"

"I'm just getting the personal phone number of Anthony Jones and then will call him."

There was a mutinous set to Ellora's mouth. "I would like to speak to him."

"Fine, then do. But please give Jonathon the details, then he can follow up and make sure all is good. I want you at the airport at 5.35 p.m. at the latest. Do whatever it takes. Jonathon, sort out the transport. Ellora." He nodded at them both. Spirals, eagles, crosses—what would connect these?

He didn't notice when the door shut behind him.

****

She blew out a breath on the other side of the door. Jonathon looked on with sympathy in his eyes. "Bit of a whirlwind, right? Are you all right?"

"Mmm." She pressed fingers to the hollows by her forehead. But she instinctively trusted Jonathon. "Is he always like that?"

"Yes. The constancy takes a bit of getting used to, along with his ability to turn on a five cent piece. When I first started, it was hard. But then you get caught up in the adrenaline and realize that there's never a dull day."

She admired the way Jonathon was tapping away at his iPad but keeping up a steady stream of chat at the same time. He put his hand out to her, gesturing inwards with his fingers.

"What?"

"Car keys, registration number, and cell number for your employer at the museum. We have your address."

Grabbing her pad, she scribbled the details down and handed them over, along with the keys hoping Jonathon wouldn't spot the shaky hands. She swallowed deeply, forcing her tunneled hearing to widen to include Jonathon's voice.

"...downstairs, Mathew is waiting for you.

Anything you need, connect with me through the car's comms."

"Thanks Jonathon."

He paused in his tapping and looked up. "You're welcome. Good luck." Brisk and business-like, he turned to his computer.

As Ellora made her way towards the bank of lifts, she had the strangest sensation of walking through liquid. Things seemed to slow, and she felt as though she had been caught in freeze frame on camera. Voices encroached...*no, no. Not now.*

What had her counsellor said to her? Concentrate on one step at a time. Bring yourself into the present and breathe. But she couldn't breathe deeply—she felt too sick. *Go away.*

She catapulted out of the slow stew of whatever it had been towards the lift, with the door opening for her. Once there, she greedily drew in breath after breath. *Stay calm. Focus on one step at a time.* She was going to do this.

In the lobby, a tall gray-haired man stood up upon her arrival.

"Ms. Radley? I'm Mathew, your driver."

Plastering a smile on her face, she shook his hand. "Call me Ellora, please."

"As you wish. This way, please."

He led her outside and into a waiting black Mercedes-Maybach. *Nice. If a little ostentatious.* After he settled in the driver's seat, he pressed a button and his voice came over the intercom. "Anything you need, just let me know, ma'am. There are refreshments to your left, accessed by pressing the drinks icon on the console in the middle. Can I do anything for you?"

She shook her head, then said no out loud. She didn't want distraction—she had too much to think about. What did she need to bring with her? Clothes, toiletries, she took out her pad to write a list when a low tone alerted her to Mathew's voice over the speaker.

"Ma'am, Jonathon has just informed me the iPad beside you is clean and for your use. As we travel, he will be uploading the appropriate research sites for you to look through."

Where the hell would she get the time to pack, inform anybody—woeful list—hand in her job resignation, *and* start her research? She should ring Anthony and tell him about the job. She didn't want to do it. Anthony was a complete honey and had had a crush on her for her three years there. She had gone on a date with him, just to see if there was any chemistry, but it was sadly lacking. Anthony was like an old cozy jumper to throw on when needing warming up.

Telling him, not in quite so many words, had proven for awkward times in the office for a number of weeks. But then Anthony had met, and subsequently married Juliet, a smart, serious woman but with a wicked line in asides. Someone who was very good for him and who lightened him up a lot. But Ellora knew Anthony would always have a soft spot for her.

"Ellora, hi."

"Hi Anthony." Her voice was high and breathy, and she forced herself to speak slowly. "I have bad news, I'm afraid."

"Yes I know. You've left the museum." He, on the other hand, sounded flat as a pancake. "I am surprised, no shocked, you didn't see fit to tell me yourself."

Damn Lee North. And super-efficient Jonathon.

She was left in a dark hole with her past employer.

"Anthony, I'm sorry. I didn't realize Jonathon would tell you before I did. You know I don't operate that— "

"Who's Jonathon? It was Lee North I spoke to." Despite the fact he clearly was upset, his voice held grudging respect.

Of course, what had she expected? Of course Lee would check her references.

"Oh, I see. Can I ask what he said?"

"Just you're working for him now and he was sorry but urgent work was taking you out of town."

"I'm sorry, Anthony. I never expected it to happen like this."

"If I'd known you were unhappy here, I would've helped out, you know. You should've told me."

"I wasn't looking for another job, Anthony. He came and found me through a bizarre state of affairs."

There were muffled noises in the background and Anthony coughed. "That was Juliet. She said to grow up and stop acting like a kid whose favorite toy has been taken away. And she's right. It's just because I will miss having you in the office. But NA is a fantastic opportunity and clearly the right one for you. You'll do well."

She swallowed past the lump in her throat. "Thanks Anthony. I'll miss you and the rest of the team too. When I get back, I'll come and visit."

Anthony's tone was gruff when he replied. "Do. In the meantime, if you need any help with anything, Juliet and I would be glad to help."

Both her ex-boss and his wife were serious and avid researchers, having been in the field for twenty years. Many was the time she had gone over for dinner, only to discover they had forgotten and had to call in a takeaway because they were deeply embroiled in some case or other. She envied them their ease and comfort around each other.

Taking a deep breath, she then called Flicka to tell her. Her best friend was over the moon for her, was thrilled she was heading back out into the world, finishing their conversation by proving why she was her best friend.

"Don't worry about the house, I'll come over later and lock it up for a couple of weeks for you—empty the fridge and the bins, anything you need doing. You just concentrate on getting yourself ready and out in time. I'll be thinking of you, and don't forget, I can come out in a flash if you need me. Anytime. I've got your back."

Those two phone calls helped focus her mind. It was hard to believe what was happening, but she doubted she would see it for the reality it was until she was actually in Greece. Greece! A smidgeon of excitement found its way through the butterflies.

Let's see, it was October, what would the weather be like? Amidst the thoughts of blue seas and white sands came *What the hell was she going to pack?* All she generally favored were the dark trousers and polo necked jumpers, which wouldn't suit sunny weather. Even if she had the time to shop, there would be no summer clothes in the stores.

The quiet car hummed to a halt, and she glanced up to see her house at the top of the drive. Mathew navigated the car until he reversed up to drop her outside the front door. As she exited the vehicle, she caught sight of her neighbors staring out of their window and smiled to herself. Gave them an eyeful, this car.

She let herself into the quiet house and went straight to the filing cabinet to find her passport and took it back out to Mathew. *First job done. You've got this!* Back inside, she ran upstairs to pull a dusty backpack out of the cupboard. Not having traveled for a while meant she didn't have the ubiquitous wheelie. She had a few hours to get her things together and she started by pulling all her clothes from the closet and throwing them on the bed.

As she hated shopping, her wardrobe consisted of a few staples: good jeans, a couple of pairs of dark trousers, a few tops, and two dresses, her new teal one making her total three. Would they be going out at all? What were they going to do about dinner—get changed or not? Her head whirled about and she forced back the red mist of panic. Breathe.

Okay Ellora Radley. If you are going to get changed for dinner, you have few options. Throw in the classic little black dress. How about heels then? Yup, throw in the boots you're wearing, they look good with jeans and trousers anyway.

Talking to herself helped. Stripping off her new dress, she pulled on the light jersey trousers similar to what she had worn yesterday and what generally was her uniform, completing it with a soft woolen polo neck. She stood in front of her full-length mirror and stared straight into her eyes. *Lorrie, you've got this.* The memory of her mother's voice calmed her at the same time as filling her with love. She could see her mother in her, her strong-mindedness and softness that combined to make her such a special mother. In her, she could see her saying it was time to get on with her life.

A couple of hours later, she hauled her case downstairs and turned to the butterflies in her tummy. Would they allow her to eat something or would she just feel sicker? She sure as hell wanted a coffee but didn't want the strong substance upsetting her stomach. Some biscotti would help. She wandered through the house, tidying as she went. Living alone, it was easy to keep clean and tidy and Flicka wouldn't have much to do.

A low tone on her phone alerted her to a call coming through. "Ma'am, it's Mathew here. There has been an accident on the road to the airport, necessitating a different route, one which will take longer. Are you ready to leave?"

Was she ready? Was anyone ever ready to throw themselves into a vortex? Time slowed once more, and as though she looked at herself in the mirror, she saw herself standing outside her body. Was she ready?

"Yes, Mathew, I'm ready." The words calmed her, and as she locked her front door, she wondered what kind of person she would be the next time she placed the key in her lock.

Chapter Four

Once they had finished strapping themselves into the first-class seats, Lee plucked Ellora's work iPad from her grasp, tapping on the screen.

"I had meant to do this before we got onboard, but we ran out of time. Hopefully, we can download before we have to switch to airplane mode. Ah…here we go."

He handed it back to her, and she saw the page open was a NA employee page, with a lot of information filled in.

"These are your login details, email address, new phone number, useful websites, source details, et cetera."

"Great thank you. There's a lot here."

"Of course. Take your time."

He watched her from the corner of his eye. When they had met at the airport, he had been surprised by her mood—she was excited and nervous in equal measures. He had to admit to being quite charmed by it.

She ran a finger down the screen, nodding gently.

"Where is it?"

"Where is what?"

"If I have a new phone number, I assume I have a new phone."

He unstrapped himself and reached up into the overhead locker to pull out a package from his carry-on luggage. "Here, newest version—as yet not hit the market—and set up for you."

Her gray eyes sparkled silver as she took it and opened it to reveal a slim silver smart phone.

"I thought you didn't like money or its trappings."

She laughed, all happy eyes. "It doesn't drive me, no, and I am happy with the older version. If it ain't broke, then don't fix it. But…"

Here she paused with a mischievous twist to her mouth. "Doesn't every girl love something new and sparkly? Especially something that will make her life easier." She rummaged further and pulled out a small dark gray zip bag. "What's this?"

"Extra battery—there may be times when we can't get to a plug socket to charge. This battery here"—he leaned over and plucked a long, slim black cylinder the size of a large lighter from the bag—"will triple the battery life. Once you plug it in, I'd recommend switching the phone to airplane mode, as it won't drain the life as fast. There is also a selection of charging leads, everything you need, in fact, for when you're on the run." He kept his tone light but saw realization sharpen her gaze.

"Are we going to be on the run?" Amusement flickered. He took a breath. Probably time to tell her.

"Some items we're asked to track down can be quite elusive and will have been in hiding for some time, centuries even. Religious artifacts, for example, ones that were hidden after, say, Henry VIII's dissolution of the monasteries in the sixteenth century." He paused, giving her time to let what he was saying sink in. She nodded along, so far so good. "Some pre-date even then. The cross, for example, dated back to the third century, and I have once tracked down a shaman drum that predates Christ." He checked, she looked thoughtful. Final step.

"The thing is…a lot of importance will have been attached to these items. They will have been wielded for great power—and why they are wanted now is not in my remit to question."

There—he definitely saw her mind ticking over now. The next question was crucial.

"Are you telling me, Lee North, that you are a treasure hunter and I your trusty assistant?" She smiled, putting a hand to her mouth as though to stop it. Her eyes widened, and he saw fear glimmering deep down. "Like, Indiana Jones? But he got himself into a lot of trouble. No, you're not telling me that…are you?" All levity departed.

"I am. Yes. Not like Indiana Jones, but it is similar, what I do. What *we* do."

"Oh." It was a small noise, overshadowed by the powerful engines on the Boeing 747 deepening. She turned from him to gaze out the window, and he settled back for take-off, allowing her space to think.

He loved flying and often toyed with the idea of a private jet. The fleet of cars he owned was kept updated with the latest emission reducing schemes, and as soon as something wasn't required, he recycled it. But having a private jet flying when there were commercial airlines doing the same route didn't make sense.

But it didn't mean he was unhappy to pay for the ease a private jet would supply. They had waited in a private bar and, minutes before the plane was due to depart, were escorted to their seats. Mathew had handled the tickets, and both had been cleared through the Greek customs before they had taken off. What was the point of having money if you didn't use it to make life easier for all concerned?

When the engines leveled off and the Fasten Your Seatbelt light went off, a steward approached. "Would you like something to drink?"

"Ellora?"

She looked up. "Still water for me, thanks."

"And for you sir?"

"I'll have the same, thank you."

After he had served them their drinks, along with peanuts and olives, the steward produced two menus. "We'll be taking dinner orders in about half an hour."

"Thank you." she smiled at the man whilst he took the menus.

"Do you eat everything?"

Taking her menu, she smiled. "I'm a pescatarian."

"Through belief?"

"I guess. I stopped eating meat about ten years ago because…" She stopped and gave a short laugh. "You'll think I'm mad."

"Well if I do, too late. You've already signed the contract. I'm not sure there's a get-out-of-contract clause for being mad."

She laughed, but there was still an uncertainty pulling straight the edges of her mouth. "Health reasons, to be honest. I like the lighter vegetarian food and fish. It seems to suit me better. How about you?"

He didn't for one moment imagine she was telling him all the truth.

"I eat everything as long as it's organic and free range, to the best of my knowledge."

"Fair enough." She read the menu. "This is a nice choice though, a couple of fish dishes and a vegetarian meal."

He took the menu, already knowing if there was a burger, he'd have it. When the steward returned, they ordered separately, Ellora ordering the warm tiger prawns on a sesame and vegetable salad.

"The lighter the better I guess, as we've a long way to go. How about alcohol?"

She tapped her fingers—topped with neatly filed nails, complete with a clear polish—on the tabletop in front of her. "No, maybe not. You get very dehydrated on a long-haul flight, don't you? I think I'll limit myself to just one after dinner." Something about her accent sounded European, which he hadn't noticed before.

"Where are your parents from?"

He noticed a flicker of pain. "Dad was from Seattle, Mum from London, UK."

Was?

"Ah that will explain it then. Sometimes your accent sounds different."

She twisted to face him. "It took me a while to fit in at school. It took months for the other kids to stop repeating what I said in plummy voices."

A certain tightness around her mouth belied her light tone—any upsetting feelings weren't just about school. What was her story? His musing was interrupted by their steward setting out their placements for dinner, followed by their food.

She dipped her head over her plate. "Mmmm, smells really good."

He agreed, but inwardly decided it wasn't as good looking as his. They took some time to appreciate the food, then she glanced sideways.

"How about you, Lee?"

"What about me?"

"Well, you know a fair bit about me from my resumé and the interview. Where did you grow up? Were your parents native to America?"

"Both my parents were Irish American." Wiping his mouth with the serviette, he sat back and half turned towards her. "But my dad passed away when I was five, and after a couple of years, Mum met and fell in love with a first-generation Irish man. I was incredibly lucky that we both liked each other from the get-go, and that deepened into a respect and a love for each other."

He stopped abruptly—not believing the train his thoughts were taking. He has just said more to this new girl than he ever had on a first date. Fortunately, the steward came over and cleared their dishes. When both refused dessert, liquors were offered. He shook his head but then Ellora ordered a sambuca on ice.

"You were saying?"

He nodded, unsure as to going further with this train. Yet he had been ploughing in ready to share with her. Damn, but she had that rare quality that invited confidences, something only the best researcher possessed.

Her drink arrived, cloudy and intense in a bell-bottomed glass. It looked and smelled good enough for him to order himself one, and she smiled when he did, clinking glasses when his arrived.

"I do love me a sambuca." She smiled, and in that moment something happened. There was more light or something—had the reading lights above them come on? A quick glance told him no. But in her smile, pure mischief had emerged in the silver shine of her gray eyes.

The slanted smile of her mouth, the brief glimpse of devilry showing in the sideways glance from under her fringe. All was...what? Beautiful? No, attractive? Well yes but not quite the word he searched his brain for. Captivating. *That* was it.

He half-smiled, and for once, settled back knowing he would enjoy having Ellora Radley by his side for the foreseeable future.

****

Ellora enjoyed the fire of the sambuca, sipping it slowly and carefully. Being in this confined space with her treasure hunting boss was proving hard. Although she had to admit that first class provided a lot more room than economy, so her tray on the arm provided some space between them. Glancing up, she saw that a curtain rail surrounded her space, with the curtain pulled on the wall in front of her where her television screen was. This was as comfortable and as private as it could get on a plane.

Her first impressions of him hadn't held up, for she had been sure he was an abrupt man with little interest other than getting his own way, not caring if he got people's backs up. But after the day, she was open to changing her mind. He was both interesting and interested. Being honest with herself, she was unsure which she preferred. The uninterested Lee was a much safer man.

A delicious feeling squiggled in her stomach— nerves, excitement, or the sambuca? *Or something else, Ellora Radley?* Something inside her was reawakening, something she had thought she had dealt with in her early twenties. About to embark on a new career with a man who intrigued her, she sure as heck didn't need this now.

Sitting back, she closed her eyes and made an effort to breathe deeply but quietly. It helped quieten part of her mind but not all. She sat up and picked up her iPad to tinker around with it. In Notes was a list of various research sites and her password, along with IDs. Perfect distraction.

Opening her search engine, she plugged in "chalice, eagle, cross" and was soon lost in sorting the wheat from the chaff. She smiled inwardly; this was not going to be easy. Gradually the cabin lights dimmed, and staff wandered through with offers of eye masks and complimentary toiletries. After a stretch of her legs, she settled down to grab some sleep. *Yeah right, with Indy to your right—no problem.* A quick peek from her peripheral told her that Lee certainly *looked* to be sleeping, so she stretched out her seat into her bed in the hope that sleep would reach her.

"Sleep well, Ellora."

"Thanks. You too."

Chapter Five

Lee, nursing a black Americano, waited for Ellora to come down for breakfast. After tossing and turning all night, he had finally given up and come down to the dining room but hadn't wanted to eat properly until she joined him. They had arrived mid-afternoon Saturday, both tired and went to their separate rooms, with only plans to meet up this Sunday morning for breakfast.

Friday, on the airplane, it had been hard to concentrate, which was very unlike him. And he was unsure why. On Thursday morning, he had woken with an intention burning a hole in his stomach—he had to find her. Not knowing who she was, there was an image in his head of a black-haired researcher—where he had seen her was beyond him. It must have been at one or another of the many conventions that their job necessitated.

Certain she was a reality, he woke Jonathon up at 6:30 a.m. to instruct him to find this researcher and to make an appointment with her ASAP. Used to his varied demands, Jonathon hadn't turned a hair and had called back sharp at 8:00 a.m. to give him his appointment time. He had smiled, arrogantly in hindsight, when he rocked up at her dusty offices thinking she'd be a pushover for his glamorous company.

Still he didn't know why he wanted her working

for him. When her PA informed him haltingly that Ellora wasn't in, he nearly exploded in frustration. Driven by something he knew not what, he had intimidated her until she left him in her office, thereby offering access to her contacts. Once he had Ellora's address, he had left in a hurry to find her.

On the way, he had refused to examine why he was so bothered about this woman, but his mounting excitement was strange to him. For he rarely became excited about anything. He had watched as the city became the suburbs, and his driver had taken him into the thickly wooded suburbs in Arlington. The drive out by Lake Michigan was wonderful, and he caught himself wondering what it would be like through the changing seasons. But the sight of a very shapely derriere bent over an battered old MG at the end of a driveway drove all other thoughts far away.

Normally, new folk would be falling over themselves to work for him. Not this lady. She seemed remarkably insouciant about the opportunity to work for a firm as prestigious as NA. He was impressed. When he had left her house, he was none the wiser as to whether she would accept. But one thing he did know for sure—now they had made each other's acquaintance, he was going to damn well ensure they had some kind of a relationship. For looking into her eyes as deeply as he had dared, there was some kind of kinship between them. Just what it was, he did not know.

Now, a mere three days later, catching sight of her entering the dining room, he was sure of one thing and one thing only—his body and mind were stirring at the sight of her.

She had reached his table. His instinct was to stand, but he held himself back, instead gesturing to the chair. Keep it professional.

"Morning." A small smile fled her lips so fast he might've imagined it.

"Hi, Ellora. Did you sleep well?" He raised a hand to beckon the hovering waiter over.

"Yes, thank you. Did you?"

"Yes, thank you." Not taking into account the wild dreams, all with Ellora as the main character. Not something to tell her, perhaps.

"What can I get you to drink?" The waiter stood patiently by them, tablet in hand.

Lee looked questioningly at Ellora.

"Coffee, please."

He nodded in assent. "A pot of coffee then, please. Would you like toast?"

"No, I'm fine thanks. I'll have a look at the specialty breads. They smell very good from here."

He dismissed the waiter with a nod and standing up, waited for Ellora to join him, and they turned as one to walk towards the buffet tables. A brief moment of time stretched around them and kept them close as something whispered inside him, gone in a flash.

Separating from Ellora, he went in search of his own breakfast. Yet at all times, he was aware of her sleek black head and where she was in the room. A tall Greek stepped up close beside her at the rack of toasters, and Lee almost smelt his interest in Ellora. Something within him snarled and stretched as Ellora gave a brief glance in his direction. He felt her confusion from here, and it joined with his.

Having filled his plate with bacon and eggs, he

headed back to their table.

"Have you found anything out yet?" Hell, he sounded abrupt, something only confirmed by the startled look on her face, but there were too many things swimming about in his head to be concerned.

"I've made progress. Despite what you said about the archives last night I read through the processes, checked my access, and sent the appropriate alerts. I guess the company's log-in details tell the archive masters who you are?"

"They're supposed to, although I have my suspicions. Most museums aren't the most high tech of places and that worries me. But all you can do is warn them."

She played about with her mushrooms and buttered some toasted walnut bread on the side. "Is online security a big risk for the museums?"

"I believe so. Some museums, the more well-known—such as yours, for example—are pretty tight on security. Others appear to be in the dark ages." He gave a short laugh. "Like their exhibitions, I guess."

Ellora chewed on her toast before swallowing, a mischievous light entering her eyes. "Imagine if the energy in the things on display infected you—I used to wander around the museum, gazing at the display and sometimes got lost in my thoughts. But afterward, I wondered whether it was lost in my thoughts or being caught up in the display. Generally, I wouldn't remember what I had been thinking, it all seemed a bit like a dream, substantial enough at the time, but dissipated the more I tried to remember it."

Clattering her cup back into the saucer, she laughed. "But where would it stop? If, for example, you exhibit Neanderthal artifacts, do you communicate in grunts and nods? Take a stake everywhere for protection? But then when you left work, would you revert to normal, or would your partner see you marching up the garden path with a stave in hand, clutching a dead chicken by the neck?"

Her smiles were contagious.

"Barging in the door, shouting, 'Get thee upstairs, Deirdre, and prepare thyself.' " She laughed, opening her mouth to continue on, but stopped. A tension thrummed through the air as his mind took the scene forward, and she wiped her mouth with her serviette and sat back. *More's the pity.* He had enjoyed seeing her lighter self.

"Where were we? Archive security."

He refocused on work. "Yes, some deserve high tech surveillance. Like I say, some museums have it, for the more valuable items."

He wondered how much she knew about the other artifacts—the ones carrying meanings for entire tribes. Those were the priceless ones.

"Valuable in which respect?"

"Mainly in the money they would command. England's crown jewels, *The Card Players* by Cézanne, the Graff Pink diamond…all obvious in their expense and worth."

He leaned forward. "But then you have the others, the items carrying worth because of their past. Did you know there is a feather, a *feather* that is worth ten thousand dollars?

"No."

"From a huia bird, which is now extinct. It was used in Maori ceremonies. What a coup for you if you have that feather in your armistice. Think about it. If you could have anything you wanted—what would you buy? After you acquired the rich toys, where would you go from there?"

She shrugged.

"To the rarities, the things not easily obtained. The artifacts that were worshipped, and inspired hundreds, thousands of people, entire tribes. For those are the priceless ones. *Those* provide the challenge." He spoke quietly, feeling the rise of warmth through him.

Her eyes sharpened on his face.

"And if you were unscrupulous, along with being very wealthy, what would stop you getting what you want?" He stopped.

"This is your job then? Tracking down items for unscrupulous dealers?" Doubt clouded her gaze.

"Of course not." Yet even as he spoke, he felt her doubt like a contagion. He carried on, more forcefully. "I return items to their rightful communities—lost or stolen artifacts during times of unrest. With all my missions, I have been satisfied I returned them to their rightful owners. Part of my criteria is I myself hand it over, thus ensuring myself of the authenticity of ownership." *Yet what about Constantin?* A niggle refused to go away.

"To get back to your question about scrupulous, or otherwise, dealers, I don't know yet about Constantin. This is only the second artifact."

He found himself enjoying talking to her. He admired her open mind and idly wondered whether she was born curious. Sometimes, it was only hardship that opened folks' minds and enabled them to be accepting of all walks and customs.

"I don't know why he is looking for the chalice. Combined with the fact I don't know a lot about him, as he operates below the surface, I'm left feeling uneasy. I'm damn well sure Constantin isn't his real name. Yet, we have unlimited funds in exchange for absolute discretion."

"What else do you know about him?"

"Jonathon checked into his background when first he contacted me. Whatever Constantin's dealings are, they are all closely guarded. He found one article praising him for his altruistic tendencies but only from years back."

"So you have taken on work for someone whom you didn't entirely trust? You tracked down a precious artifact to place into his hands?"

Lee didn't like the accusatory tone and felt himself bridle.

"There's more to it than that." *Like what, North?* He changed the subject, pinning her with his eyes so she could not do anything other than follow this change.

"What have you found out so far?" He sat back in his chair, ignoring the swirl of his stomach as he faced up to the fact that he was being judged and found wanting.

"It's complicated, as the concept of the chalice has had different uses, and many different faiths have one in their armoire of artifacts. You have the classic— Jesus using the chalice at the Last Supper and hence at Christian Mass. Wine meant to represent his blood is sipped from chalices. Some stories say this chalice was used to collect his blood, but then the story gets mixed up with the Holy Grail from Arthurian legend. There is a lot to sift through. As of yet, nothing about eagles, crosses, and swirls."

He nodded. There was something pulling at his memory, and he tried to track down the root of the thought, but it was proving elusive.

She finished eating and pushed her plate from her, looking up in gratitude as the plate was whisked away and more coffee poured. At his nod, the waiter did the same for him and disappeared with quiet steps. Both picked up their coffee and took a sip before settling in.

"I've looked up the symbols themselves without any connection to a chalice." Her gray eyes sparkled silver as she placed the cup in the saucer with a clink, maintaining a steady eye contact. "Eagle. We have the obvious of the bald eagle being a symbol of America, representing freedom." She paused. "It doesn't feel right for here though—the chalice being clearly European and being forged in Neolithic times. Another belief is that eagles are metaphorical for the ability to fly high and be able to see problems from a distance, and deal with them before they manifest themselves. A personal favorite of mine talks about eagles being known to convey messages and prayers to the Great Spirit—the Great Spirit being a Native American term. But what is that doing on a seemingly Christian artifact?"

His mind whirled with all the possibilities. "What about the swirls?"

"I've searched up ancient religious swirls. Upon initial look, these appear Celtic and are called the *triskele*. If I have it right, of course. There are three swirls all interconnected at their center—kind of like three legs or arms coming out." She clicked on her iPad and swiveled it around to show Lee the screen. "This symbol was used in Neolithic times and is carved in the entrance rocks of Newgrange, which is a passage tomb in Ireland older than Stonehenge and the pyramids. I feel more convinced with this representation than the eagle symbolism."

"This is throwing the search far and wide. We have, what, Christianity, Celtic mythology, Arthurian mythology, and shamanism?"

She looked sharply at him. "Do you know much about shamanism?"

"A bit. What about the cross?"

"Searching for anything about a cross is just like looking for a needle in a haystack, so until we get some traction on the other symbols, I'm not getting too excited about that one."

Slowly, she focused her gaze on him, and in the depths he saw something fleeting, gone before he identified it. But it made his stomach lurch. He eyed her.

He nodded slowly. "Good work so far. How much do you know about shamanism?"

She glanced sideways and sat back with a wry smile. He found he missed her open look.

"I don't know. I've read the basics. But something inside resonates with the words. I feel like it's something I already know, but I just don't know how. It's like…" She looked around the room as though looking for the words. "Like déjà vu, only instead of vu, it's déjà knew. Ha." She laughed.

He stared. She was a constant surprise. A warm flush ran through him, and the more he thought about it, the more he realized he knew exactly what she was talking about. He felt the same, only it was that he had somehow known Ellora before he met her. Déjà knew. He laughed aloud, tickled.

The sound broke the spell and she pushed her hair back from her face, showing him a faint flush. She broke eye contact and with grace and economy, she rose from her chair, pulling her purse from where it hung on the back. "Shall we head to the executive lounge? And on the way, I'll grab the Mac."

"I'll meet you there." He shot back his cuff to check his watch. "I want to make some phone calls."

Before his first number was dialed, she had shimmied through the restaurant doors.

"Philippe, how are you?"

"What do you want, Lee? More trouble?" Belying the words was a joking tone. The two men went back a long way—treasure hunters experienced enough to know the times when two heads were better than one, when to back off, and when to watch the other's back.

"Exactly. I'm on the trail again."

"What can I do?"

"I'd prefer to do this in person."

"Sure, are you in Athens?"

"Yes, I flew in yesterday."

"Excellent timing, my friend. The annual masked ball at the Acropolis is on tonight, come along. Imelda will get an invite for you. Come, we can have a chance to talk and you can see who else to mine for information."

"My assistant, Ellora Radley, is with me."

"Bring her. Tonight, Acropolis, nine thirty. I'll see you there."

He disconnected and sat, tapping his phone idly against his lip. He couldn't have asked for a better start to this trail. All the important people in the world would be there tonight. Would Constantin?

Chapter Six

"Tonight? We are going to a ball, at the Acropolis tonight? Seriously?" Her blood froze.

"Yes, the masked ball."

Lee practically drawled the words, a gauntlet clearly shown in his direct gaze. They had been working together, going through files and archives for the past three hours, and now he saw fit to tell her?

"What time?"

"We're due there at nine thirty. I'll meet you in the lobby at nine. I need to check on the guest list. Oh, you need a mask, by the way." He rose.

"Wait, Lee..."

He looked back and cocked an eyebrow.

"Um, never mind." How did she sound so relaxed? Calm was the furthest thing from her mind. What the *hell* was she going to wear? She waited until he had departed the executive lounge, then rose and hurried over to the mirror. Large worried gray eyes looked back, scouring her hair.

Her hair, what was she going to do with her hair? Although to be fair, that was probably the least of her worries. Nothing she had brought with her would do— yes, she had the black dress, but this was a ball, for pity's sake. She wouldn't go, she'd make her excuses. *But it's a ball...at the Acropolis.*

A passing waiter stopped, "Are you all right,

61

miss?"

"I'm fine, but thank you." She smiled, then stopped. "Actually, I need some help please."

Name badge marking him as Markos, he was a handsome twenty-something with dark eyes and darker hair. "Of course, what would you like?"

"Some local knowledge. I've just been told I'm attending a ball tonight, and I have nothing suitable. Do you know of any place open on a Sunday?"

"At the Acropolis?" Markos's eyes widened and a look of respect came into them.

She nodded, nerves gathering force within her at his reaction.

Putting his iPad on the table, he perched on the sofa in front of her. "Not a lot is open on a Sunday."

This day was getting worse.

"But my aunt owns a boutique two streets away from here. I'll ring her and see if she will open."

"Please, please do."

He rose and went to speak to his manager at the desk, and soon both men were looking over. The older man nodded, and Markos pulled out his mobile phone. He spoke and nodded enthusiastically, gesticulating wildly. She forgot to breathe as she watched him coming back. This was insane, the way her life had changed dramatically since banging her head—she almost laughed aloud—perhaps she had entered an alternate universe, and actually, her body was lying unconscious in a hospital bed somewhere.

"Yes, miss, she is going there as we speak. Now…" He sat again. "There is a beauty salon in the hotel. I have checked, and they will stay open late so they can squeeze you in at seven."

"Markos, I could kiss you. Thank you for your consideration." Thank god for Markos and her savings, which would be almost depleted. She thought with regret of the new engine on order for her MG, then pushed it from her mind with the realization of her new salary. Hell, she could have a new dress, a new hair style, *and* a new engine if she wanted.

She stood and Markos accompanied her through the lobby and out the round doors. She blinked in the bright sunshine as he pointed her down the street.

"It's called Bella's and is on the left-hand side two streets away. You cannot miss it."

"Thank you, Markos."

"For a beautiful woman, anything." Taking her hand, he bowed over it and dropped a quick kiss on the back of her palm. "I look forward to seeing you later."

Laughing at the mischievous look in his eyes, she took off, hoping against hope something suitable was waiting to be found in Bella's. Did they sell shoes too? And what about bags? And wraps and *oh*, her mind was going to explode.

Hurrying along, she saw a woman ahead unlock a shop. She quickened her pace and caught up just as the door was swinging shut. She blocked it and smiled at the petite woman, mid-fifties she guessed, pitch-black hair in a bun with a blue flower to the side. Dressed in a flowing caftan, she was pretty with a wide smile.

"I am Marianne, you must be the lady from the hotel."

"Yes, yes I am. Thank you for opening for me. I really appreciate it."

"Markos told me you were going to the ball tonight. It is a very big affair, and you must be dressed appropriately. He is naughty, no? The man who is taking you? Most people spend months planning what they are going to wear and getting their masks made."

Whilst she talked, she was walking around Ellora, eyeing her up with a professional air. "Good. You have a neat and easy-to-dress figure. Sit, sit." She pointed to a dusky pink velvet chaise lounge laid out in front of the floor-to-ceilings windows. To the right were racks and racks of brightly colored items, but the high ceilings of the shop decluttered the space.

"As we don't have time to do the, how do you call it, bright colors and feathers and bows?"

Relief. "Flamboyant?"

"Yes, flamboyant." Marianne rolled her tongue around the word in delight. "We must go classic."

Great, classic was perfect. Ellora rose to look through the dresses hanging in groups around the shop.

"No, you sit." Clearly things operated differently here in Greece. Obediently, she sat back.

Marianne chatted on, her voice increasingly muffled as she stuck her head through the different racks, telling her about the various celebrities she had in the previous week. Gulping, Ellora rose to check the prices on the dresses close to her. *Phew.* Having a low value euro was going to stand her in good stead here.

"Now take a look at these."

The woman was good, and she relaxed infinitesimally. She had a collection of dresses, ranging in colors from black through to red, which she hung on an empty rack beside her.

"First impressions?" Marianne snapped her fingers. She rose, feeling ever so slightly heady. Never before had she been out shopping for such a luxurious dress. In fact, never before had she had a personal shopper. Tentatively, she ran her fingers through the various materials, enjoying the slip and shine as she pulled each one out. The red was a no-go, she would never wear such a bright color. Marianne tutted as she shook her head.

"Red would be the best for you, your coloring. You're making a mistake."

"Not for me, Marianne, red is too much. Now, this, this is much more up my street." She took out the dark turquoise satin and held it against her.

"This is good—go, try it out."

The dressing rooms were behind Marianne, large and airy with white blinded doors. Feeling as though the satin would be the one, she only took it in. Her suddenly very ordinary clothes shed, she stepped into the dress, pulling it up over the hips. A 60s-inspired dress with a square neckline, dropped waist, and a flared skirt, she knew the minute she put it on she didn't want it. It was too much for her, despite the color being good.

"Come, let me see." The imperious tone in Marianne's voice propelled her out the door. Standing with her arms crossed, Marianne's gaze narrowed. "No, I don't like. The color, yes. The style, no, it is not you. Here." She scooped up the black silk that Ellora had only skimmed over in her decision to eschew black for once, and pushing past her, hung it up in the dressing room.

On the hangar, it looked a little limp, but she shrugged out of the satin and pulled the silk over her head, struggling to find the arm holes, hidden as they were within the wide scooped neckline. A delightful shiver ran through her as she zipped up the side, feeling the silk hug her curves yet not too tightly.

"Come." Again, Ellora almost fell over herself to obey Marianne, but as she sashayed—for there was no other way to walk in the dress—she caught sight of herself in the mirror beyond and stumbled to a halt.

The scooped and ruched wide neckline came to a halt just on the bones of her shoulder, dipping to her collarbone. Below the layers, the material fell to her waist, not clinging but not loose—just right—affording her the ability to move with ease and then fell to the floor in a graceful fold. Only by looking very carefully would anyone see the panels sewn in, and with movement, the dress caressed and kissed her legs. It was simply divine and she couldn't take her eyes off it.

Marianne clapped her hands. "You are beautiful. Very beautiful." She laughed as she looked at Ellora, her color now high. "Accessories, we need accessories. What jewelry do you have?"

Her heart sank. "Beyond my crystal bracelets and rings, not much else."

Marianne held one arm folded, balancing the other elbow on it, and tapping a finger idly against her mouth. "Well, let us see. We need a mask first. Perhaps no jewelry would suffice. Being so pretty, you don't need it. Nor is there anywhere a lot of flesh which would need distraction. Have you shoes and a bag?"

"I have both, plain and simple. Nude patent high heels and a simple envelope clutch."

"Good, good, they will go well." Marianne started through the back of her shop, then stopped. "Come, you must pick."

Together they headed out back and through a small

doorway secreted into the wall. She gasped as Marianne switched the lights on. Masks of all shapes and sizes glittered and glimmered, ranging from the sheer provocative to the full-on headdresses, the kind you would expect to see in Buenos Aires for the festivals. Marianne laughed at her amazement. "Would you like to try one on?"

She felt like a kid in a sweet shop. "Yes, please." Taking the largest and most ornate one, she carefully pushed the green and red feathers back.

Marianne cautioned, "Stand firm, for it is heavy."

She stood like a statue, feeling an immense weight settle on her head. "Wow, it's heavy. Why would you put yourself through it?"

"Take a look at yourself and you'll see."

Cautiously turning her head, she forgot to breathe as she stared at the exotic creature looking back. It wasn't her, it was some exotic bird of paradise—haughty, aloof, and mysterious. She felt a squiggle in her stomach as she stared into her own eyes, not recognizing herself.

It was mocking in a *you don't know when you have it good* kind of way, and shivers started down her back. A shadow passed through her own eyes as she watched, and suddenly the weight of the headdress pressed too hard as she felt a lack of oxygen in the air.

"Please, Marianne, take it off."

Marianne seemed to hear the high-pitched panic and in smooth and well-practiced movement, swept the headdress off.

"You are pale."

"I'm okay." She passed a hand over her eyes, squeezing them shut, trying to shut out the shadow she had seen. "Do I have to wear a mask?"

"For the ball, yes, you do. There is an unmasking at midnight, after which you have the choice of whether to wear it or not."

"Just something simple then, please." *Something that doesn't change me into something I don't recognize.*

"How about this one?" After scouring the shelves, Marianne showed her a simple mask fastening at the back of the head. "You would need to get it fitted at the hairdresser, but after the unmasking, you then fasten this rod to the side so you can place it up or lower it over your face. It would be better should you not have to carry it all night though."

"You're right." She squashed the uncomfortable feeling and allowed Marianne to attach it for her. Taking a deep breath, she glanced in the mirror only briefly. If she had to wear a mask, then she would, but she was scared to see a shadow once more. It sufficed. Quickly she pulled it off to Marianne's disappointment.

"My darling, I did not see it properly."

"Sorry, Marianne, my jet lag is catching up with me." Yes, that must be it.

"You poor dear." Marianne patted her familiarly on the arm. "We must get you finished in order for you to have a quick sleep before tonight. So…" She stepped back. "You do not need jewelry, except perhaps for a thin diamond bracelet on one arm and long drop diamond earrings, as your hair will be back off your face. Do you have such an item?"

"Er, no, Marianne. Do I look the type to wear diamonds?"

Marianne didn't smile, returning her look instead

with a concerned gaze. "I cannot have you at the ball without the proper accessories. The man who is taking you, would he buy them for you?"

She laughed. "It's my boss, Marianne, not a date."

Marianne frowned. "You cannot be looking this good and not be on a date. This boss, what is he like?"

Ellora felt warmth suffuse her. "About thirty, I guess. Tall, broad, amazing amber eyes, sharp cheekbones." Conscious her hand had crept up to caress her own face, she blushed harder. Marianne looked pleased.

"Definitely we need the diamonds. Bon." She nodded. "I will lend you some."

"Marianne, no. Absolutely not."

"Absolutely you will. There will be cameras." She gesticulated wildly. "You might be in the magazines; you have to do it properly."

Looking at the other woman, now with her hand pressed to her heart, she capitulated. Then the nerves started anew. "Cameras? Magazines?"

"Come, nerves are not the accessory to wear with this dress. This dress requires confidence, and clearly it is your dress. Yours to wear. You were meant to come and fetch it today. It fits you perfectly, and more so, it brings out something mysterious and something special about you. Wear your head held high, and do not let me down."

As Marianne spoke, she was getting changed, her mind whirling. Yes, Marianne was right, but god help her, she had never worn such a dress before, never been in such a situation before, and her head spun with her new boss, new job, and jet lag.

Marianne bustled about, pulling a dress carrier over

69

the dress for her. "I shall ring the hotel and tell them to send a courier to pick this up for you, along with the mask. The diamonds shall be there once I get home to send them out."

Once she was dressed back in her lovely comfortable clothes, she went to settle up. Seeing her hesitation, Marianne placed an age-spotted hand on hers. "You are beautiful, both within and without—do not forget it. Break free. There is something about you, Miss Radley. We will meet again. If you need me, come to me." The last words were spoken gently, and Ellora looked at her sharply, but Marianne's attention was on her till.

With tired legs, she made her way back to the hotel. She had forty-five minutes before her hair appointment at 7 p.m.—just time for a power nap, followed by a glorious shower. She idly contemplated going downstairs in her dressing gown for her appointment, but her insides shriveled as she pictured bumping into Lee. *Lee.* What would he be wearing tonight? A tuxedo? Her insides flipped at the thought of him in a tux and a mask. *Best not to think about it.* She'd be confronting the reality soon enough.

****

Lee placed his phone on the table with a sigh. He hadn't been able to find anything out about the chalice. Something wasn't right. Normally it was hard uncovering details, but this? This was practically farcical.

He picked up his whiskey. Nine on the dot and they had to leave in fifteen minutes. He resisted the urge to rub his frontal lobes where his mask pressed. Since arriving in the bar, he had received deferential treatment—clearly, he was someone important enough to be going to the event of the year. Only two other guests, both male, sported masks.

He watched as they stood to greet their guests, tall blonde women dressed in burgundy and indigo. Attractive women were always rendered beautiful when wearing masks, although he didn't care much for the over-the-top nature of these two. Wondering what Ellora would be wearing, he recognized excitement in his anticipation. A hush fell.

The most beautiful woman gazed around the bar calmly, faint smile playing on her lips. Impossibly sleek in a dress which clung in all the right places, she stepped out with confidence towards him, a clutch in one hand, the other holding up her skirts. His vision narrowed in on only her, his hearing muted to only the sound of her breath escaping her lips, and something deep inside him growled in appreciation. Nostrils flaring, he picked up her scent as she moved ever closer, an unrecognizable scent but now filed away under *hers*. Hers and hers alone.

It was mild and heady all at once. Time slowed as silver eyes sparkling behind the rich black velvet of her mask gazed deeply into his, long-lashed dark lashes briefly shading her gaze. A look that took eternity, he felt her reach out and know him, just as he knew her.

He stood and kissed her on both cheeks, making an enormous effort to step back and appear composed. She called to mind a panther—sleek, smooth, and impossibly beautiful. Hair piled high on her head with escaped tendrils made her appear taller. Long drop diamond earrings like shooting stars swayed nearly caressing her neck, and he quelled the impulse to reach in and drop a kiss in the hollow of her neck.

"You are beautiful, Ellora." He had known of her beauty, of course, but tonight, it was like he was seeing a new person.

"Thank you. You look good too, Lee. I like your mask." She gave a light smile and turned her attention to the bartender whose attention was glued to her.

"Sambuca, please."

"Certainly, single or double?"

"Single thanks, no ice."

Glancing around, Lee realized everyone watched her. Scowling, he stood closer and leaned on the bar, shielding her from prying eyes. *She was his.*

The bartender placed a shot glass on the polished mahogany bar, and with an expert flick of his wrist, upended the bottle, filled the glass, and pushed it to Ellora.

"Thank you." In one smooth movement, she picked up the glass and threw the shot back, her neck almost swanlike in the light. An ache woke within him and he swallowed deeply. *Haul those thoughts back Lee my friend. It's work tonight. Work only ever with this woman.* He acknowledged the words, but they rang false. There was something about her which spoke to him, made him feel like a missing piece of the puzzle had been found.

Conscious she had asked him something, he pulled his attention back. Gambling it was what time they had to leave, he shot back his cuff to see the time.

"Five minutes."

"I like your mask. Where did you get it?"

"I'm always prepared. Masks, handcuffs, you know the way."

Emotion tensed through the air and he heard her catch her breath. He stared into her eyes, wondering had the same image appeared in her head as in his? Judging by the dilated pupils, he figured it had. Her scent appeared once more and he inhaled greedily, yet circumspectly, feeling his body stir and move towards her at the same time as a hand went out to her back. Encountering only bare flesh, his mouth went dry. Lowering his head to her ear, "Is your dress backless?"

She pulled back only enough to meet his eyes. Heavy lidded, they were hypnotic. Without withdrawing, she nodded. Moving the hand on her back around her waist, he searched and found her right hand and gently tugged on it. Surprised, she let him, stepping back and allowing him to unravel her. He had thought the dress magnificent upon seeing the front, but as her creamy back was revealed to him, he had to stamp hard on the desire threatening to burn him up. Had he ever felt the need to devour a woman as he did her? Actually, had there ever been any other women before Ellora Radley? Hearing a low cough, he swung irritated to the courier standing there.

"Excuse me sir, but your car is here." Damn, the ball. He was going to have to share her with half of Athens when all he wanted to do was immerse himself in her. Feeling something fierce rise in him, he nearly growled at the courier when he saw how he was smiling and ingratiating himself to Ellora. Who, to give her credit, didn't seem to notice. Instead, she smiled and placed a hand on his upper arm.

"Let's go."

As one they turned to the door, their steps falling into place together instantly. Unable not to, he allowed his hip to touch hers as they fluidly moved.

Just enjoy this moment. And enjoy it he did, walking into the lobby and feeling all eyes on her, this glorious creature gliding by his side. The limousine's driver stood with the back door open, doffing his cap when they approached.

"Mr. North, Ms. Radley." He handed Ellora into the car and walked around to get in the other side. When he got in, she had arranged herself against the creamy leather, half turned towards him.

"It is only five minutes away, sir. Help yourself to a drink." The partitioning glass rose again, leaving them in privacy.

"Would you like a drink?"

"No, thank you."

"I've had a look through the guest list, and it is quite comprehensive. You network and I'll take up the trail of the chalice tonight."

She nodded. "I shall leave it to you then to ask questions. I'll just make contacts and find out what I can about the running of the archives."

"Good. I might ask you to do some follow-ups if I find someone we can trust."

"Would they open up to me?"

"As you're with me, yes. You might have more luck than me, too."

"And why would that be, Mr. North?"

"If the person in question is a man." He gave her a half smile. "Actually, you may be getting attention from both genders tonight."

She smiled and turned to watch as the car slowed to join the queuing cars dropping off their guests. Glancing past her, he saw ancient Greek columns bedecked in lights cleverly placed behind flowers, casting a mystical glow upon the Acropolis. He also saw Ellora swallow, and the way she plucked at her clutch.

"Ellora, there is no need to worry. I know this is all new to you. Just stay by my side until you feel comfortable and you'll be fine."

She nodded, but her sparkling eyes were overshadowed. Reaching into her clutch, she pulled out her lipstick and compact mirror, quickly painting already glossy lips. Watching her, he was conscious of a paradox—he wanted to see her entire face at the same time as delighting in the mystery the mask cast.

The car purred to a halt, and she winced as the flashes of the cameras filled the air. "Don't worry, the photographing only lasts as long as it takes to walk up the steps."

Judging by the worried look she gave the red carpeted steps, he knew she was calculating how long it would take.

"You'll be with me. And once they"—he nodded to the paparazzi—"understand we're nobodies, they'll leave us alone." *Hopefully.* He gave her hand a reassuring squeeze before stepping out his side of the limo, indicating to their driver he would open Ellora's door for her.

As she stepped out, just like he knew they would, the cameras swung to face her. Security from the Acropolis stepped forward and nodded to him, relaying in a professional manner should he need them, they were there, but otherwise they would remain in the background.

Ellora placed her hand in the crook of his arm, and

out of the corner of his eye, he saw her shoulders go back and her head hold high. *She rocks!*

Chapter Seven

"Who are you?" A reporter in a red dress fired the question. Lee smiled vaguely in her direction, both neglecting to answer. Once he calculated they had stood there for enough photos, he gently squeezed her hand in the crook of his arm to alert her to the fact they were on the move and stepped out once more together. Her hand was light on his arm as she maneuvered the steps, again holding her dress high in case of tripping.

When they reached the summit, replete with vast white and gold gates ahead, he whispered, "Ready." As one, they tuned in to each other and out to face the crowds, Lee using the opportunity to place his hand on her lower back. A shiver ran through her. Flashes popped in their faces, and after one long second, they turned and headed through the gateways.

A gasp escaped her. "It's beautiful." Her eyes were wide as she gazed around, the ruins being lit up cleverly with creeper plants and roses draping the columns. Without a roof, Orion strode across the night sky, the three sisters keeping a close eye on procedures. At the far end and to the right was an orchestra playing Vivaldi's *Four Seasons*, and there were speakers camouflaged behind the columns. Impeccably dressed waiters and waitresses stepped throughout the crowds, weaving their way with trays held over the heads, white-gloved hands holding them aloft with ease. Two servers proffered their trays.

"Champagne, rose champagne or a non-alcoholic cocktail, madam, sir? Or I can get you something else if you'd prefer."

Ellora wrinkled her nose and he smoothly interjected, "A sambuca for the lady and a whiskey, no ice for me, please."

She smiled. "Ice with the sambuca, please." The waiter bowed and walked off, whilst another took his place with a tray of canapés.

"Not for me, thanks." He waved the waitress away, Ellora following suit, and taking her hand, moved them away from the entrance. Now they had made their entrance and people knew they were together, he wanted to remain low-key. He guided them over to the touch screens to enter their names in order to see where they would be seated for dinner. He quietly groaned when he saw where Philippe had sat them.

To be fair to his friend, he was trying to be helpful, for Julian Zenon was the person to ask about the Acropolis's archives. But he was a loud man, fond of a drink, and he didn't want the entire table—a quick count saw there were twelve—to overhear their conversation. Although Ellora was beside him, a fact he didn't know whether to be glad of or worried about, Zenon being a man known for chasing skirt. Yet to his right was his wife, a formidable and statuesque woman, who displayed territorial traits whenever attractive females were in the area. It could go either way.

The waiter returned with their drinks and he raised his to hers in a silent salute. She nodded back and took a sip.

"Why sambuca?"

"Misspent youth. Why the whiskey?"

"I like the burn."

She held his gaze longer than was strictly necessary, enabling him to witness shadows lurking behind the crystal clearness.

"Is everything okay?"

She bit her upper lip. "Yes. I'm good. What's the plan?"

Seeing Philippe in the background, Lee stood back and nodded to him. The other man smiled and came over.

"Lee, I wasn't sure it was you. These masks confound me sometimes. Good to see you again." The other man grabbed him by the forearms and pulled him in for a bear hug, pounding him heartily on the back. "And this must be Ellora." He took the hand Ellora offered and, bowing over it, dropped a kiss on the back of her palm. Standing back, his appreciation for Ellora was clear in his gaze before he glanced to his right to a tall redhead who had stepped up.

"Lee, you know my wife, Imelda."

She gave him a warm smile before lightly pressing her masked cheek to his.

"Of course, Imelda, how are you?"

"I'm wonderful, thank you. And this must be Ellora?" She proffered a slim hand to Ellora who shook it warmly. "Oh come, here in Athens, we kiss." Doing the same cheek thing, she then tucked her arm into Ellora's. "You are beautiful. Shall I show you around and introduce you to everybody? Bye-bye boys, do miss us."

Imelda blew them both a kiss and took Ellora off.

"Thanks for arranging this, Philippe. I appreciate

it."

"Have you seen your table? I hope Zenon keeps quiet, but two people dropped out this morning directly after your phone call and Imelda filled the gap. I hope Ellora doesn't bring the worst out in him. Just your researcher, you say?"

The sharp planes in the other man's face told Lee that nothing escaped him. Hence why he was such a good treasure hunter. "I've only known her since Friday."

Surprise showed in the quick frown. "You two look as though you were made to be together. Are you sure, or are you just kidding me?" The other man's voice was teasing, and he found it hard not to laugh.

"I'm pretty sure this is the first time we've met." *In this lifetime, anyway.*

The other man's eyes held a knowing look. "Okay then, let's see who else can I introduce you to. Anybody you want to meet?"

"Zenon is covered. How about Diablo? And Philippe, do you know a man called Constantin?"

Philippe gazed unseeingly to the right. "I know a few, yes, but none involved in this world. One is a gardener, the other a fisherman. It's a very common name."

Much as he had thought. "Have you heard anything about a third century chalice recently?"

"You'll have to give me more—chalices are quite commonplace."

"One with eagles and swirls engraved upon it?"

Philippe pursed his lips and inclined his head slightly. Lee took the opportunity to glance around the rapidly filling room and spotted a few acquaintances. A sudden impression of being watched assailed, and he glanced upward into the rafters. Nothing but a slight shadow shifted.

"Can you tell me anything more?"

"Not yet."

"Eagles are quite commonplace in the spiritual world. Could be shamanic, and the swirls too. How much do you know about their beliefs?"

"A bit."

"After the ball, have breakfast with Imelda and me. The pair of you. Imelda is the one to speak to regarding shamanic practices. In the meantime, I'd point you in the direction of the Siberian curator. I'll speak to Imelda and ask her who else would be worth talking to."

"Thanks, can we make it brunch though? We only flew in last night and Ellora is shattered, so I don't think we can come straight to you after the ball."

"No problem. Sure she's just your researcher?"

He laughed, avoiding the question. "Thanks."

As both men scoured the crowd, they saw Ellora and Imelda emerge from behind a column, laughing. They made a striking pair—Ellora all in black, tall and panther-like; Imelda the same height, red hair piled on her head, her clingy deep green velvet dress the perfect foil for Ellora's black silk. Heads turned as they made their way through the crowd to stop by a group of men, who quickly stepped back to allow them in.

"They can go places we'd never get to, my friend." Philippe smiled, and clapping him on the back, led him into the crowd.

****

Imelda's ready laugh, her easy chat, and her

welcoming nature were intoxicating. After they had visited the powder room, Imelda had leaned into her. "Philippe told me you were here working with the delicious Lee. You lucky girl." She had sighed, smiled, and turned her direct green gaze on Ellora. "I am happy with my Philippe."

Ellora glanced up at Lee, chatting to Philippe. Mistakenly, she had thought she'd never be able to pick him from a crowd of dinner jackets and masks. Even with her eyes closed, she'd be able to see him, as his unmistakable presence seemed to shine and beckon.

Earlier, upon entering the bar, something inside told her to pause in the doorway and breathe before entering. Which was just as well, for when she actually turned her gaze onto him, all the oxygen in her lungs departed. Immediately. Standing tall, broad shoulders filling out his dinner jacket, the perfect cut telling her it was bespoke.

The mask—where the hell had he gotten that mask—a neat black one, the slanted cut sitting high on his cheekbones. As she got closer, amber eyes turned as the holes cut in the mask made his eyes appear all knowing and powerful. Inside, she quivered with anticipation of being near him, of smelling him, of stepping into his presence.

How she managed to hold it together, she would never know, but Marianne's words about confidence being the only necessary accessory to this dress flitted through her mind. The touch of his bare hand, the whispers of words in her ear, all had created delicious and fiery feelings in her belly. And now, only now, when she was safely apart from him did she dwell briefly on them. Only briefly, he was her boss after all.

How the hell was she going to do this?

"Darling, who shall I introduce you to? Oh, I see Zenon, he's sitting at your table, beside you. Let's start there."

Imelda led her expertly through the crowd, greeting most with a smile, sometimes stopping to say hello, but never staying long enough for Ellora to join in. As she approached the group of men, she whispered in Ellora's ear whilst never taking her eyes from their target. "Zenon, he's a bit of a creep. It's a good idea to let him know we're friends, hence the introduction. Behind his front is a very sharp mind. He controls what comes in and goes out of the archives, so if possible, befriend him. But be careful, his wife is formidable and won't take too kindly to you."

She straightened her back and lifted her chin. If she had thoughts of home and best friends and warm fires with nothing *formidable*, then she sure as heck wasn't going to show it.

She was done up to the nines and with a mask on. Dressed to kill, if the look on Lee's face when she entered the bar was anything to go by. And it was rather exciting to wear a mask. She was whoever she wanted to be. Right now, she had to rise to the occasion and use the mask—be the intriguing creature that Marianne intimated.

"Bring it on, Imelda."

Imelda measured a glance; whatever she saw must've reassured her, for she brightened and carried them onwards.

"Gentlemen, how are you all?" In a clear voice designed to travel, Imelda announced their arrival. Upon seeing both women, the men hastily stepped back, allowing room in their circle for the new arrivals.

"Gustav, Dirk, Julian, Martin, I would like you to meet my very good friend, Ellora Radley, from the US. Ellora, these are the only gentlemen in Athens you need know."

Graciously working her way around the circle, Imelda smiled and air kissed them all. From the corner of her eye, Ellora saw more than one man make a futile grasp towards her but Imelda managed to dance effortlessly away from more contact than was strictly necessary.

After she had met four sets of narrowed eyes, Ellora found herself beside the man called Julian. He turned to her fully and grasped her hands between pudgy fingers, raising it to his lips. "Julian Zenon, at your service, Madam." He planted a squidgy kiss on her hand, and she had to quell the desire to pull away and wipe it off. Much as she couldn't shake it, she could just see him clutching a fat cigar and was sure he would normally be seen with one. In fact, glancing around the group, they all looked like cigar smokers, slightly overweight with their waistcoats straining to hold their barrel-like stomachs in. But it wasn't just the physical nature of the men, there was a pack-like mentality and she just knew these men were linked.

Unspeakable acts of cruelty were their common domain.

Glancing around once more, the air softened, and once more, the men looked just like normal, slightly misguided men. Still vaguely nauseated, she looked to Imelda for her cue. Seeing the way she stood slightly out of the circle, yet employed her hands and gestures to full effect—which made it look as though she was immersed fully with the men at the same time as bringing her space—she took a half step back.

"What brings a beautiful American like you to our shores?"

"My new boss is an antiques dealer, and I am his researcher. Sometimes he requires me to join him on a trip. And, I have to say, I have no objections at all." She smiled briefly, planning the next question. If she had him pegged right, he wouldn't listen to what she said anyway but was just waiting for the opportunity to talk about himself. Lee had said he would be asking the questions tonight, so it was down to her to start building relationships. Handing the conversation over, she gave him control. "And what is it you do, Señor Zenon?"

"Please, call me Julian." He bustled on, clearly impressed with his own authority. "I run the archives here." Pale eyes watched her, putting her in mind of a baleful cat. "If you like, I can show you around."

I'll bet you can. She nodded noncommittally, hoping he wouldn't push her, for alienating him this early would be a huge impasse. "And what is normally kept in the archives?"

"My dear, do you know much about antiquities?"

She plastered an ingenuous smile. "Not a lot. We do have a show we can stream online, what is it called? Antiques Art Show or something? No, you don't know it?" If she had angled it right, he would be affronted at her implication that he only did something superficial. He would want to show her his importance, and she wanted to keep him talking.

Julian shook his head impatiently. "No no, my dear, they only hunt valuable resources. No, *my* archives are full of resources, which are valuable for an entirely different reason. They are full of the kinds of things with immense cultural significance; therefore, no price can be on their head. Think, Miss Radley, and I'm sure you can call to mind several things you wouldn't sell for love nor money."

Eh no, Fatty. Don't patronize me. But he had responded how she wanted him to.

She widened her eyes. "I guess, looking back at what my parents left me, I wouldn't allow those things to be out of my belongings. Things like their wedding rings."

"The very thing." He boomed his agreement back to her. "Wedding rings. They don't cost a lot, now do they, but the value is in what they represent. Power comes from what we as humans attach to things. A stone, a cross, all are meaningless until somebody attaches importance to them."

"Yes, I see. But why would anyone else think they're valuable? Take the wedding rings, for example. Priceless to my parents, but no one else. What would be the point in saving them?"

"Would you not value them?"

"Well, yes I would. But only because of my parents. I certainly wouldn't put them into a vault to save."

"I see your point, young lady. But what if for generations these wedding rings had been used? Your great-great-great-great-grandparents, for example, saved up all their money and bought them. Then they got handed down throughout the generations. And let's say none of the marriages broke up, everyone was happy, and life was good. Now would you attribute any power to them? Or if not, but if you were getting married, would you not want those rings for yourself and your spouse?"

She nodded. "I'm getting the picture. Your vaults are full of items of similar importance."

He smiled. "Now imagine it's not just your family who place importance on these objects, imagine it was entire communities, perhaps even countries."

She nodded obediently along, but something rebelled inside her.

"Taking into account what you've just said, how much power do these things have if they are no longer with their communities? Take for example, oh I don't know, a cross. If it were used in religious ceremonies by say, the Vatican. If it were here and no longer there, would it have any power? Does any power an item has still have it if the person or people who imbued it, as it were, is not with it? Going back to the wedding rings, no one would know upon looking or touching them that I deem them to have such power. Therefore, the rings don't have power."

"You're saying power only exists because people believe it?"

Back down. "I'm only talking about artifacts. Not power in general."

This man's eyes gave her the creeps. Droop lidded with deep wrinkles around them caused them to appear embedded in his head like stones, incapable of showing any expression. He opened his mouth to reply when, like magic, she felt Imelda appear behind her.

"Gentlemen, I must take Ellora away as the bell for dinner is about to be rung. Until later." She treated each man to a bright smile before directing Ellora away.

"I overheard a lot. Beware of him, he will try and

trip you up. If you and Lee stumble at all, he'll be on you like a ton of bricks. He thinks he's one of the most powerful men in Europe, so keep the conversation light and away from personal beliefs."

"Okay, thanks. He did dive straight into the deep and meaningful."

"He knows exactly how to turn the conversation emotional and will endeavor always to do so to get you on the back foot."

As Imelda predicted, three light chimes sounded throughout the Acropolis, and the loud hum of conversation lessened as folk split up in search of tables. Ellora breathed deeply. Her conversation with Zenon rattled her—she wasn't looking forward to sitting beside a man who enjoyed winding people up.

She said goodbye to Imelda, promising to come and look for her once the main course had been cleared away and wended through the gleaming round tables clad in cream tablecloths with golden cutlery and ware. Gracing each table were identical bouquets of perfect cream roses, and the glassware all had a very thin line of gold around the rim. Place names sat by the fanned napkins, and Ellora found her excitement moving up a notch; this was going to be fabulous.

She caught sight of Lee moving toward her from the opposite direction. It felt like her entire body smiled in response, and she had to remind herself to keep her feet on the ground, despite feeling as though she was flying. His supple body moved with an agile grace, and she felt a flicker of recognition as her eyes met his.

A recognition that soared across the expanses, the ages, the whatever, and slowed whilst she and Lee connected once more. Yet simultaneously, a shadow touched her only to float onward, and she shook her head, disoriented. A near stumble could've been catastrophic if it weren't for the fact of Lee being right there, beside her before she quite knew how.

"Is something wrong?" He held her at arm's length, eyes scouring her face.

"I'm fine, Lee, just jet lagged I'd say." *I hope.*

"Come, this is our table." He pulled out her chair and she subsided gratefully into it, smiling at Lee when he sat.

"How have you gotten on?" She pulled her napkin onto her lap and leaned towards him in order to speak quietly. Or at least that is what she told herself.

"We'll see. I have been speaking with a couple of Philippe's contacts, both of whom are in the relics industry. I didn't bring up the actual chalice, but they happily spoke about the power possible to wield with one of these artifacts in hand."

"Such as what?"

"Control, mainly. All depending on how many believe in it as to how much control."

"Interesting. My conversation with Zenon was all to do with power. And how certain objects only had power because of what the community gave to it, and without the community, there was no power."

Lee smiled assent to the wine waiter hovering with both red and white wine. "Which would you like?"

Opening her mouth to reply, she inwardly cringed to hear Zenon's voice approaching. Introductions were made to his wife, Juliet, a stunning woman who clearly had plastic surgery, as she seemed in perpetual surprise. But it was a relief as Zenon smoothly moved into a bland conversation based around Athens and what to do if you were a tourist.

Dinner proceeded in a haze of well-mannered serving staff and wonderful tasting food. This parallel world she had entered sure knew how to gild the lily. She was happy to let the conversation flow over her, interjecting every now and then, but enjoyed sitting back surreptitiously admiring the man to her left. She raised a glass of the finest red and took a sip. *Good work, Ellora Radley. Wait until Flicka hears of this!*

Chapter Eight

Lee doubted Ellora had any idea how good she looked. Most men, and a few of the women, watched her circumspectly as she chatted and smiled with the best of them. How unbelievable he had met her just over forty-eight hours ago—she felt a big part of his life already. *Crazy.* She was hired as his researcher, but somehow she seemed, with one smooth move, to fill a gap within him, one he didn't know was there. But now he was aware of her, not only when she was with him, but when she wasn't. His dreams since he had met her had increased in vividness, but it wasn't all the newness. It was oldness about them together that held him mesmerized.

Aware she had just stifled a yawn, he leaned in closer. "Would you like to go back to the hotel or stay until the unmasking?"

She smiled. "Thanks for checking, but I'm sure I will be fine. My body clock should be fine for this, after all, we're coming into our evening now. Plus, the unmasking will be very exciting."

"I'm glad you'll be fine, but let me know if not. We only have another half an hour until midnight anyway."

"You should go and mingle then."

"Come with me?"

As an answer she rose to her feet and after saying

their goodbyes, they headed to the bar where a good many of the crowd were now gathered. The orchestra had packed up after dessert, and coming onstage was a Greek band who had a one hit song ten years ago and now toured doing covers of popular songs. There was a new energy after the good food and beautiful music, and a lot of the guests were tapping their feet, looking forward to dancing.

Reaching the bar, he checked what Ellora fancied, unsurprised when she said sambuca. Both with drinks in hand, they stood facing the crowd, talking quietly.

"What did you get from Zenon?"

"A load of power talk. It was tedious to the extreme. The only thing worthy of note is the fact I'd say I could get me, if not us, a personal invitation into the vaults."

He grimaced. "I'm not letting you into any vaults with that man on your own."

She laughed. "Don't come across all protective. I can look after myself, you know, and have done for years."

"Oh, and before I forget, Philippe and Imelda have invited us to brunch. Normally the tradition after the ball is to stay up all night and then go straight to breakfast in our glad rags. Although I thought we'd need bed in the interim."

Pursing her lips, she nodded slowly. "I'd like bed."

He stared. She was his newly hired researcher, for Pete's sake. *Get your mind off bed with her.*

He swallowed. "We'll leave after the unmasking."

Eyes bright, she acknowledged him and then froze in the act of raising her sambuca to her lips.

"Ms. Radley, Mr. North. What are you two

plotting?"

Zenon was back, and judging by the tone of his voice, well into his cups too.

What a strange question.

He kept his answer banal and short and sweet to discourage further conversation. It didn't take a genius to figure out that Ellora had had enough of this man. A quick glance at his watch told him they were approaching midnight. The band picked the beat up with an old U2 track, and soon the dance floor was flooded. Ellora raised an eyebrow and gestured to the dance floor. Before he was able to respond, the three men she had been speaking to earlier arrived en masse.

He cursed to himself and moved in closer to escort her onto the dance floor. But he hadn't a chance. The four surrounded them, raising glasses and effectively closing their exit. At their arrival, Zenon changed tack.

"Lee. You don't mind if I call you Lee, do you?" Zenon fixed him with fathomless eyes, awaiting his nod. "Ellora tells me you're an antiques dealer. What kind of antiques?"

He ran smoothly into his dual life. "Generally old English antiques find their way across the pond. Nothing dramatic, all quite standard. Quite a few turn out to be fake, which is where Ellora will earn her wage."

"Do you often work in Europe?"

"Occasionally."

Zenon raised an eyebrow. "Last time you were out of the US, I believe you were tracking down a cross. Just last year, wasn't it? Tell me, what happened to that cross?" He now sounded sober as a judge.

Philippe was right—this man knew a lot. But how?

Silence surrounded them, not bothering him in the least. He felt like proffering a measuring tape to him, or at least giving him his statistics. There was something about this man, something he didn't like at all. Perhaps it was the eyes, the feeling you could drop into them and never emerge. He allowed the silence to lengthen, not bothered about answering the question. To add insult to injury, he took out his phone and texted their driver to be ready at the front. He did not like the way this was going.

Degree by degree, Zenon's face turned florid. He gestured as though in disgust, and a crony picked up the conversation.

"What has been the most valuable object you have recovered?"

"It would be a writing bureau from Hemingway. His family had placed it in safekeeping but over generations had lost it."

"Impressive."

In his peripheral vision, he noticed Ellora kept fiddling with her drop earrings. Something wasn't right here. Behind her shoulder stood the grand clock, ticking down the minutes to midnight. His teeth set on edge. Zenon moved back into his line of vision.

"What brings you to Athens?"

"Catching up with old friends." He scoured the crowd in front of him, looking for Philippe. Back up would be good.

"Have you ever been on a treasure trail, Mr. North?"

"I'm happy with my antiques."

"Strange, but you don't look like most antiquarians."

He summoned a laugh. "We weren't introduced properly. What is it you do again?"

"I run the vaults below us. In my directorship, we have managed to acquire a vast range of treasures—hence my question. I am always on the lookout for those who can track down other artifacts for me."

"Where do they come from, your treasures?"

"All over the world."

He clenched his jaw. The man in front of him would be a dangerous adversary. But Zenon turned to Ellora, running his fingers lightly up her bare arm to settle on the small of her back. Behind Lee's eyes was an explosion of red, and he breathed in deeply, reaching into the circle where Ellora had become penned in. Yet with lightning speed, she smoothly swung to Zenon, tipping the end of her sambuca, ice and all, over his front.

"Oh Julian, I am sorry. You made me jump." Genuinely horrified, she stopped a passing waiter, asking for a cloth.

An ugly mottled flush crept above Zenon's collar line and his mouth tightened. Lee watched the other three men, all of whom were oddly silent.

"No matter, my dear." He forced a laugh. "Let me get you another drink." A waiter materialized at his elbow proffering a cloth, and Zenon asked him for drinks. Zenon took it and looked at Ellora who kept his gaze.

"I'm glad it was sambuca, and nothing to stain your marvelous waistcoat. Tell me, where did you get it? It's very unusual, not just design but the material used."

Lee glanced at the waistcoat. It was flamboyant,

with peacocks gracing both sides and complimented the man's mask. Or commiserated with, he wasn't sure which.

"My wife designed it and subsequently got it made."

"I must ask her where, for it really suits you."

In the background, the minute countdown until the unveiling commenced. Lee glanced around. They were hemmed in. To move now, at the last minute, would make it obvious they didn't want to be seen. Yes, these men knew what he looked like from the internet, but they had not seen him in person, and more to the point, did not know yet what Ellora looked like. He cursed himself for allowing them to get caught here. Although, looking at the chain of events, he doubted he had had any choice. The four men had moved in and weren't allowing them to go until they got a good look at their faces.

He glanced at Ellora, who was smoothly chatting with Zenon. Feeling the weight of his look, she returned it. Understanding of their situation was as clear in her blue eyes. And then the answer came to him.

"Ten, nine, eight, seven…" The crowd chanted deliriously.

Lee reached out and met Ellora's hand and gently tugged her towards him. She capitulated easily, and he pulled her against his chest.

"Five, four, three, two…"

Cupping her face in his hand, he gently rubbed his thumb over her slightly parted lips, hearing and feeling her gasp. Gazing into her eyes, he dropped his lips to hers.

"One!" The crowd roared its delight. Fireworks

crackled and roared in the heavens above.

But all sound muted as Ellora's lips came to life below his, moving slowly, supple under his, moist and inviting. Cupping her face in his hands, he explored further, nibbling at her bottom lip at the same time as running one hand onto her smooth bare neck. The feel of her skin below his hands enflamed him further, but he held himself back yet, wanting to delight in the delicacy of this, their first kiss.

He felt her impatience and returned his lips fully on hers, whispering to her. He didn't know what he said, but he felt compelled to communicate with her on all levels.

I know.

Her voice, soft and gentle. But rational thought had departed with the delight of the feel of her. Without pressing her against him, he still felt her curves as though she were imprinted on him. Her lips moved seamlessly with his, opening and welcoming him into her, holding nothing back. Restlessly he pulled back, then unable to help himself, tasted and delighted in her once more.

Time did its delightful warp and stretched around them, protecting them in their passion as they exchanged kisses and promises.

Until something awoke him and transferred the waking to Ellora. Continuing their kiss, they were both very much aware of what was going on around them. Whether it was the fact they were joined at the lips, their thoughts seemed to be in sync. He reached for her hand, and as one, they broke their kiss and foreheads pressed to each other's, smiled, then turned and practically ran for the door, keeping their attention on each other at all times.

Yet a part of him kept an eye out and he felt the four men had moved away, understandably uncomfortable at being in their presence, but watched with narrow eyes as they made good their escape.

Still running, they exited the building and lightly stepped down the steps, holding hands up against the flashes and collapsed into their car. Behind blackened windows, they relaxed.

Ellora looked delectably edible—wide eyes with dilated pupils, pink lips swollen from their kisses, her curves smooth and soft under the sheer silk dress. Yet now was not the right time. This was something he wanted to develop, not race into as he had with other women. She deserved more. He looked at her, and as he felt his entire body yearn towards her, he hoped she would understand.

****

Insane. Deliciously, delightfully insane. Toe curling, firework hurling, light igniting insane. His kiss, the feel of him below her hands. And what made it more insane was the fact it felt very sane. But a sanity she had never known before.

Under Lee's intense gaze, she waited for her entire body to break up into crystal pieces and float to him to be consolidated into his beautiful presence. Something else told her no matter how awesome their kiss, they were going no further. Deep within her, she acknowledged the rightness of the move, whilst the part of her inhabiting her skin wept with disappointment. *And yet, when the two of you do happen, for happen it will, it will be worth waiting for.*

Taking breath deep into her, she felt herself

disentangling all that delicious emotion away from him, and they subsided against the cream leather.

He opened his mouth to speak, and she just shook her head. She needed time to regroup. Feeling her mask still on her head, she reached behind to unfasten the catch. He followed every move, but she refused his outstretched hand. Her mask came off easily, and she gently rubbed where it had laid against her skin. He copied her and took his mask off and they sat quietly, both masks in their hands millimeters apart from each other on the cream upholstery.

A curious sensation surrounded her. She checked herself out, she was breathing normally, deeper than usual, her limbs were relaxed, her mind was quiet. Peace. She was at peace. She smiled and looked at Lee, unsurprised to see a mirrored image.

After a few minutes, the car slowed in front of their hotel and the courier sprang to open the door for her. With a contented sigh, she left the car, waiting for Lee to join her.

"Nightcap and a recap?"

She shook her head. "Not for me. I'm too tired now. Come to my suite about eleven, and we can discuss tonight before we head for brunch with Imelda and Philippe."

She just wanted to be alone. Scratch that, she *needed* to be alone. To dwell on their kiss.

"Sure. Let me walk you to your room."

She placed a hand on his chest. "I'm fine. You go sleep."

She turned and walked to the lifts, feeling more woman than she ever had before. Her dress swirled around her legs, and she leaned into the sway of the skirts. God, she loved the feel of the material, running a hand over her side and her hip as she waited for the lift to arrive, giving a little wiggle just to enjoy it more.

With a ping, the lift arrived, the doors opening with the mirrors framing her. She didn't recognize the tall and glamorous woman staring back and paused before stepping in. Over her right shoulder, in the reflection, she saw him. Standing and drinking in his fill in of her. There was beauty and longing in his look, and holding it, she stepped into the quiet interior to swing around to join his gaze until the doors closed and cut them off.

Pressing a hand to her stomach, she leaned against the mirrors. She didn't want to label this. Just wanted to go with it. She floated as though in a bubble to her room, peeled off her clothes, took down her hair, took off her makeup and, eventually, subsided into her super king size bed. All the while not thinking of anything but the space in the look between them. Fortunately, the weight of the duvet held her from floating off into space.

But she floated into her dreams, waking the next morning with the same sense. Stretching and reaching out, she felt...what? After a couple of minutes of idle wondering, she named it. Blessed. She felt blessed.

Her phone beeped from its charging station. Time to get up. Excitement swirled into her tummy. She had no clue what was going to happen today—it was all to play for. How delicious. Protecting her hair with a shower cap, she hopped under the power shower, allowing all jet lag to fall from her. Time to be concise and succinct.

After feeling delightful in her dress last night, she was loathe to put on her old clothes, wanting instead to embrace the new her. She stared at the old her, chewing her bottom lip. Glancing at the phone, she saw she had over an hour until Lee showed up. Hurriedly, she pulled on trousers and a top and raced out to Marianne's shop, who looked up in delight as she tumbled through the door.

"Marianne, I need your help. I want a new wardrobe. All in half an hour, can you help?"

Marianne clapped her hands in delight and thirty-three minutes later, Ellora was back in her room, a stack of clothes with her. Not having had the time to try things on, Marianne said to take them, return the items she didn't like. She had also had a wonderful time filling Marianne in on the ball, Marianne hanging on every word.

She hung each of the four outfits up facing her. Which one to wear today? She was drawn to the navy shirt dress with white polka dots, adding white tennis shoes to complete the look. An image of her bank manager shaking his head came to her, and she shoved it aside. She could afford it. She was a new person, *remember*.

Prompt as ever, Lee knocked on her door at 11 a.m.. The appreciative look on his face made her hectic morning very much worth it. He himself was dressed in an open-necked white shirt with dark chinos, a casual blazer thrown on top and her body seemed to yearn towards him, then, like a pet, relax into his new presence. They strolled down the corridor and into the executive lounge.

"Would you like some coffee?"

"No, I'm okay, thanks. I'll wait. The Greeks drink coffee like it's going out of fashion, so I have no doubt it'll be on tap."

For once, she didn't need the kick caffeine gave her. They sat on the sofa facing each other.

"Last night—what were your impressions?"

"Okay, I didn't like Zenon at all, he gave me the creeps. Hence the drink."

Lee smothered a laugh. "You seemed so genuinely remorseful I thought it must've been an accident."

"Perhaps because I was genuinely horrified at what I'd done. I'd do it again, mind, but I knew if I didn't persuade him it was an accident, he would make a dangerous enemy. Did we pull it off?"

"I don't know. Perhaps if we hadn't pulled our stunt to get us out of unmasking in front of them, then it would be no problem."

His eyes darkened, but whether it was because of the threat they might feel from Zenon or in memory of their kiss, she didn't know.

He smiled and turned his amber gaze on her, causing delicious squiggles in her stomach.

"Did you see them as we left?"

"From the corner of my eye. They looked mad, Zenon holding court and the other lackeys listening."

"It wasn't a coincidence they were beside us for the unmasking. Zenon either runs the show or is second to someone who does. He has a need to know everything and everyone in this industry. What did you tell him about us?"

"Only what we had agreed. How about you?"

"He pried quite a bit, excusing it by saying he was looking for treasure hunters."

As he sat there, musing over events of the night before, she felt her heart sink. "Perhaps the one thing we didn't take into account is the fact that you, um, actually look like a treasure hunter. Not an antiquarian."

Understanding flared in his eyes. "You mean I wasn't wearing, what did you say? A tweed jacket with leather elbows?"

She raised an eyebrow, amused. "I'm not just talking about your style, Lee. It's your whole attitude, your looks, your presence."

At his carefully blank expression, she muttered, "You know what I mean. Don't make me spell it out."

She felt the words rising in and she knew they were going to tumble out. "Oh hell, you're Indiana Jones."

A surprised laugh burst from him and she sheepishly smiled. "Surely you know what I mean."

Lee's phone beeped loudly and looking at it, he frowned. "Philippe, saying come to their house for breakfast, not the café we had decided upon. Apparently"—he stood—"trouble's afoot."

A short car journey later and they pulled up to large ornate gates, a camera to the left tracking them. Their driver pressed the intercom and introduced them as Ellora and Lee.

Noiseless gates swung open smoothly, and the car purred up the sweeping driveway, past a semi-circular green and to the steps leading to the white double front doors.

"Trouble, here we come."

At Lee's snarl, she jumped a little inside. Was this adventure about to become real?

Chapter Nine

As they approached the top step, the door on the right opened, and Philippe stood there, smiling.

"Come on in. Lovely to see you again." He stepped back, allowing them access. Imelda stood just past him, dressed in a cream pantsuit, her hair elegantly piled on top of her head, sunglasses perched on top. Her husband, in contrast, wore pool shorts and a pale blue tee. Both seemed a bit preoccupied and, once they were inside, told the servants to serve brunch out on the terrace.

"My dear, you look wonderful." Imelda tucked her hand in Ellora's arm and gave her a warm smile. "Don't look so worried, however. All will be well."

The men walked in front, and hearing her words, Philippe snorted. "Lee can be the judge of that."

Pace quickening, they walked through the high-ceilinged marble hallway and around the table in the middle, which bore a big and bright bunch of cream and peach roses. Clearly, treasure hunting paid off for Philippe. What was Lee's house like?

Bright sunlight greeted them from the wide-open doors at the far side of the hall, and it was through them they stepped.

"Oh, how wonderful." She exclaimed before stopping herself. For in front was an Olympic sized topaz colored infinity pool. Beyond the rim lay the ocean, white flecked waves tossing and turning.

Imelda smiled. "We can take a dip afterwards if you like. Although Philippe doesn't like us to do that—apparently he grew up with the maxim of never swimming after food until an hour has passed."

Despite Imelda's best efforts, the mood between the men remained somber as they sat down at a long wooden outdoors table. Quietly moving in, the servers arrived with plates laden with fruit, pastries, and pots of coffee.

"Please, help yourself. Eggs Benedict will soon follow, but let's start here."

Lee interjected, "But what about—"

Philippe held up a hand. "Not until after we eat. Business on an empty stomach is poor hospitality indeed."

Ellora tucked into fresh melon and warmed croissants, magnificent coffee being plentiful. The promised eggs and muffins arrived, and the talk was all about the ball on the previous evening. Imelda entertaining them with gossip, both salacious and non. Ellora was in fits of laughter many times and if it weren't for the fact unwelcome news was sure to be coming, she felt completely content. Especially when she looked at Lee, admiring the square cut of his jaw, now lightly flecked with stubble.

Pushing his plate away, Philippe nodded to the staff, who had the table cleared and fresh pots of coffee and cups out in no time.

"I hear you two gave quite the performance last night." Philippe put his coffee cup down with a clink and alternated Lee and Ellora with a stern stare. "I had warned you, both of us did in fact, about Zenon. You do not mess with him."

"Do you think we had a choice?"

She heard Lee's words, and despite knowing and having agreed to the kiss, she still felt them hit her stomach like lead bullets. With a heroic effort, she ignored the ensuing ripples and concentrated on the conversation. She leaned in. "Plus who's to say we were messing with him? We were just having a kiss."

"If that's what you call 'just a kiss', then old man, your boat's come in."

Imelda leaned forward and put a hand on his forearm to stop her husband from further embarrassing Lee and Ellora. After a glance to him, she continued, "Have you seen the Monday newspaper?"

Reaching behind them, Philippe pulled the widely circulated newspaper from the steel table behind him. There they were, locked in each other's arms, whilst fireworks lit the night sky over the ruined wall of the acropolis. She stared, it was a fantastic photograph. Couldn't get any more romantic. She glanced shyly at Lee, who stared at Philippe.

"What's the problem?"

"After you left in such a hurry, Zenon told his men to follow you." His glanced switched to Ellora. "But I guess you know—otherwise you wouldn't have pulled such a stunt. And thinking about it, it was ingenious. But Zenon can't abide not knowing who is in town."

Philippe glanced over his shoulder and pulled his chair further in to them both. "Last night, word went out one of the artifacts, a chalice, has disappeared from his archives."

"What kind of chalice?" Lee's voice was sharp.

"I don't know—this information wasn't passed

out."

Only the twitch in his jawline would've told anyone Lee was perturbed by this news.

"Did you ask anyone the questions you asked me last night?"

"No, I didn't trust anyone enough."

"Well, that's something."

"And Zenon thinks we've got it?"

Philippe spread his hands out, shrugged and sat back in his chair.

"We were followed back last night; he knows where we're staying." Lee's eyes narrowed. "I'll bet our rooms are being searched."

She froze, what had they left in their rooms? A quick inventory, her new clothes but nothing else valuable. It would be information they were after and they both had their iPads and phones.

She met Lee's gaze calmly, as though big men riffling through her smalls was nothing to freak about.

"Do you think it's true—the missing chalice, I mean?"

Philippe shrugged again. "It's hard to say. But Zenon is a proud man, and I doubt he'd cast doubt on his own abilities to look after the archives unless there was something serious afoot."

Lee was deep in his own thoughts. "Philippe, did you give my description of the chalice to anyone?"

"A few discreet enquiries, but only to those I trust implicitly."

"And Zenon, he has a lot of money and power?"

Philippe only nodded.

"Did you give out any names?"

Philippe smothered a laugh. "Friend, of course

not."

"Have you any other news from last night?"

"For now, you know all we know."

Lee nodded imperceptibly and stood abruptly. "We must go. I don't want to place you both in danger by being here, and we should check out of our hotel and decide our next plan of action."

Surprised, she placed her coffee cup on the table and stood to leave.

"Just one more thing." Imelda spoke slowly, waiting until she got a nod from her husband. "Come, let's walk." She held her hand out and directed Ellora past the pool and onto the vivid green of the maze, impeccably cut bushes showing the square within.

Once within the shade of the trees, Ellora spotted a bench deep within the maze. It was to there the four headed.

"I have a gut feeling about the chalice you are seeking. The symbols all speak to me of shamanism, but as the artifact itself is a chalice, it surely is inherently Christian. When Christianity and Shamanism met was a dangerous time. Be careful." Imelda spoke just above a whisper. "Many prized shamanic artifacts were destroyed or disappeared. If this is what I think it is—shamanic—then in order to have survived, it has to be capable of great power. Also—" And here she paused, a frown appearing between her eyes. "I don't think you are the only person looking for it, Lee."

There it was again—shamanism. Glancing at Lee, she shared a quick nod with him. "Imelda, I need to know more about shamanism. Can you help?"

Imelda nodded without surprise. "Of course. Come, let us walk whilst the men talk. I'll be as brief but as thorough as I can. Shamanism is the oldest spiritual worldwide practice. Centuries ago, artifacts were found in places from Siberia to the Andes, to deep inside Australia, Borneo, you name it. All similar and all being used for the same ritual at a time when travel wasn't possible. Where did these rituals come from? They involved the wise man or woman of the tribe entering an altered state of consciousness to communicate with spirits for advice and for healing. Are you with me?"

She felt a kinship with her words. She nodded.

"There are many different worlds the shaman frequents, depending on the nature of what their tribe needs. The main three are this world, the lower world, and the upper world. In the lower world, you meet your power animal, who is a bit like a guardian angel. We all have power animals, whether we know it or not. They provide guidance, counsel, and courage. One of the first stages of shamanic work is to journey inwards to find your power animal."

Panther. Where was that thought from?

She drank the information in greedily, feeling the words patch up something inside her.

"The upper world is where spirits in human form provide guidance. Key amongst the shamanic culture is asking for healing for someone or something, and this is where this is requested. Also, shamans help traumatized spirits pass over to more peaceful places. Still with me?"

"Absolutely. Your words are giving me the strangest feeling, as though I know exactly what you're talking about, although there is no way I do."

"I have studied shamanism for many years now,

and I'll only say this more to you. I feel you have a natural ability to enter altered states of consciousness. Has anything strange happened to you before?"

"Like what?"

"Perhaps you entered altered states of consciousness before—drugs, maybe?"

She laughed. "Never."

Imelda nodded. "Good, for that way is not to be trusted." She paused in their strolling. "Singing, chanting, drumming, dancing?"

She was in the process of shaking her head when she stopped. "Dancing, yes absolutely. I love dancing, and whenever I'm feeling low, I go out and dance. What is it they say, dance like no one is watching? The odd thing about it is once I've stopped, I cannot remember the music nor the dances."

"No, not odd. It would indicate your conscious mind has departed, your ego has left, and your subconscious is communicating with the spirits in trance." Imelda stopped and took Ellora's arm, turning her to face her.

"There's something else though—you need to protect yourself if that's what you are doing. Low level possessions can happen if you're channeling without knowing it."

"Ellora?" Lee's voice came to them. "We need to leave."

"Wait, Imelda. What do I do?"

"See if you can come back tonight, and we can talk further. Bring Lee, he needs to know too. Tell him what I've told you."

"Why are you telling me?"

"Because there is something about you telling me

110

you have a natural ability to do this. And it's important work. Also, it just might be something to do with the chalice."

"Ellora?"

"Coming," she called back, adding to Imelda, "I wish we were able to talk more."

"Just bear in mind if you do find the chalice, you may have a strange reaction to it. A powerful shamanic tool in the hands of an amateur might prove more dangerous."

She paused. "If you do find it, reach straight out into the spirits' world and ask to be protected by them." Imelda grabbed her arm tightly. "Promise me. Also promise me you'll come back as soon as you can, and we can expand on this further."

Pulling her into her arms, Ellora felt her rapid heartbeat. She nodded against the hug.

The men were speaking together as surreptitiously as Ellora and Imelda were. Lee nodded to her, and she fell into hurried steps with him. They took leave of their hosts, Ellora regretting already the loss of the other woman's company.

She waited until they were in their car before questioning Lee. "The chalice—"

He shook his head briefly, and she stopped.

"What would you like to do with the rest of the day? We should head out to a nice Greek beach to take photos. Let me check sunset times." The look in his eyes was wary as he gave her a slanted look.

Endeavoring not to look at their chauffeur, Ellora nodded along. "Wonderful."

They passed the remaining journey deep in their own thoughts, she ran through what Imelda said.

Excitement rushed through her at the thought of finding her power animal.

Markos greeted them both as they came into the lobby and made their way up to their rooms.

"Can I come in, Ellora?" Despite being out of earshot and eyesight of anyone, Lee spoke quietly, a warning look in his eyes.

"Of course."

The door opened with a green light and a click, and Lee held it as she went through, heart thumping at the thought of what she might find. A quick scour around told her nothing had been moved—or at least it seemed so. Everything was a little too precise, but it was impossible to remember how she had left it. Unease gnawed at her bones.

"Shall we have a coffee?" Lee's voice cut into her thoughts.

"Um." *No, the last thing she fancied was a coffee.* But a quick look at his face told her he was up to something. "Yes, let's."

With his hand under her elbow, he guided her over to the table and holding one finger to his lips, turned the kettle on. Only when the boiling was well underway did he speak, quietly. "Get your things together. We're leaving."

Her heart thumped uncomfortably against her chest. "Where are we going?"

"Not sure yet. Philippe has a car waiting for us outside the back door."

The whistling of the kettle came to an abrupt stop and a dark look crossed Lee's face. He gestured to her to gather her things.

"How do you take it again? Coffee, I mean." He

slanted her a mischievous look, but one belied with worry.

"Surprise me. Oh sorry, coffee—white, no sugar please." Lee hummed to himself as he ensured he made a lot of noise with teaspoons and cups whilst Ellora ran lightly around the room.

"Here." Lee handed her a cup, and she thanked him, nodding she was ready.

He took a sip of his own and groaned. "Awful stuff. I may have some filter in my case. I always take some just in case I can't get a good coffee. Rare in Greece, I know, but carrying ground bean has saved my neck more times than once. Shall we go to mine?"

He took her heavy case with ease.

"Why am I not surprised you brought your own coffee? Okay, let's go." Striving for a light tone was hard, trying not to let her voice emerge squeaky.

He opened the door and they stepped outside, leaving the key inside.

A few short steps and they were outside his door, where they ran through the same charade, this time with her making filter coffee. His room was immaculate and rather austere, whereas her room had the air of someone occupying it. The housekeeper would have been hard-pressed to find remnants of anyone here. As the aroma of fresh beans filled the air, she discovered she wanted some after all and, taking a sip, had to agree with him. "This is delicious coffee. Where did you get it?"

He looked up from his packing. "A lifetime of research has gone into my coffee. I'm glad you like it." He warmed her just by looking at her, and she clutched that feeling deep inside.

Once all packed, he gave a whirling gesture with

his hand, indicating they should keep talking. "Where shall we go? What beach?"

"I'm in your hands, Lee. I don't know the area at all. Like I said, surprise me."

He grinned and grabbed her hand. "Unorthodox I know, but what do you say we take a shower before the beach rather than after?"

What was he up to? She forced a low giggle from her too tight throat and followed as he went into the wet room. Putting his mouth close to her ear, he whispered "Turn all your mobile devices off." She nodded and backed out, rooting through her bag for her phone and iPad. Soon the roar of the power shower was heard, and he called, "Come on in, the water's perfect." He emerged from the bathroom, leaving the door open and she followed him to the door. Ever so slowly opening it, he looked outside and then moved through with the two suitcases. Holding her breath, she followed, waiting whilst he allowed the weight of the door to close without a sound.

"Relax." He mouthed the word and she took his cue. They attempted to walk unhurriedly toward the exit door next to the lifts. It got farther away with every passing second. A low whirring alerted them to the lift being called. Upon reaching the lit neon sign, he sped up and pushed her through the door just as the arrival *ping* sounded like a bullet. Blood rushed through her at a rapid rate. He caught the door from swinging inward after them. They paused. Heard heavy footsteps.

"Quick." Ellora grabbed her backpack from Lee and hefted it on her back.

They took the stairs two at a time. Pausing at the end, she looked around blindly for any other door than the one leading them into the lobby. He caught up with her and pulled her behind the staircase, where there was a door with a bar across it.

"It's alarmed. Still, we have no choice." Placing all his weight on the bar, he burst through it. She followed, hot on his heels. She held her breath, awaiting the siren-like sound, but when none was forthcoming, blew out. Bright sunshine greeted them, and a beige 4WD.

Chapter Ten

Lee flipped something in his hand and the car unlocked with a chirrup, the boot yawning open as it did. He hefted their two cases in.

After looking all around and seeing nothing untoward, Ellora swung into her seat as Lee threw himself into the driver's. He started the engine before shutting his door. With a screech, they took off.

"Damn, we're in a one-way system. It'll take us by the hotel."

Ellora spotted the sat-nav system seating squarely between the pair, which looked like an updated version of one she knew. Between glancing at the street names and mapping where they were, she confirmed there was no other way to go and flicked it off.

Cursing, Lee directed the 4WD in the hotel's direction.

He glanced over. "I don't want to run the risk of bringing us to the attention of the police. Are you okay?" As they rejoined the main street, the traffic forced them to a crawl.

"Me, yup, absolutely. Never been better." *Alive.* Her blood pumped through her veins; her senses were on full alert. *The thrill of the hunt.* Except they were the hunted. Hunted by whom? With a glance at Lee and his look of intense concentration, a new thrill surged through her. Whatever happened, Lee was by her side.

"Put your sunglasses on." Lee had his large aviators already in place.

"Don't look at what's happening." He checked her mirror and pulled the car into the outer lane, placing at least one lane of traffic between them and the hotel.

"Good point. I always think if you give your energy over to something, someone will pick it up." She tried to stop the tendrils of unease morphing into fully blown cramps.

They crawled past the hotel to see police cars pulling up, sirens blaring. Traffic was practically at a standstill.

"Shit."

"Are they looking for us?"

"I'd say so."

Keeping their eyes on the road, the car inexorably inched its way past the hotel. In her peripheral vision, she saw Markos, a disbelieving look on his face, chatting with a man in uniform. Suddenly feeling very visible, she sank back into her seat, thanking the universe and all in it. It seemed to take forever, but eventually they had the hotel in their rearview mirror.

Lee's eyes behind his shades constantly flicked from the road to the mirrors, the light ticking in his jaw showing his unease. Strong arms clad in turned-up shirt sleeves maintained a steady hold on the steering wheel whilst muscular thighs in chinos flexed as he went through the gears as the terrain and the other traffic dictated. Good distraction. She turned in her seat to gaze out the back window. When there was no sign of anyone following them after a couple of miles, they both relaxed.

"Do you know where we're going?" she asked as

she settled into her bucket-like seat.

"No, but someone does." He reached out and turned the sat-nav on. After a couple of seconds calibrating where the car was, the light tones of the sat-nav emerged, saying something in Greek. She changed the settings to English to hear "Turn right at the next set of traffic lights."

Lee threw her a half smile. "It's somewhere we can lie low for a while." Pressing a couple of buttons, he sighed. "But we'll be about an hour out of the city. Never mind. Just enjoy the ride." Taking his right hand off the wheel, he settled his arm along the window, shifting farther back in the seat.

"Okay, now you can tell me what's going on."

"It's complicated. And before I saw the scene at the hotel, you were going to get the first available flight back to the US. I'm sorry you've been dragged into this—I had no idea what we were getting into." A world-weary air settled around him as he looked apologetic.

"Don't worry, Lee, I'm having the time of my life." Heck, she wasn't lying. "But tell me what price I'm going to pay?"

"Apparently, word is out I'm looking for the chalice."

"And?"

He sighed. "What I think is happening is that the chalice we are actually searching for has now been said to be missing. And since all of Athens now know we are looking for it..." Stopped at a red light, he ran a hand through his hair, ruffling it.

"Wait." She sat upright. "Are they saying it was us?"

He nodded sideways before pulling away from the lights. "We didn't exactly help with our abrupt exit and not unmasking. To compound matters, there's a rumor going around about me dealing in black-market goods. Who? Philippe? Constantin?" He drummed his fingers on the steering wheel.

"Why run then? We don't have the chalice, and we can prove that."

"Can we? We are new in town, with no power protecting us. Zenon, on the other hand, runs the place. I have no doubt if we turned ourselves in, they would find some way of finding the chalice in our belongings. No, there's something more to this."

"Like what?"

"I don't know. But we need to be careful until we do know."

"Is Constantin Greek?"

"He sounds American."

"If he's who you are speaking to."

"You're right, and who's to say he's using his real name."

"Are Zenon and Constantin the same person?"

"I think not. Constantin has an understated presence, even on the phone. He speaks like he's used to being listened to. Zenon, on the other hand, is loud and pompous, as though the only way he can get people to listen is by being louder than they."

"Possibly an alter ego? Good disguise?"

He slanted her a look. "Possibly. The impression I received from Constantin is he is a dapper, elegant, quietly spoken man."

"Totally the opposite then."

"Quite. But you never know."

"Could Zenon work for Constantin?"

"That's the most likely situation."

"Does Zenon know who you are?"

"He knows we are here for some good reason. Because there is something more sinister afoot and I don't know what it is. There at the hotel was overkill. He was flexing his muscles, but why? And what would have happened had we still been there? Where would we be now? Negotiating our release with Zenon? Did he want us in his power?"

She half turned in her seat, all the better to watch him. "Has this kind of thing ever happened before?"

"Not to me, no. But to others, yes. It's a very claustrophobic industry, everyone vying for attention and control. Successful treasure hunters are viewed with dispassion, suspicion, and jealousy. We are the outcasts."

Without looking over, she saw easily why the men of last night would be jealous of him. His presence, his charisma filled the car, and whereas she found it immensely exciting, perhaps some men might not be quite as thrilled.

"Lee, how dangerous is this? What happens to successful treasure hunters?" She laughed. "Where do the treasure hunters themselves hide? You yourself said there weren't many around anymore."

He glanced at her for a short moment. Then releasing a big sigh, he switched his attention back to the straight road.

"Just because there aren't many in the business. The majority retire early on—it's a lucrative business and one for youth and strength. Others get too involved with what they're hunting, refuse to accept they can't find it, and carry on their lives hunting down elusive, perhaps not even real, artifacts."

The apartment blocks and shopping malls were changing to expanses of green and open spaces. Lee dropped the gears to accommodate a wide curve, and they embarked on a smaller, stony, treelined road which the large vehicle took well within its stride. His grip tightened on the wheel.

"Philippe thinks it's something to do with the cross. It's coming back to haunt me."

"Why, what happened?"

"I'll tell you more when we get there—let's get this figured out first."

"So what would the cross have to do with it?"

"Philippe just thinks it can't be a coincidence that trouble dogs Constantin's requests."

"Constantin is the common denominator. I wonder is there anything connecting the cross and the chalice? One appears to be thoroughly Christian whilst the chalice we're not sure about. What do you know about them both? Historically, I mean."

"You know all I know about both, but let's look at it again. The cross was in the hands of monks who, for want of a better word, sang to it. It was an artifact used in the religious wars, and so it dated to the 800s. The chalice, we don't know. Why would Constantin want them both? I'm reluctant to think so as they are completely different to each other."

They fell silent, each contemplating their situation, and for a time, she relaxed. She was safe, cocooned in this large vehicle effortlessly eating up the miles, muting the sounds of the outside world. Opening her laptop, she soon became immersed in the archives from the British Museum and scoured the images and text before her, looking for anything with the search word "chalice."

"Anything?"

"Nothing clear for what we're looking for. But there is this painting that I can't take my eyes off. It's a sixteenth-century painting and depicts witches burning at the stakes. And I don't know why, but there's a pit of snakes squirming in my stomach." She glanced away, swallowing deeply. "I need to close it, perhaps it's because I'm concentrating whilst on the road—it could be making me travel sick."

She laid her head against her rest, allowing her eyes to close and breathed deeply. Soon she felt him drop the gear, and she opened her eyes as they pulled up in front of a log cabin, deep in the woods.

"This is it."

"I feel like we're in a movie or something. Is this our hideout?"

He nodded. "We need to lie low whilst we figure out why the police were swarming all over our hotel. Then what to do about it."

"How about Philippe and Imelda? Are they going to help?"

"No. They are too visible in Athens to be anything other than exemplary. Philippe gave us this cabin, which is where he and Imelda used to come when they were dating, before they wanted the press to know about them. It's safe. Like I say, all we need to do is figure out everything else. Simple."

A love hideout? She had to acknowledge a slow turning over inside her at the thought.

****

Lee cursed to himself, repeatedly. What the hell trouble had he gotten them into? Him, he didn't care less, but Ellora?

You have arrived at your destination.

I know.

Ellora blinked, a long languorous sweeping of her lashes, and for a brief second, he saw a fleeing shadow before the sense of a feline came to him. Frowning, he broke their gaze to reach into the glove compartment for the keys, ignoring her proximity. More importantly, ignoring the sensation of a low heat being lit under his skin.

"Let's get inside."

She nodded, and he stepped out of the car to fetch their cases. Together they went up the wooden steps onto the porch gracing the front of the low lined cabin. The key went in without a hitch, and the door swept seamlessly open, inviting them in and around to another door. She gasped, and he turned to see delight in the curve of her lips.

The L-shaped room was dominated by a red shag-pile rug, stretched out in front of the inglenook fireplace with a long, low corner sofa, creating an effective barrier to the kitchen, which was decked out in black and cream marble with grey flagstones. Opposite the wall with the fireplace was a cross between a ladder and wooden stairs, leading up to the mezzanine floor, which looked to house only a super king bed.

"This is gorgeous." Ellora's hand was over her mouth as she wandered around, pulling the heavy blinds up. "Wow."

He stood in the center looking around the small but immaculate cabin. Hot blood swarmed through him, but not from any outside fear. He and Ellora, here on their own in what was clearly a love nest. He felt the knowledge coursing through him, as though it were running through well-worn grooves—grooves he had not yet made. *Focus, North.*

He heard her low laugh behind him. "Hadn't you better go and do manly stuff, check the heating and electricity, light the fire, chop some wood, build a treehouse?"

He should, but he just didn't want to leave her. "I will, all in good time. I just want to see what's in the cupboards too."

Separating, they went through the cupboards.

"Rice, pasta, noodles in mine," she called. "How about yours?"

"Canned stuff, tuna, sardines, tomatoes. Herbs and spices." He poked about a bit more. "Coconut milk."

"Not bad. The fridge is going to be empty." Opening it, Ellora nodded. "Thankfully. But the electricity is on." She opened the door below the fridge. "Excellent, a freezer." It was full of frozen vegetables, along with a bag of chopped onions, and strips of chicken and frozen cod.

"Good for Philippe and Imelda. They know how to do things."

She smiled. "They sure do. So I'm very good at the basics—you know, scrambled eggs and that kind of thing." She bit her lip.

"I can cook and enjoy it." He looked at her. "I think perhaps a Thai green fish curry?"

She nodded. "Sound delicious."

"Stick with me, kid, you'll be fine." He would enjoy cooking for them both tonight and took the cod from the freezer. "I'll check out the rest of the cabin first, and outside too. Come with me?"

Mad, but he just didn't want to be without her. Security, he decided. They ascended the ladder and stopped to look at the vast bed stretched out in front. It was a super king futon mattress on a low base, bedecked with a creamy feather duvet and cushions with wild hares looking knowingly at them.

"You were saying?" He looked at her.

"Um, I was?"

"Maybe it was me then." Images of them tumbling around each other, tasting and trying out, flooded him with a cool mist, and in an attempt to halt the inexorable hardening of his body, he went and looked out the bay window. Below it stretched a ladder, clearly a fire escape. Over on the other side of the room was a door they hadn't seen from below.

Clearing his throat, but still not relying on his voice, he gestured to it and they both carefully stepped around the futon, trying to ignore the white elephant in the room. Through the door was a luxurious wet-room. They stopped and stared.

A panel midway through cordoned off the shower jets, with jets themselves embedded in it, along with three from the ceiling. The other half was a step up and looked as though it was an entire body dryer, with the far wall mirroring everything back to them. On the walls were stacked soaps, moisturizers, massage oils, and heck knew what else.

"Oh my god."

He looked at Ellora, her dark eyes reflecting his whirling emotions. "No wonder Philippe smiled when he gave me the key. Come on."

He grasped her hand, and without looking further, marched them both back through the bedroom and gestured to her to go first.

With a similarly focused air, she went ahead and grabbed her jacket.

"Where are we going?" His voice was thick as he joined her, but he didn't care.

"For a walk. We're safe, right? From the police and Zenon?" Her voice was defiant.

"Yes, we're fine. This place is off the grid; no one knows of its existence."

"Right, let's go."

Picking up his jacket, she threw it at him.

"Are you okay?"

"I'm about as fine as you are, I'd imagine, Lee. Fresh air and good exercise are what I need right now."

Shrugging into his jacket, he grabbed a bottle of water from under the sink and put it into his deep pocket. In two short strides, they were out the door and she stood on the porch, breathing deeply.

He watched some kind of battle within her and understood. He felt the same. He reached out to touch her and tell her, but she swung to him. "I know, okay. I don't think I'd be feeling this quite as intensely if you weren't too."

With her cryptic remark, she went down the steps and took a right into the dense woods. He set off after her. Oaks, pines, and firs grew haphazardly. A dense undergrowth made quick going very difficult, but she had no problem weaving her way through.

However, the concentration needed took his mind off her lithe body moving in front of him, and this he was very thankful for. She paused in front of the dark mouth of a cave but after peering underneath, took back off again. She kept a good pace up, only pausing when they came to a clearing. From the sides of the woods, rose a hill, clear of anything but grass. He halted beside her. She was puffing and pink suffused her cheeks, making her look pretty and carefree.

He waited until she caught her breath before saying, "This is odd."

"It looks like a fairy mound to me."

"What's that?"

They wandered around the base. She chewed on her bottom lip before expanding further. "Apparently, in the Celtic countries, they have quite a few. In Ireland, it's where the Tuatha Dé Danann, whom I believe were shamanic, were confined to when they were defeated. Or they were driven underground. Either way. But the hills don't allow anything to grow on them besides grass. I wonder what's the story behind this one."

She gave him a peculiar look, carefully hidden by thick lashes. "Are we allowed to walk on it?"

"Well yes, I guess."

They headed up the hill, on top of which was a limestone rock, standing upright. She paused by it and ran her hand over the smooth exterior. "Can we sit on it?"

He shrugged and she perched against it, dreamy eyes looking away to the east.

"Do you know what Imelda told me?"

In a few words, she recapped their conversation, and he felt a knowledge awaken. "You know, I can understand it. The whole power animal answers something I didn't know was a question. I bet I can guess what your power animal is."

His words dropped into the silence, an odd silence. Glancing at the sky, he saw the sun well into the west. They were in the gloaming.

She looked almost luminescent in this light, her eyes foreshadowed, her mouth curved gently. A light wind blew a strand of hair free. "Imelda said you have to enter an altered state of consciousness." She gently ran her fingers over the stone. "But here it wouldn't be difficult to do. Chanting or drumming or dancing does it." She glanced self-consciously at him.

"Well, sing, chant, or dance all you want, Ellora."

"No, I can't. I don't know what I'm doing. Moreover, you're here. I'm not sure how much of a trance I could enter, knowing you were watching me. Imelda said something about leaving your ego behind. And my ego at the moment is jumping all over the place in frustration. It wouldn't let me go easily."

He stifled a laugh at the serious expression juxtaposing her words. Yet still he understood.

Dusky pink and pale orange greeted the sun as it went down behind the trees. A low, warm, vibrant color graced the air, the kind which only appeared in the gloaming. She glowed with health in it, her skin clear, the few freckles across her nose standing out, generous lips curved, graceful neck huddled into her jacket.

"You are beautiful." The words were out before he had thought them.

She fastened her eyes on him. "If I am, it's only because the beauty in you brings out the beauty in me." Her words were low and murmured and her eyes widened as she said them.

"Thank you."

She works for you, North. Rein it in. Okay fine. He carefully schooled his face and looked out at the horizon before turning to her.

"Let's go."

She nodded and, taking a deep breath, faced the dying sun and breathed out. She took his hand, and they more carefully made their way back to the cabin. Darkness fell, cold swarmed in, and he cursed himself for allowing them to wander far. But she unerringly made her way back, and before cold had set in his bones, they were climbing the porch steps.

Chapter Eleven

"That was great. I needed the space and the exercise." Ellora took off the jacket and hung it in the small space between both doors, taking her boots off too.

Lee divested himself of his burgundy coat. Unfortunate, in her opinion, as the color highlighted the amber in his eyes and complemented his tanned skin, with the dark stubble creating shadows but drawing her attention irrevocably to his lips.

"I'll light the fire."

"Nice idea. I'll see if I can find their drinks cupboard."

"I'd be surprised if it wasn't well stocked."

"I agree."

Opening all the cupboards, she eventually came across one filled with bottles. "Look at this!" There were several bottles of both red and white wine, sambuca, brandy, and some mixers. "Which would you prefer tonight?"

"Let's open a Malbec, shall we?" He was crouched in front of the fire, blowing at the kindling. She stood watching, pulled in by the movement of his back and for a second, she was the kindling, being gently blown on by him. As the fire whooshed into life, so did her excitement. How was she going to resist him? *This was a perfect set up. This amazing cabin, bed, wet-room.*

Why are you resisting him, anyway?

Damn good question, whoever you are. Because as soon as I allow myself to be vulnerable with him, I'll no longer be in control. That's why.

And what's wrong with not being in control?

I might fall apart without control keeping me upright.

Do you have a choice?

"Are you okay, Ellora?" With a sudden jerk, she put a full stop to her conversation. Chatting back to the voices was something she had never done before. But never had they seemed this insistent. Yet not threatening, instead comforting. And as she focused, she realized it was but the one voice. A nice voice.

"Ellora?"

She startled. "Just opening the wine." She injected a light tone in her voice and, scrabbling around in the cutlery drawer, opened the wine.

"Let's leave it breathe a while, shall we, whilst I start on dinner."

Lee started clattering around the small kitchen. In her head, the image of the witches burning beckoned.

"Do you need me?"

"Not for this, no." He smiled and she felt herself reach out of her body. *This man was ticking all the boxes—even those she didn't know she had.*

"I'll log on to those archives then."

Sitting in front of the kindled fire, she reloaded the website she had been looking at in the car and was soon lost in her searches. After a while had passed, Lee reappeared, holding two glasses of wine and handed her one.

"Whilst we're waiting for dinner, I want to tell you

about the cross, and how my involvement with it ended."

She took a sip of the wine. "This wine is delicious. Perfect. Right, go for it."

"Remember you spoke about the energies of ancient artifacts? Well, there was something so strong about the cross. Holding it felt like a huge responsibility, and once you managed to put it down, the images wouldn't or couldn't leave your mind. And, oh I don't know, it felt *Irish*. I can't explain that only to say, you know when you look at something, because of the artwork, you know where it came from? Celtic swirls, similar kind of thing."

"Was it decorated in a Celtic fashion?"

"No, it was plain and simple. I guess the silver could have been Irish, though. But to view it, there was nothing about it saying Irish. It was only when you held it that you got a sense of it. But I'm jumping to the end—you need to hear the start and, most importantly, the middle."

"Go on."

"We followed the trail to Ireland, to the Wicklow Mountains. Beautiful part of the world. There is a monastery, Glendalough Monastery, one of the most famous in Ireland but now pretty run down, comparatively speaking. When we questioned the prior about the cross, he closed up like a clam."

She watched him carefully and turned herself to face him, no emotion going unchecked. She wanted to know this man, wanted to see how he played out with the thoughts going on in his head.

"Not unusual, certainly, but there was something more to this man's reaction. He seemed scared. Not just a normal scared but a hyper reaction. I wouldn't have been surprised if he had run screaming into the woods.

"Prior Albany wanted us to leave as soon as he heard what we were searching for. We withdrew, naturally, to the boundaries of their land and then came back under cover of darkness. Through the windows of their church came strange lights. We crept closer and heard a low humming. A type of Gregorian chant, I think. The more we could hear, the deeper into my bones it got, and it was quite unpleasant. A bit like the feeling you get inside when you hear chalk screech on a blackboard. When we checked the windows, we saw about a score of monks, all facing the altar chanting. Not so unusual, you'd think. And chanting to a cross. Again, not unusual. Until you saw the cross itself. There were tendrils of black smoke curling around it and in time to the chanting. And when they stopped chanting, it flared up and they bowed as though they were hearing or seeing something holy. Insane though it sounds, there was a call and receive to it—you know the way in music, one instrument calls and another answers? I'm nearly sure this is what happened."

"So, just to be clear—you think the cross was a method of communication?"

"Mad, but yes." He looked almost sheepish as he ran a hand through his hair.

"Well, here's to the crazy ones! What did you do?"

He smiled at her briefly before continuing.

"Throughout our search, we had collated evidence the cross had been commissioned by the Vatican, and hence it had been appropriated. We just did what anyone would do, broke in there and put the terror of the law on the prior's back. The monks reacted as though in a daze and almost dissipated through the doors. The prior? Not so good."

He stopped and gazed into the fire. He gritted his teeth and, closing his eyes, dashed a hand over his forehead. "In fact, to this day, I am not certain whether he was possessed. The way he looked at us was though we had committed him to a long and torturous death."

He transferred his gaze to her and in his eyes, she saw a deep yearning, for something she knew not what. Understanding?

"When I went to take the cross, when I actually touched it, the prior fell to the floor screeching, beseeching us not to take it. We ignored him—after all, it was an important artifact to be returned to where it belonged. I wrapped it in the special cloth, which Constantin had couriered to us. As we did, a silence fell, and it was only then I realized there had been a constant whirring going on in the background. But welcome though the silence was for it, not for the prior. He screeched louder, pressing his hands against his ears. It felt as though what was silence for us was noise for him."

He sighed and his shoulders bunched tightly. Sitting farther up, he dropped his elbows on his knees and ran his hands through his hair.

"He went insane. We couldn't quiet him and had to leave him after calling out the other monks to assist. Then we left with the cross. But the screams followed us. Nightmare."

His voice held echoes of the trauma, and she moved closer, her heart expanding with compassion for him.

"There was nothing else to be done, Lee. As you

say, the cross had been stolen and needed to go back."

He turned shadowed eyes on her. "The more I get to know about Constantin, the more I wonder. Perhaps the cross was the cornerstone of something he didn't understand, is capable of wielding great power, and he just wanted it for himself? How do I know I wasn't his puppet?

"For the monks who had dedicated generations of prayer and power to the cross, perhaps it's their mouthpiece to God. But what do they do without it? More importantly, what does it do without them?"

Watching him rack his hands further through his hair, she ached to bring him peace.

"What happened then?"

He stared so intently into the fire, Ellora was sure she'd see a small red flame run over the edges of him, like a lit paper. Eventually he took a deep sigh and sat back, putting his arm over the back of the sofa.

"The cross was rumored to have special powers. The energy crackled from it. When I touched it, I felt almost as though it was repelling me. Needless to say, I shrugged it off, and once it was in the sack, it seemed to quiet. We drove to Shannon, went through the necessary customs, which had all been organized from Chicago, and got the next flight to New York out of there. But shortly after the plane left the airport, an engine stalled."

Shock spread seeking cold tendrils. "What happened?"

"Fortunately, we were not high. The second engine cut. Cabin pressure dropped, and the plane plummeted."

He spoke calmly, and she could not detect an iota of fear.

"Folks panicked, as you can imagine." He shook his head in remembrance. "It was horrid—you could taste the fear. But then just as we were about to crash into the Atlantic, one engine came online again, and we actually glided onto the water."

"Wow, you were lucky."

He smiled grimly. "More than luck." But the words were spoken fast and so softly Ellora she wasn't sure she had heard correctly.

"The rescue boats were there within minutes. There were no casualties. There were some evangelical voices praising the Lord, bit of weeping and wailing, but we got back on land. Put up at the Shannon Resort Hotel whilst waiting for them to drag the hold and get our luggage back." He cast a wry smile. "Funny thing is, there was no cross to be found.""

"Had the hold been damaged?"

He shook his head at the same time as not taking his eyes from hers.

"But what happened to it?"

"I don't know. I called Constantin immediately. Obviously, I had been keeping him up to date, and he was aware we were on the way back and what flight we were on. I prepared for him to go ballistic. But you know what?" At her head shake, "He didn't. Oh, don't get me wrong, he huffed and puffed, but it all seemed for form's sake. Then he said okay."

"Interesting."

"There are a couple of options here. Constantin wanted me to track the cross. But it was my first commission. I did as he said. I found it. But perhaps he didn't trust me enough with it. Once I found it, he sent someone in to get it."

"But you're implying he caused the plane crash."

"No. But he had men following me, both in the air and on ground. And when there was an opportunity to take the cross after the crash, they did."

She nodded slowly, taking it all in, hard though it was.

"And the second option?"

"Probably more difficult to swallow. The one in which the cross didn't want to leave Ireland and it escaped the hold and is somewhere at the bottom of the Atlantic on the coastline of Ireland."

"Okay." She drew the vowels out as she blew out a long breath. Her brain scrabbled to keep up with what was going on, and part of her wanted to return home.

Aware that he looked with concern at her, she struggled to pull herself together. This was strange, but then her life hadn't been in any way normal. Crosses having souls, duplicitous businessmen double dealing? It was just a level she hadn't been aware of before.

"I'm fine. Don't worry. It's all mad. But I have a lot of respect for madness." The words fell out of her before she knew what she was saying, but she was rewarded by a laugh from him.

"My mother used to say the same."

Warmth spread through her, and she welcomed it without examining it.

"A fat check arrived the next day."

He stood and paced through the room. "As for the prior, I checked on him the following week, rang the Order and asked for him. He was admitted to a mental asylum."

She narrowed her eyes and saw the shadows he was dragging around with him. But they weren't his—

they didn't belong to him.

"Lee, that's not your fault."

He stopped in his tracks, facing away from her. She saw his shoulders rise and fall and then he swung back. "I know."

Despite the words, his eyes remained shadowed and in her mind's eye, she allowed the grandfather clock to tick ten seconds before unfolding her legs and standing. If he didn't want to talk, then fine. She rubbed him gently on the shoulder. "I'll check on dinner. Where shall we eat?" She rummaged around in the cutlery drawer.

"In front of the fire." His low voice rumbled beside her, and she struggled to stay upright on suddenly weak legs.

"Great, here you go." She passed the forks over, along with the bottle of wine. "How about music?"

Music was the only thing missing right now.

"I have no doubt there is a music system squirreled away somewhere. You serve, and I'll figure it out." He disappeared around the corner, and she leaned against the countertop in relief. Hunger, that's what it was. *Yes hunger, but for what?*

****

Lee stood in the middle of the room. What was he looking for again? Being in close proximity with Ellora scrambled his brain. He laughed to himself, it was actually two extremes. For there was no doubt in his mind some things he saw with more clarity now she was with him—take the episode with the monks, for example. She seemed to have cleared away any doubts and confusion. And yet for each moment of clarity, came clouds of confusion. Like right now.

Music. He busied himself opening doors and soon came across a set of speakers, if he recognized them correctly, and would be Bluetooth enabled. Great, time to play his own music. Rummaging through his bag, he pulled out his second iPad, the pay-as-you-go data-enabled one.

"Ellora, you're sure your phone is off?"

There was a moment before she replied, "Yes, dear!"

Smiling to himself, he powered up the iPad and soon had it connected to the speaker. Now what music? He wanted something soothing and nonintrusive for dinner and chose a playlist which started with Snatam Kaur; he had heard her once before at a coffee shop and the sweet tones had created peace in the spaces between his thoughts. Soon her voice filled the air as he filled their wine glasses.

Ellora appeared at the corner of the kitchen. She looked as though someone had switched a light on in her. "This is nice."

She disappeared again. Hearing the unmistakable sound of dinner being served, he went to her.

"Anything I can do?"

"Serviettes are the only thing we're missing."

Lee found some in the kitchen windowsill and pulled the blinds down. He took them into the sitting room, closing the blinds in there too, and lighting the corner lamp, enjoying the shadows being chased. After a moment, he shimmied up the ladder to light the bedside tables. Arriving downstairs, he liked the effect they made, creating a glowing space for them both to retire to. *Yeah but to do what?* He ignored the thought. They had dinner to get through yet.

Ellora came around, holding two steaming plates.

They settled themselves on the sofa, each half turned to the other. She sat cross-legged, placing her plate on her knees.

"Eat!" He gestured to her, and they fell silent as they appreciated the good food.

Immediate hunger depleted, she put her fork down and took a sip of wine. "I've been thinking about the chalice and wondering what Constantin would need it for. I mean, what is a chalice but something to drink from—i.e. blood of Christ. I guess it's too big a leap for it to be the Holy Grail?"

"Interesting."

"If it is the Holy Grail, then that would be a phenomenally powerful artifact. "She returned her attention to the meal. "This is delicious, isn't it?"

He nodded with his mouth full. Somehow, he thought anything would taste delicious around her.

"Which led me onto what Imelda was saying about entering an altered state of consciousness and made me realize—perhaps the chanting put the monks into trance, and so they were communicating with someone or something?" She played absentmindedly with her last bite.

"Look at the place in history for chalices. They have an integral place in religion, with Christ having drunk from one at the Last Supper. But this one, the images you have described, I can't see them as purely Christian. Why were they on it? What was its role in life?"

She placed her cutlery on her plate and pushed it away, gaze on the fire.

"You said the date was around sixteenth century,

didn't you? The religious wars kicked off then. And if these symbols are shamanic, perhaps they were employed in the wars? Think about it…"

She stopped again, eyes following the flames as they leapt and danced with her. Watching her and the way her mind worked was mesmerizing. She thought unlike anyone he had ever met before. This boded well for the future.

"Perhaps another way of looking at shamans would be as witches. And we all know what happened to anyone deemed to be a witch. Let's just say that the chalice was in use for normal Christian activities and then used to try to lure shamans and witches into confessing their so-called sins."

"You mean like a marketing ploy? Come all ye faithful and see the changes we have wrought within our church. If people were drawn in by those images, then they were exposed as witches and, what, burnt at the stake?" He spoke flippantly, but there was a slow changing over in him, the kind heralding realization.

"Yes, exactly."

They stared at each other, both minds ticking over.

"So do we have any answers?"

"What are the questions?"

Lee finished his meal and collected the plates together. Standing, he mused aloud, "Where is it now? Why are we being framed for taking it before we actually took it? Who is Constantin? If he is connected to Zenon, why send us on the trail only to expose us?"

"He must be trying to expose us in this world. But why? Maybe he thinks you are dangerous and pose a risk to his business. He's trying to rid himself of you."

"But why? The clue must lie with the cross."

"Did you see too much? The chanting for example. Maybe that was something he was running. Maybe he set something in motion, and then couldn't stop it. You said yourself how attached they were to the cross. Can you remember whether he said anything about trying to get the cross away before you?"

"Definitely not. I think you're onto something. Funny, I always thought it was strange, but had it filed away as a not-to-be-explained thing. If that's why he did this, then it backfired."

He turned and took the dishes into the kitchen and started washing up.

"Let's sum up, then." Ellora followed him in and busied herself putting things away.

"Constantin hires me to track down a cross. I find it amongst an almost cult-like gathering of monks, who are behaving strangely. I tell Constantin. As he's up to no good, he thinks I have seen too much and now need dealing with."

"Yes, or he wants to recruit you to the dark side. Bring you in and show you what's up."

"He might have used a lighter hand there, then."

Washing up finished, they looked at each other. *What now?* "Coffee?"

"Nah—too late for me. I'll have a chamomile tea." She put the kettle on, and they both wandered back through after Lee filled his wine glass.

Ellora put another log onto the fire. They both watched the sparks flying up the chimney. Crackles sounded as gas pockets burnt fast. With a sigh, she sat on her haunches.

"So have we solved it?"

A heavy thump inside him brought cold blood

swarming through him. They were in danger. And whereas before, it was no bother being in danger—now he had brought someone else into danger with him. And not just anyone else—beautiful Ellora.

He dropped to the rug beside her and took her hand.

"Ellora, I don't want to say this, but I will. As your boss, I'm ordering you to go home. Get yourself out of this. I have inadvertently brought us both into danger."

The fire flared, or was it her eyes?

"No way, Lee. I'm not going anywhere."

"Not your choice, I'm your boss, remember."

"So that's all our relationship is, a working one?"

Damn, she had him there. But what could he say? If he said no, then there was a higher likelihood of her persuading him to allow her to stay. If he said yes, he could pull the boss ticket and she would leave.

He hesitated. "Yes."

She unraveled herself into standing and paced the small place behind the sofa. Watching her, his heart ached—but for what, he knew not.

She stopped and then turned to him. Facing her, a light within him flickered and dropped low. "I want to register that I don't think it's a good thing for me to do. I think you need me here, and not just my amazing researching skills either. On your own, you will be more vulnerable."

No, with you I am more vulnerable. The thought flashed viciously through him, making his blood heat because she had to go.

"Lee, you have brought me into this—how can you just let me go? I'll worry so very much about you."

"I've been in similar situations and know what to

do. Ellora, not only will you be safer, but so will I. I've been undercover before, remember?"

"But what about…?" Her voice quailed and he knew his shot had hit home.

"What about what?"

"Our journey so far together, the things we have uncovered. I just kinda assumed we were in this together. And by together I mean, well, the obvious…" She faltered and then moved rapidly onwards. "But also in order to figure this out, it would take the two of us. Yes, you know how to track artifacts, but I know how to think about it all and to get us there."

He stood and walked around the sofa to her. "You are right, in both your assumptions. And maybe you will be able to help me virtually, and I certainly hope you will—otherwise I'll stop your pay. But for your own safety, and hell"—he ran a hand through his hair—"my own peace of mind, you need to be safe."

The last remaining light within him flickered and died, and his heart sighed. Her eyes mirrored his feelings, but she stuck her chin out.

"I don't agree." She turned her back on him and went out to the kitchen.

Using a private VPN line, he dashed off a message to Jonathon about getting Ellora home. Whilst he was thinking about it, he placed their passports, money, and spare phones back into the backpacks, easy to grab if they needed to. Force of habit from being in dangerous places, not knowing if he'd wake up and have to run or fight.

When he returned his attention to the room, Ellora had sat back down in front of the fire, a steaming cup beside her. He sat beside her.

"I'm sorry."

The look she gave him was bright with unshed tears. "What for?"

"For it ending like this. For it starting like this."

"I think you are making a mistake."

"I know you do. But I have to do this. If anything were to happen to you, I would never forgive myself."

"But what about you?"

"I'll manage."

She nodded and took a deep breath. Blowing the air out seemed to clear the air in front of them. "Nothing we can do about it tonight anyway."

Lee refrained from telling her he had already set things in motion. "Let's sleep. Why don't you sleep up there, and I'll stay down here?"

She bit her lip and huge, expressive eyes looked back. "Perhaps I'm being naïve, but could we share the same bed? I'm not sure I want to sleep alone tonight." The mood shifted between them.

Warmth spread through him. "We can give it a go, why not. If I can't stand being beside you in bed because I want to jump your bones, delicious lady, then I'll come back here."

Her smile spread delight through him, and she drained her cup. "Right, I'll head up then."

"I'll just finish here, tamp down the fire to put it out, and then I'll be up."

Gratitude for the space he was affording her to get ready for bed was obvious, and she headed up the stairs. With an immense effort, he didn't watch as she went, instead gathering the cups and taking them around to the kitchen.

After washing them up, he came back and checked

the fire. It was only smoldering, so he placed the fire blanket over it, waiting until it was clear it had all gone out. This was a timber construction, after all, couldn't be too safe with fire.

"Music?" he called up as he heard her come out of the bathroom.

"Whatever you like, your choices have been spot on."

He mused over his collection. Perhaps some Mari Boine, a Norwegian Sámi singer who transported him somewhere every time he listened. He would enjoy the experience with Ellora. Going to the front door, on a whim, he opened it and looked out. Night was thick and dark over the trees, and as he looked, unease kicked off inside him. Shutting, bolting, and barring the door, he tried to shrug it off. No one knew they were here, besides Philippe. All was safe.

Still, the unease stayed with him as he readied for bed, then eased himself beside Ellora, whose peaceful face told him she was close to sleep. She murmured something, then reached out with her arm, folding herself into his arms.

Hugging her close to his heart, he felt a song in his blood. One he didn't recognize, but which he knew. He felt awareness leave her body as she relaxed into sleep. Hoping the same would happen him, he drifted off on the music.

Chapter Twelve

She was drifting in a beautiful river, naturally breathing underwater. Something was by her side, and turning her head, she saw Lee. The look on his face mirrored the feeling inside of perfect peace. Fronds of green passed them, and a beautiful golden light infused her. The light grew bigger until they both rose to the top to a clearing in the woods. As they emerged, she turned to Lee only to see a tiger by her side instead. Laughing, she shook herself, watching in amazement as drops flew from her. With a jolt of something akin to joy, she saw herself. A panther, long, low, sleek. We are Pride. *With a look at Lee, they turned as one and ran through the woods, feeling wind upon her face as the trees were left behind for a vast pasture lying out before them. She had never moved this fast. She stretched into all four limbs and shook her head in glory. A streak beside her told her Lee was keeping up and enjoying it just as much. Stopping, panting, they stood at the far end, rejoicing in their bodies. Until a dark scent pervaded the air. Both tensed and Lee looked, his amber eyes reaching deep into her blue gaze. He shook his head sharply.*

She opened her eyes to see him looking straight into hers. "Time to go. Now."

Without speaking, she sat up and threw on her jeans and top as he did the same. Once done, they stood in silence, listening. With a funny pang, she yearned for the clarity of sound she had in her dream. But something felt wrong. She gestured to the stairs, but Lee shook his head, going over to the window. *But her things?* Had to stay here. He had a small backpack already plastered to his back and handed her hers. The case was too unwieldy to bring down the ladder outside.

Cold air flew through the window, and she shivered. She'd miss the warm wool coat and, reaching inside her case, pulled another jumper from it and wrapped it around her waist. At the window, Lee looked back and cursed quietly. Going back to the bed, he pulled the duvet back and folded it at the end then gave a decisive nod.

He hesitated at the window, clearly not knowing whether to lead the way or to stay in case danger arrived before they could both get out. She shimmed under the low window, gasping as wind buffeted her. With her heart in her mouth, she felt for the rungs of the ladder and, after testing each rung, placed her weight on it. A loud creak rent the air, and she froze. Nothing happened and she whispered up, "That was the third rung." She made it down without further mishap, and soon the sound of the window closing came to her and he appeared, a large mass in the darkness.

He grabbed her hand. "Come." They jogged alongside each other away from the house, both unerringly going in one direction. Warming up quickly, after about five minutes they slowed to a walking pace.

"What now?" She kept her voice low, knowing how sound could travel in the dark.

"I don't know. Maybe head to the cave we saw earlier. Wait until sunrise."

She nodded and they changed direction, doubling back and across. They fell into a fast pace and soon arrived at the dark mouth. Lighting his phone up, the two bent low and entered it. Made of sandstone, it was soft and rough at the same time, the floor covered with sand. There was a groove against the far wall, and it was there they sat.

"What the hell?" Ellora knew she sounded panicked but couldn't help herself.

"All I know is we couldn't stay there any longer. Something woke me. It's almost as though I could smell danger."

His words broke something in her mind. "We did. Remember? When we were the large cats?" Her words tumbled from her in excitement. "Weren't you there?"

Silence was her only answer.

"We went through a river, remember, and emerged in a clearing. You as a tiger, me a panther?" Frustrated she couldn't see him, she flicked the torch on the phone and the cold white played shadows on his face, making him looked shocked and worried. But heck, it had felt real. And to wake like that, his eyes looking into hers, exactly as in her dream had convinced her it was real.

"Go on. Tell me what happened."

In for a penny, in for a pound.

"We ran, you and I, as large cats. Through the woods and across a huge field. It was glorious, feeling the speeds we could go to." She laughed in hindsight at the joy she had experienced. "I know you felt it too. You had to have. Then we were just looking at each other, and suddenly, we smelled danger. You felt it first and told me in your eyes. I opened mine, and there you were, looking at me. Just the same as in the dream, if a dream was what it was."

"I woke up looking into your eyes like you had just blinked, and you were present and in the moment with me."

She felt a rising sense inside her. This was important stuff, bizarre but important. As she recognized it, she felt as though something stamped upon it as though to minimize the importance. *Not for you.*

She gave a brief shake to throw the thought away. "What *was* the danger?"

"It must be the police or Zenon coming to look for us."

"But how would they have found us?"

"Only one way—Philippe must've told them."

His jaw was set at a stubborn angle, and she saw the muscle tick against his ear.

"You're jumping to conclusions. It couldn't be. Not Philippe. You've known him for ages. Why would he send us off to his fabulous hideout and then give the police the heads-up? He wouldn't, Lee. It must be someone else."

Lee stood, narrowly avoiding the cave roof. "I don't see how."

"Maybe there is no danger, we're just letting it all get to us." *Yet that would give lie to her dream and to the knowing part inside her.*

"Maybe." He nodded slightly to her and paced to the mouth and back again. "There's only one way to know for sure."

"Ask him?"

"I go back and watch the cabin and see what happens. If we did overreact, then great, we can get our stuff. But if we didn't, we'll need to rethink."

"I'll come with you."

"No, you stay here." His tone told her he wouldn't be moved.

"But what happens if you get into trouble?"

"I won't. I'll stay in the trees. Ellora, I need to do this, and you need to stay here. I'll be back."

"And what happens if you don't?" She knew her voice was cool, but damn this. She didn't want to be apart.

"Call Jonathon on the pay-as-you-go phone. Tell him I've disappeared and to get you out of here. We can't use these passports, but we could get a train somewhere. Here…"

He reached into his wallet and pulled a credit card out and gave it to her. "The number is three-one-seven-oh. Use it."

"Lee, let me come with you."

He stopped in the process of putting his wallet back and went into a crouch in front of her. "Ellora, if both of us get captured, then where'll we be? Notwithstanding, I won't place you in danger, two of us in the trees would be hard to hide. Me on my own is much easier."

Desolation threatened to overwhelm her, but she reached deep inside. He was right, at least she would remain free and be able to help him. She gulped and nodded. "Be careful."

"I'll be an hour, two at tops." He went to leave, then turned and advanced on her, eyes glinting in the cold light. She stood to meet him, and he wrapped her in his arms. "Don't worry. Now I've found you, I'm not going anywhere." She nodded against his chest, feeling him move back. She pressed her lips hard to his cheek, then dropped a kiss on his mouth. Anything more would be torture. She stepped back.

"I'll be counting the minutes."

And he was gone.

She was left alone in a cave in the gloom. Silence grew and stretched around her. Her eardrums quivered with the effort of listening, and she felt a particular heaviness in her ears. *Crazy kid. You can't be on full alert. Step down.* She breathed deeply, placing her hand on her diaphragm to feel her belly fill and drop. Lying to better accommodate her breath, she hummed—what song she knew not, but it was deep—and after five or so minutes of it, she relaxed. Allowing her body to sink into the earth below her, she drifted off into some place, neither here nor there, not waking nor sleeping. But she felt safe, worried but safe. An image interrupted her— the one she had been looking at in the car before she felt sick. Moving herself to be more comfortable, she took her iPad from her bag and powered it on to look at the screenshot she had taken.

It was quite terrifying, really. Two young women being burnt at the stake whilst onlookers crowded. Both women had been depicted with hook noses and pointed chins—was this a correct likeness, or was the artist influenced by the women's supposed trade? As she stared, she felt herself being pulled towards it, and it was as though the flames leapt higher as she gave the print more and more of her attention. The more she looked, the more she saw. The men who were afraid for their womenfolk burning. The women themselves, appearing to be accepting of their horrible fate. No children, thankfully, for that she could not have borne.

Beside the women lay a pile of cloaks and belongings; were they next to be burnt? A small item grabbed her attention and she enlarged the heap. *Yes, there.* A small bowl was nearly buried underneath—but not just any bowl. She enlarged it even more, rendering it to a blur but being able to see the shape of the markings. Swirls, Celtic swirls. And a cross. And the start of something which curved around the bowl. Her heart leapt into her mouth. For she was sure, one hundred percent, this was their chalice.

When she heard noises coming from the brightening entrance, she only allowed herself to think it must be a fox or some animal on an investigation. When the entrance fully darkened though, she sat up in excitement. It was Lee, it had to be.

"Ellora." Never before had her name on someone's lips sounded as beautiful. She struggled to her feet and threw herself at him. Outstretched arms caught her and soon she was in a warm safe bear hug.

"What happened?" Once she felt her heart return to normal, she had to know.

"We were right."

Of course. She pressed a hand to her mouth.

"I got there still pretty much under cover of darkness and climbed the great oak. Standing against one of the limbs, I was invisible. Fortunately. For the place was like honey to a swarm of bees…the lights were all on, and there were three SUVs parked up outside. Our bedroom window was open, clearly they had seen the ladder.

"They knew the place, for one went unerringly to the ladder and two went to the front door. Then the leader emerged, talking on his walkie talkie. 'They were here but they're gone. Bed is cold, fire is cold. You can tell Philippe he'd better come up with something more.'

"They didn't hang around and took the car. I don't think they took anything else, but I didn't want to chance going back in."

She was dying to know more, but now wasn't the right time. Lines etched on his face spoke of disappointment and betrayal.

"Come here." She sat and patted the ground beside her and with a sigh, he lowered himself. She grabbed his hand. "Maybe he had to tell them. You don't know what's going on, after all."

"You think?"

"I do. You've been friends with him for a long time."

"And he was genuine about letting us have the cabin." He fell quiet and she stroked his hand, shifting herself to face him. She let him muse for a while. "You know what? I really liked Imelda too, and I generally have a good instinct for people."

He moved restlessly. "I need to see him."

"What, and ask him?"

"Well, what else can I do? As you pointed out last night, I need to find the chalice and I won't do that by sitting here. In want of a different direction, I'll go down this one."

She noted the use of "I" with a pang that had nothing to do with danger. "You'll be walking into the lion's den."

"Perhaps. But you are right—I have known them for a long time. He might be in trouble. He might know information I need. I realize the gamble, but without any other direction, I think it's worth taking."

A sudden dip in her stomach told her this was the right thing to do, with the ensuing flush of excitement rushing through her.

"And I can talk more to Imelda and find out more." The words were out before she quite knew she was saying them, darn it.

"Ellora. I've set things in motion for you to be safe. I'm not changing my mind. Once Jonathon gets back to me, we'll know more. For now, you stay."

It was better than nothing, and she was going to make damn sure he wasn't going to dump her in Athens too. Slowly, slowly, catchy monkey. She schooled her face to be blank.

"Okay, how do we do it?"

He glanced out the cave mouth, slightly chewing his bottom lip. "We have nothing with us except for money and passports. I wonder have they put out a missing-persons alert for us? We need a car."

"Well, you find me a car. I'll make it work for us." No problem to her, she hadn't spent the last ten years tinkering with engines without learning how they worked inside and out. *Score one on the indispensable list.*

"I thought you might be able to." Admiration lit his eyes. "Keeping low, we avoid people and get a car. Easy."

"Okay, but before we go, let me just show you something." She passed him the image.

He took it. "What am I looking at?"

"It's the chalice."

She watched him flick over and around and through the image until eventually, his eyes settled and grew rounder. He peered closer. "You're right—only it's not the chalice. It appears to be a bowl?"

"Yes! And maybe this is why we couldn't track it down before."

"Excellent. Where was this?"

"Ipswich, England, sometime in the mid-seventeenth century."

"We had to start somewhere. So it was what was deemed a witch's possession. Interesting. This contradicts the earlier thoughts of religious icons."

"Normally, you might think so. But when you take into account Christianity's high jacking of many pagan rituals, perhaps they highjacked their worshiped objects too?" She stood, being too excited to remain still, and started pacing through the small room. "Let's look at extremes here—let's say this bowl was what sentenced them both to death—they must have used it for something. But what?"

He turned to watch her in the ever-increasing morning light.

"Good work, Ellora. Let's walk and talk now." He stood and held out a hand. She slipped hers in and allowed him to pull her against his long lean body for a fraction. *Yummy*.

They both exited the cave, she blinked in the bright sunlight. Out of cover of the cave, nerves fizzed her stomach. "Lee?" She kept her voice low.

"Mm?" He was checking out the path.

"Do you not think those men might be out looking for us? Did you actually see them leave?"

He nodded and put an arm around her shoulder, rubbing gently. "I did. And the car. They were saying we were long gone. Fire cold, bed cold, and there was no point without the dogs."

As though on cue, in the far-off distance, a dog barked, followed by the racket that could only be a pack.

Her blood ran cold. "They came back with the dogs though."

"Okay, we've still got a head start. We're okay. Come on." He grabbed her hand and they half ran, half slipped down the trail to the cave.

"Which direction are we going in?" She didn't like the way they were headed.

"We should curve around where the cabin is, as we need to get past it anyway. If those dogs are following our trail, they will stick with it anyway. And the direction of the cabin is the only way I know which ends with civilization. This here"—he gestured expansively at the huge trees—"I have no idea where they end. Going in deeper is only going to lead to trouble."

"The dogs won't pick us up as we go past them?"

"We won't be close enough. If we're lucky, we'll come across a stream."

She shivered. A cold dip was not quite what she wanted. Mind, being dragged into custody was not a viable option. She scoured the trees, looking for weeping willows as their presence indicated water and hopefully a stream. They fell into a fast pace with each other. For morning time, there were few squirrels about, but generally it was quiet. As they moved through the trees, she realized just how quiet.

No breaking of twigs below their feet, no scampering of animals flushed out by their approach. Silence seemed to follow them, surround them even.

She welcomed it as she would an invisibility cloak and wrapped herself up in it but stayed alert. The trees thinned out and maybe because of it, she heard barking. They stopped and listened.

"It sounds as though they're going away from us, which would make sense."

Ellora nodded. "Look." She pointed ahead and to their right. "If I'm not mistaken, those branches look like the boughs of a willow. It's slightly out of direction, but let's check it out."

They followed what looked like an animal trail over a tussock and heard the sounds of trickling water. After a couple of minutes, a small stream wended its way merrily around and through the hollow in front.

"What do we do?" She narrowed her eyes as she looked at the stream. "Immerse ourselves?"

"Wade through it."

Relief lightened her mood. "Great. I thought we were going to have to strip and dive in." She shivered at the thought.

Splashing noisily, they crossed at ankle height of the water. "Good job too, as the water isn't deep enough to cover us and it's damn cold."

Once on the other side, Lee said, "Be careful to stay out in the open, avoid dense thickets, that kind of thing."

Good point. After about another half an hour of trekking, they stopped and listened. Still faint sounds of dogs but getting closer. They set a faster pace.

This is weird. Being on the run from hounds. How the hell did this happen? Her stomach rumbled. Lee held a hand out to stop her, and she suddenly became conscious she was trudging through the forest, head lowered and on autopilot.

"Are you okay?" His velvet-warm tones wrapped around her, and she resisted the desire to snuggle into him and forget about life.

"I'm okay. Let's just get there, wherever there may be. I am hungry though."

"We need an old farmhouse with tractors and cars parked outside and an open window into the kitchen, in which lies a loaf of bread just out of the oven and cooling."

Her mouth salivated, and she laughed. "Yeah, and a pot of honey from their beehives sitting alongside a nice yellow pat of butter, complete with a sign saying, "Help yourselves.' "

"Don't forget the coffee!"

She inhaled as though she were drinking up the smell. "Scrumptious." But it had worked. Yes, she may be hungry, but she could cope. She glanced up at the sky. "Midday must be soon, judging by the sun."

They fell into step together. "I'm excited about the illustration." She had forgotten about it in their run, but now she was flooded with delicious awareness.

"So not a chalice, but a bowl. Let's think...bowls, chalices, goblets. Well, they're all to do with the water element. Liquid to be drunk."

"And what else can you do with liquid in a bowl?" Her mind raced as though it knew it was about to come up with the right answer.

"Aside from drinking it?" Lee sounded amused.

"Scrying, Lee, scrying! A definite witch-like thing to do!" Her voice had risen in excitement, and a detached part of her wondered, was she herself sounding witch-like? The thought amused her at the same time as it knocked a piece of jigsaw puzzle into place, somewhere inside her.

He laughed delightedly. "So that was why those women were being burned? Because they told the future with this bowl?"

"Who knows, but why was it in the frame if it didn't have anything to do with it?" She thought back to the two women. *You are my friends now.*

"I think you're right."

Without realizing it, the two had been on a path, one which now opened up into a dirt trail. Glancing at each other, they silently made a pact to be quieter. Lee walked in front of her, his head continually turning as he checked where they were going. Trees became increasingly sparse until on both sides there was a high hedge growth. The path had developed well-worn grooves, with a grass verge running in the middle. To their right appeared domesticated fields, plowed and turned over for the winter.

Rounding a corner, in the distance they could see the farmhouse. Long, low, and white, it stood out against the horizon, a distinct lack of trees to provide cover. Keeping quieter, they approached it, ducking by the hedgerow whenever possible. A scrambling in the bushes stopped them in their tracks, and they froze. She was sure Lee must be able to hear her heart, as it threatened to leap out of her body through her throat. With a *whoosh* and a loud screech, a pheasant launched itself into the air, and she stumbled backward until she felt Lee grabbing her, her head feeling so light she felt as though it was about to float from her shoulders.

"Give me a minute, please."

Her voice emerged pale and wan, and Lee had

concern in the planes of his face as he watched her. "Do you want to wait here, and I'll come back for you?"

"No, don't worry about me. I just need some more water. And chances are I'll get it there more so than here."

"Let's keep going then." The farmhouse was beginning to take shape now. A long line of washing hung outside in what must've been the garden, an endless garden with a couple of red wooden sheds. As of yet, they couldn't see any vehicles.

"Choices—we march up there bold as brass and ask for help. Or we go covert, get something to drive and hopefully something to eat." Lee scanned the house. "It doesn't look like there's much going on inside the house."

A deep roar rent the air, and they shrank against the hedge as it subsided into a low throb. He peered through a break in the hedge, quickly sinking back by her. "The tractor is heading out to some fields. It doesn't look like a large farm, no livestock, for example. There are no outdoor playthings or signs of children around, so hopefully it'll be the farmer and only his wife inside."

"Baking bread and making honey?" She nudged him playfully. "Or maybe she's off saving the world somewhere."

"Either way, we're going to have to go for it. Now there is no cover, we're going to have to walk up there. If there's a car, we head straight to it as though it's our own. How long does it take to hot-wire?"

"All depends on the type of car. The older, the easier it is."

"Okay." He straightened and grabbed her hand.

"Let's go, Ellora Radley. Head up, shoulders back. We have business here."

They strode out from the path and onto the property's land. She scanned the blank windows for movement, anything. The washing flapped in the wind and a lonely crow swooped over their heads, cawing. "Hot damn, announce our arrival, or what." Lee sounded irritated.

"I like crows. Let's follow him."

The crow disappeared around the far end of the house rather than the near one.

"You sure?"

"Yes." She couldn't quite say what it was, and perhaps it was only her empty stomach talking, but her instinct was adamant.

"Okay."

Cutting across the garden in front of the washing line, Lee kept his head turned towards the house whilst she watched the crow. They reached the far corner and went around. In front was a garage with a side door. Lee strode down the side of the house and peered around.

"Bad news, no cars."

But the crow was sat atop the garage and Ellora tried the door gently, hoping it wouldn't be locked. They were in luck, for soon they were in the gloom. Alongside a car. An old dark-green mini.

"Excellent," she whispered, "this one is easy." She walked around it, running her hand over it. "And it's in good shape too."

"Let me check the garage door."

Despite the loud thumping of her heart, it rose in spirits. For in the garage lay out any and every kind of tool she would need. First, she grabbed a broad but thin knife, then reaching over to the hooks on the wall, pulled a leather biking jacket from its wire hanger. The knife she inserted in between the car door and the car, and once she had a tiny space, she shoved a wedge in, broadening the gap to allow the coat hanger through. Once the gap was wide enough, she straightened the wire hanger and sent it in to pull the lock up. The wire wasn't strong enough. *Damn.*

Seeing her fluster, Lee came over. "How's it going?"

"I just can't seem to get through to the lock." Her hands were clammy, the coat hanger slippery.

"Here, let me."

He pulled it back up and doubled the wire before sending it back again. With a click, the lock released.

"There you go, kiddo," he said as he opened the door with a flourish. "Do your thing."

She shoved the seat back and peered under the steering column. "Have you got your phone handy, with the torch?"

Within a couple of seconds, she had a bright light showing her the panel below. "Great, this is old enough to be prized off. Excuse me."

She scooted out, only to lie herself back on the seat in order to access the panel with ease.

"Are you okay there, or do you need a hand?"

No way, mister. This is my territory. You already had to get the lock for me. "No, no, I'm fine, thanks." *At least she'd better be.*

Putting her back into it and using the palette knife, she eventually got the panel off. "We are lucky this is an old car. The newer models are equipped with so many locking mechanisms and alarms, we'd never have gotten this far." She huffed as she pushed the panel out the door.

"Now for the serious stuff." She muttered under her breath as she clocked the three different colors—which one was the ignition? The brown one. Yes! Quickly stripping the battery wires, she entwined them and stripped the ignition wire of about an inch of cable.

She whispered, "Lee."

Perusal of the doors complete, he came over.

"I've got it. How're the doors?"

"They're well oiled. Do we close them after us? If we leave them open, then it's obvious the car is gone. But can we take a chance on waiting whilst I close them?"

"I think so. This baby should be quiet enough. And let's say you were in the house and you heard what you thought was your car start up. You'd go to your window and watch to see if you'd imagined it or not. A pause before we drive out of here might work in our favor."

"Okay. I'll open them, you drive out, I'll close them, hop in, and then off we go."

He walked from the car, and Ellora set to. The minute the doors opened, she started the car, wincing. But it was a gentle roar, and she placed it into first gear and took the hand brake off.

Gently pressing the brake, she brought it to a quiet halt outside the doors. Lee closed them and clambered back into the passenger's seat, making the already small car miniscule.

"Ready?"

He nodded and she put the car into first gear, and it

hummed quietly under her feet.

He banged on the dashboard. "Way to go, Ellora. Gentle down the drive, then floor it."

She pressed the accelerator, and the car crept away from the house.

By the time they had covered the hundred yards or so until the gates—thankfully open—she had the car in second gear running at ten miles an hour. Lee had twisted in his seat and watched the house carefully.

"There doesn't appear to be any movement at all. We might be in luck."

Glancing very briefly in the mirror, she agreed, but it was only on the open road that she allowed herself to relax. As soon as she did, her stomach rolled in an almighty rumble. She felt him look over. "Do we stop at services—I seem to remember one on the way out— or do we go to a shop? We need to eat. And coffee, man I need coffee."

"Have a look in the back seat, is there anything we can use? Jackets, hats, scarves, anything?"

He leaned closer to her to look to the back seat and she could feel the heat of him. Despite empty stomachs and nerves and adrenaline, there was a deep tugging within her for him. For his closeness, for his smell, for the security of being in his arms, even for a brief moment.

"And ta-daaaa!" He flourished a farmer's cold weather hat in the air, the kind with warm flaps pinned over the crown, able to be tied under the chin. "Exactly what we need."

"Okay then, you can do the shopping. Supermarket or services?"

"Supermarket. Most services have cameras and are

quite small. Once this car has been reported as missing, then they'll scour the services. How's the petrol, by the way?"

"Nearly full. It was the first thing I checked."

"Okay, let's head to the supermarket."

She nodded. "But be quick, right? Grab coffees and pastries. Don't do a weekly shop, darling."

He grinned an easy wide-mouthed smile. "What— no wine? No sambuca?"

Seeing a sign for the supermarket, Ellora flicked on the indicator and took a road opening into a large discount shopping area. "Where to park? Out on our own or amidst other cars?

"In the middle."

"Okay. But far enough away from the entrance." As soon as she saw something suitable, she pulled the little car in and allowed the engine to die.

Chapter Thirteen

Lee pulled the hat over his head and grabbed the fleece-lined jacket. Yes, he looked too hot for the weather, but so what—he could be an invalid or something. The aroma of coffee surrounded him as soon as he stepped through the sliding doors and he growled in appreciation before stopping himself.

Checking out the delicatessen counter, he grabbed a basket and piled in sandwiches, pastries, fruit, and water. When it came to his turn for ordering, he placed one for four coffees. Making the coffee took forever and he had to keep fighting the desire to look at his watch. What was he going to do about sending Ellora home? Jonathon hadn't replied—or if he had, the message hadn't come through. But if it was safe enough, he had to send her back. He'd never forgive himself if anything happened to her. But then would she ever forgive him for sending her home? He was in no uncertain mind about how she felt about it. Perhaps it would be the death knell before they had ever taken off. But still, better a dead relationship than a dead girlfriend. Where was the damn coffee? If their time was limited, then he wanted to be with her for as long as it they had.

Finally receiving his coffee holder laden with cups, he took back off through the supermarket, scanning the car park as he went through the doors. For a brief second, he thought the car had gone, but then he espied it. As he approached, he saw her reach over and open the passenger's door for him. He subsided into the car, expelling a long breath of air.

"I thought something had happened and you'd had to move."

"Likewise, I thought you took forever—maybe we should lighten up." She smiled sideways. "Eating and coffee should help with the nerves. Are we okay here or should we move?"

"Here, undercover of the other cars."

Silence and condensation filled the car as they both ate and drank. Finally, with a groan, she laid her head back. "I'm done. I'm full. I'm not sure I can ever move again, in fact."

He handed her a second coffee, laughing as her eyes widened. "I figured we could both use two each."

"I like the way you think, Lee North."

"We are about twenty minutes away from Athens now. How do we play this…"

She stared at the steam on the windscreen. "I don't know. Options are we walk straight in there and confront them, or we call ahead and try to set something up."

"Not good options. Remember the security of the place, and also I'd imagine their communication would be compromised."

"Good point." She stared out the window. "Break in?"

"I doubt it." He drummed his fingers on the side of his coffee. Doubt shadowed his mind. "And if we do get in, how would we get out again? Bear in mind we need an escape."

"Should we try to meet them elsewhere?"

"Of all the places they'll be looking for us, the Acropolis certainly isn't it."

She nodded slowly and he saw the steely glint renew in her eyes. "Okay, should we try to see Imelda?"

"I don't know if we can trust her."

"But we don't know who we can trust and we need answers."

"Do we? Right now, I think we need the chalice."

"Shall we just march on up there and ask to see it?"

The dryness in her words nearly made him laugh.

A brief flash of merriment lightened her distracted gaze before her eyes opened wide.

"Wait a minute, the lady who runs the boutique down the road from the hotel had an entire room filled with masks and hair pieces and wigs, ready for the masked ball. Maybe we could go there and get kitted out in a disguise?"

Good idea. "Do you trust her?"

She bit her bottom lip and her troubled eyes captured him. He could see her mind working hard. "She was very good to me, but she is the aunt of one of the concierges. Yes, I'd say yes. There was something about her—it was almost like she could see my soul when she looked at me, and I don't know about you, but I trust those few people like that with my life."

"Right, let's make our way to town. We'll both go to the shop, and if anything happens and we decide we don't trust her, then we'll think again."

She half smiled before her mouth became downturned again. "I'm not going to ask what you mean."

"Something is going to happen today. One way or another."

It was a sobering thought, and he could see her excitement and adrenaline wilt. He waited to see what would happen next. Her chin lifted and her shoulders went back. "Let's do it." She reached under and started the engine and soon they were headed into town.

"Ellora, I just want to say—"

She held a hand up quickly before returning it to the wheel. *Don't.*

****

All too soon, they were wending through now familiar roads. Ellora had been lulled into a false sense of togetherness by a full stomach, replete caffeine levels, and enjoyment of the drive. Rain had started, and the near hypnotic swish swipe of the windscreen wipers had taken her mind and treated it to a sparkling future with the man by her side.

Now they were back on familiar territory, her low-level nausea returned along with unease. After parking on a quiet back street, Ellora led the way to the shop. The streets were quiet in the rain and the dip after coffee rush before the lunch time workers left their desks. She saw Lee scanning the doorways they passed, scouring the corners for cameras, and she pulled her jacket farther over her head, not for the first time thanking the weather gods for giving them both a reason to hide their heads.

Stopping under the small porch door, she stopped. "We're sure?"

"Sure we have no other option, yes." He nodded and pushed the door open, standing back to allow her to enter. As the bell tinkled, Marianne came out of the back office, hand flying to her mouth as she saw Ellora. Any fears she may have felt were soon allayed by the concern in Marianna's eyes.

"Quick, quick, come in."

She ushered them into the changing room area.

"The police were around here asking about you. I said you were a beautiful young girl with no need to steal anything." Marianne patted her cheek. "And is this the man they were asking about? Lee North?"

Lee watched Marianne as Ellora introduced him. What he saw reassured him; a strong, compassionate woman who, even though scarcely knew them, was looking at Ellora as though she were her long-lost granddaughter. There was also an air of oppressed frustration around her.

"I don't like the way this town is run by him." She chinned towards the door. "He thinks he owns the place. Pah. You know what I think?" She glared at them both. "He has the chalice himself. I don't like that man, never have. But what are you going to do? The scale of the search for you is wide. You've been on television, you know."

Ellora swayed and reached behind her for the low-lying sofa. Lee caught her as she sank back and gently lowered her into the cushions. He glanced at Marianne, seeing soft concern in her eyes.

"We have to find the chalice ourselves. So, Zenon has it?"

"But where?" She gave an expansive shrug. "I know not. I don't know this chalice, what it looks like. The press is not showing images of it as they are asking for help from the public."

"Can we trust you, Marianne?"

"But of course. I have good instinct when it comes to people." She paused, her face soft. "And as I said to Ellora, she has a good connection to the spirit world, and you do too." Still holding Lee's hand, she picked Ellora's up and held both close to her expansive bosom before closing her eyes. "You two are strong. You are protected by the spirits, like a great oak tree. Remember this. Allow yourselves to go places you haven't been to, but always remember to thank the spirits for their help and protection."

She opened her eyes, the turquoise in them fading back to a normal blue. The tiniest of shivers went through Lee, almost like someone had quickly brushed him all over with a magnet.

Glancing at Ellora, he saw she looked bigger, stronger somehow.

"Marianne, we had something strange happen to us in the woods. Can I ask you about it?"

He hadn't known Ellora was going to look for clarity on their dream.

"You can try—I might be able to help, then again, I might not. Wait one moment."

Marianne left the room and soon the sound of her locking the door came to them. Lee looked at Ellora, "Are you sure about this?"

"Since we don't understand what was going on, we need to talk to someone who might."

Marianne came back into the room. "How can I help?"

"We were staying in a cabin in the woods." In a few brief words, she told Marianne about the dream. Lee forced himself to remain quiet and watched as Marianne reached out and clasped Ellora's hand.

"Go on, this is your power animal." Marianne looked pink with pleasure. "I've still got it. I was right. I thought you two had a strong connection. Your power animals have come to get your attention. A clear sign you are meant to do something important. And together. I have not heard of this before."

"Marianne, can you tell us more about power animals?"

"In shamanic terms—you've heard of shamanism?"

Both nodded. "Well, a power animal is like a guardian angel in Christianity. Your animal protects and guides you, contributes toward your power, and each have certain attributes to bring you. Everyone has a power animal, some have more than one. Both of you being large cats show a deep affinity with each other. Panther and Tiger are similar, strong hunters, yet gentle. Both show strong family ties, are loyal yet can be ruthless. You need to look into the qualities these animals bring you. Also remember they are there when you need help."

"How do we ask them for help?" Ellora's voice was breathy and her eyes sparkled.

"Have you felt them since then?"

Ellora nodded. "Out in the cave, I definitely felt something. I was safe, for sure. When I was in the dark too, I felt I wasn't alone and the dark wasn't dark, more like bathed in bright moonlight, although it was a very cloudy night."

"Panther was with you. Normally I would say for you to do a journey—go into trance and visit the lower world to ensure Panther is your power animal. Then when in the lower world—the wonderful pantheistic world—you see whether an animal comes to you three times. Each time, thank the animal and move on. After the third time, ask the animal if he or she is your power animal and then if the answer is yes, talk to them and ask them how you can honor them in your everyday life.

"Spend some time with them, see if there are any messages for you in the spirit world, then thank them, retrace your steps, and come back into this world. Then you must see what ways you can honor and thank them in your daily lives. Perhaps, as both Panther and Tiger are endangered, you could sponsor the species. We can do a journey now if you like in order to acknowledge them and bring them formally into your lives. I can beat the drum for you."

"This is fascinating, Marianne. How do you know it all?"

"Oh my dear, long story. I've always been involved in shamanism, in all my lives." Marianne twinkled at Ellora. "And I can see both of you have been too. You just don't know it yet. Before we journey, I don't think this is what you came to my door for. What can I do for you?"

"Ellora mentioned you had wigs and clothes and we were wondering, can we disguise ourselves here and perhaps take more clothes with us?"

Marianne laughed. "You can, yes. But you don't need my help."

"How do you mean?"

"Well, what have we just been talking about? Your power animals? Shape shift into them."

Ellora burst out laughing. "But won't a tiger and a panther attract a lot of attention?"

Lee gazed over. That was her question? Not "What the hell are you talking about, woman?" Ellora seemed to take it in her stride, easily. But man, he was struggling. How could their bodies just shift into something different? Weren't they made of skin and bones and all things impermeable? How did it change? The night before, he had enjoyed being in another's body, but it was just a dream. And now? Now they were actually considering going into the lion's den—at this, his lip curled at the old saying—with nothing other than illusion to protect them? And yet, a knowing unfurled within him. This was right, this was the thing to do.

Last night, his dreaming self had changed. Not his reality. *But who was to say what was and wasn't reality? His thoughts and experiences?* He was sure of Ellora's response; as there was nothing to prove it wasn't impossible, it was therefore possible. Perhaps the only limitations on this exercise was the constriction of his thoughts. Set them free and who the heck knew? He settled back to watch the women, deep in their discussion.

****

Marianne laughed. "You have much to learn, yet know a lot already. It is a strange combination, but I can't give you the answers, only show you what is possible. Tiger and Panther, your power animals—honor them."

"Can we be invisible as we are?" Ellora couldn't quite believe her ears. Yet a glance at Marianne's implacable face reassured her.

"Yes, in your human form you can, but it takes practice and power, attained over many lifetimes. As

175

your power animals have come to you, you should avail of their help."

"But how will we, oh I don't know, open doors?"

Marianne's laugh was light and amused. "Do not worry. I will guide you to your power animals, you will welcome them and ask them whether they are your power animals. Once you have confirmation, you will journey back with them and from here, go on as Tiger and Panther."

Simple!

"Hang on a second." She stood, conscious her voice rose with her. "Don't tell me we are going to change into animals and go to the Acropolis and find the chalice?" She dashed a hand over her forehead. "Really?" She paced around the room.

Lee rose and walked over to her. As he did, the air tensed slightly, and an awareness sprang into her bones. A primal awareness. Her sense of smell woke, and she could smell something strange, yet familiar.

He took her hand, and the hairs rose on the back of her neck. All that framed him, the room, Marianne's concerned face, the clothes on their racks, faded into a blur whilst the bones in his face stood out, the intensity in his eyes aflame in an otherwise white face. As she stared deeply, the color of his eyes seemed to fade from deep whiskey to diluted whiskey to a shade without color, then they were deep whiskey again, but it wasn't Lee looking out. Well, it was, because she'd know him anywhere, but it was a different version, a different time. Her ears hummed and droned, getting louder and she put her hands up. *Stop.* "Stop!" she shook her head and the loud buzzing mercifully subsided, and she was left holding Lee's hand. The Lee she knew in this lifetime.

"We've done this before, Ellora. This time at least we will know what's happening. Don't forget—what has not been proven impossible may not be. Who's to say?"

Marianne returned from wherever she had gone, with a drum in her hand. A round drum, very like an Irish bodhran—something which Flicka played—and beautifully crafted with an image of a bear on it. She looked from Marianne to her drum and back again, and caught some kind of a connection, almost like an invisible thread was between the two. Marianne looked at the drum with the same fondness with which a person would look at a child. Seeing the two of them together closed the door on any more doubts.

"Your drum is beautiful."

Marianne lit up as she thanked her. "I made her years ago, and she has been my constant companion since then. Before we go any further, I want to talk to you both about protection. You are safe here and will be safe, but just in case you ever need it, it's useful to know. When I need protection, I envisage myself in the heart of a tree, a big tree, and around the base are my spirit warriors guarding me. You are rock solid and secure in this place, but still can move and do what you need to do. You need to be adamant in your protection, almost as though you are stepping into the tree, your protection rising around you like a sap. Got it?"

She could do that; she nodded and felt Lee beside her doing the same.

"Now, shall I guide you, or can you two journey to your power animals yourselves?"

She swallowed and looked to Lee. "For the purpose

of what we're doing, it might be good to be guided, thank you, Marianne. Will we be able to converse?"

"With each other, yes. But only after you come back with your power animal. Both of you will experience different things, and then come back to me. Once you go onward in your animal form, you will know what each is thinking. This is the way of communication between the two of you. Don't get used to it though—it stops as soon as you come back into human form. Shame, as it's a much more effective way to communicate—emotions are felt as well as the words and so nothing is lost."

After pulling out some mats from behind the sofa, Marianne gestured to them to lie down. Ellora arranged herself on the flowered mat, gently touching feet with Lee.

"What will happen to our bodies, our clothes?"

"You will change into your power animal as you are and change back as you are. Don't worry about clothes, you're not turning into the invisible man where his clothes dropped when he changed."

As she spoke, she played the drum in a low consistent manner. The deep voice of the drum changed the air in the room, and it became thicker. Ellora breathed more consciously and after a couple of minutes, felt her limbs relaxing into the ground. Suffusing her was a curious languor mixed with excitement, as though she knew what she was doing; yet she had no clue. Beside her, Lee breathed slowly and deeply too. Almost as though she had caught their relaxation, Marianne spoke slowly and steadily, all the while keeping the drumbeat constant.

"Become aware of your dreaming self and allow it

to rise up as though getting out of bed from your body. Your body is safe here, and you are attached to it with a silver cord. When you feel ready, let your dreaming self sit, then gradually stand. Leave this room. In the next room, you will see a wonderful golden mist. Walk into it, feel the cascades of light surround you. Raise your face and feel the little pinpricks of light fall on your cheeks and forehead like morning dew. Pause and enjoy the refreshing energy. When you are ready, go out the front door, which now leads onto a bridge. The bridge is high with wooden carved balustrades, and as you cross it, you allow your hand to lightly run over it."

All the while, Marianne maintained the beat and Ellora's heart rate kept pace. Marianne's melodic voice captured something deep inside and set it free, exposing her but lightening her at the same time. The images described unfolded in her imagination, a film reel in her head, and she could perfectly see herself coming out of her body, through the mist, and across the bridge.

"Once across the bridge, you see a clearing, beyond which is an ancient forest. Walk through the clearing, and soon you are amongst the company of old trees. They welcome you with gentle sighs of wind through their branches, and your feet follow a well-walked path. Soon you come to what must be the most ancient tree in the forest. Go up to it, place your palms on it, and greet it. As you bow your head to touch your forehead to the bark, you see a gap by one large root, a gap big enough for you to fit.

"Ask the tree whether you can go through this entrance and once he acquiesces, walk over and slip into the gap. You descend into an earth corridor, again a well-used one. Running your hand against the sides, you feel the shapes of animals and symbols drawn there, some centuries ago, some recent. Still you go down. Breathing in, you smell the dark loamy underground of the earth and the walls feel crumblier under your fingers. Sunlight appears at the end of the corridor."

Ellora's hands twitched as she touched and breathed in where she was. She firmly put the part telling her this couldn't happening into a box and shut it. This was no time for doubt. Once it was done, she could question everything but for now—right here, right now—she had to give it her all. Otherwise would be the point? The beat of the drum smiled with her.

"The light is getting bigger, and you see it is the mouth to this corridor. You emerge, blinking in the beautiful sunlight. Once your eyes are accustomed, you see a vast mountain range to your right, before which are miles of pastures with long grass, tall, deep green firs stretching up the deepest of blue skies. This plain teems with animals. To your left is a forest, and right in front of you the path leads. Look for your power animal. Say 'My heart's friend, I am here, where are you?' Walk where you feel led. After an animal approaches you three times, ask is it your power animal. Take your time."

Marianne stopped speaking, but her drum spoke louder and more insistently to Ellora. She could see the wind in the trees and felt the gentle kiss and welcome of this beautiful land. As she walked the path, the freedom in not being in her body whispered and sung to her. Curious to know what she looked like, she glanced at herself, seeing a vague outline of her body. Yet as she did, it disappeared like dust, falling to the path. At the same time, she became aware of eyes watching her before a panther stalked beside her. She smiled at the beautiful, sleek animal, admiring the bunch of muscles as she prowled, the surety of the placement of the large cat's paws.

The creature's deep blue eyes looked deeply into hers before, with a flick of her tail, she disappeared. With a wrench of her heart, she watched her go but carried on her path. The thrum of wings had her looking up, and she saw a golden eagle swooping above her. Rustles in the bushes beside her spoke to her of more presence, but she kept onward toward the sound of water.

The dusty path opened out into another clearing, this one with a great, still lake. To the left of the lake, graceful giraffes pulled leaves from the trees, chewing carefully. One swung its great head to her, and she nodded to it, admiring its markings and beauty. Drawn to the lake, she went to the side and leaned over to see what was reflected. The sky glistened in the water, and she saw her vague outline, as though seeing herself in a rain-soaked window, but Panther appeared beside her. Her heart leapt within her, and she acknowledged him this time again. *My heart's friend, where are you?* The smile in the creature's eyes warmed her before she turned to look beside her, but once more he was gone. She stood and shook herself and carried along the path.

In the background, the drum became more insistent. "It's time to come back with your heart's friend. If you have not been visited three times, stand still and fling your arms out to welcome your power animal into your heart."

She turned in a circle, her arms wide. *My heart's*

friend, where are you? In a blur of speed and night, Panther leaped into her arms, switching into bright air, and evaporated like a cooling mist onto her skin. Behind Panther, she caught a glimpse of a pride of panthers watching approvingly, almost like proud parents watching their daughter marrying.

Are you my power animal?

Of course. I have always been with you. Greetings, dear heart.

"Follow your footsteps back. You're traveling quickly now, into the entrance of the cave, which leads back up through the corridor."

The drum filled her ears, much as Panther filled her heart with joy. She sped up the corridor and through the gap into the ancient forest. Stopping, she turned and thanked the tree.

"The trees stand back, allowing you speedy traveling. You cross the clearing and see this door. Stepping through it, you see the golden mist and feel the particles caressing you and your power animal. Again, you're through it. Gently holding on to your animal, lower yourself into your body."

Marianne gave one last loud beat of the drum, and Ellora took a deep breath, inhabiting her body once more. She stretched into her limbs, felt her heart respond as her dreaming self returned with Panther. Her belly rose and fell as she breathed.

"Stretch into your body, and wriggle your toes and fingers to get your presence back. Once you feel yourself occupying your body, open your eyes slowly, and when you feel you can, sit up."

It was an exquisite feeling, reinhabiting her body, at the same time as she mourned the freedom of moving without the cumbersome lifting of limbs. Sitting up, Ellora gazed at Marianne. Lee was a large presence beside her, yet she didn't want to look. Marianne knelt beside her and, nodding to her, cupped her hands and breathed into Ellora's crown, speaking then quietly to her. "This is blowing your power animal into you. It does not need to be done, but I like to do this. Take a few moments and feel Panther."

Marianne did the same to Lee, and Ellora found her sight changing and her sense of smell become sharper. The far corners of the room blurred, and what were once vivid masks and outfits now lost their brightness. Almost black and white but not quite. Her head spun, and she felt sickness rise in her. Like a claustrophobia.

Marianne's voice broke through to her. "Breathe deeply, stretch into your limbs. If any senses are more compromised, such as your sight, it will result in some other sense being strengthened."

Not trusting herself to move, she took deep breaths and experimented with her limbs and her blood moving about this quadruped body. Her heart rate was quite high—but then again, adrenaline was scorching through her. Sounds out in the street came clear through to her, and she flicked her ears, thinking a car was about to come through the door. Marianne's eyes followed hers and again she spoke quietly.

"Allow your senses to acclimatize. Do not force it. Walk around and feel what it's like to be in your animal's body before you go out."

Ellora looked at Lee but couldn't see him. All she got was a vague, shadowy sensation of a large cat beside her. She shook her head and tried again, feeling her head round in a circle rather than what she was used to. Shapes took form, and she gasped as the outline of a big and strong tiger took place. Yet the whiskey eyes, they were Lee's. Once more, she shoved disbelief aside. *This was happening. This was important. Go with it. But I can't do it.*

Yes, you can.

She stood, amazed as her arms went to the ground also. Yet they weren't arms, they were strong, black legs. Opening her mouth, she scratched a sound out. Nothing like anything she had ever heard. She tried again, opening her mouth wider and trying to locate her stomach. A growl emerged, followed by a faint purr. Taking a pace through the room, she stopped. It felt as though she walked on cushions, with the hairs and whiskers on her feet checking out the ground. Weird and like walking on a firm yet not too hard mattress. All four legs moved in accord, and inside her she felt amusement. *A feline kind of enjoyment.*

She straightened her back—whatever else, she wasn't in this on her own. She could get used to this. The nausea subsided, leaving room for excitement to thrill through her. Walking around the room, she purred at the stability at the lower point of gravity, supported by four limbs, not two. The scent of Lee told her he was with her, and she looked to see his large presence by her side.

He nuzzled her, and she nuzzled back, and before she knew it, they were pouncing and clawing and nipping each other but with gentle teeth. They rolled over and over, she gasped in the sheer freedom of being in a powerful cat's body, enjoying the feeling of Lee's hard strong Tiger against her. Over and over they tumbled, until she pulled free and stood, panting.

Shaking her head once more, she let out a roar, and Lee joined in.

Marianne had now faded to a vague shadowy outline, but Ellora could see her smile. "You two can see each other in your cat form, but no one else can see you, unless they are present as power animals. Highly attuned people might be able to make you out in a vague form but nothing else. The only thing you need to avoid are other power animals. Now, any questions? No? You are ready."

Lee looked.

Ready?

Absolutely.

As one, they turned and bounded through the shop and out into the street.

Chapter Fourteen

Lee wanted to laugh. The sheer exhilaration of being in this body was nothing less than magical. It was mad, it was crazy, but it was happening. It had happened before and would happen again. He looked at Ellora, loving her sleek smooth Panther. He should've known how impressive she could be.

Be careful.

Why?

I can hear your thoughts, much like you can hear mine.

Now she mentioned it, he could hear whispered words zooming in and out.

Okay. Where are we going? To Imelda or straight to the vault?

I vote for the vault. Let's find the chalice.

Good thinking.

Out on the street, the world as they used to know it carried on but again, with only vague outlines.

You know what this is like? She turned her amazing sapphire eyes on him.

No, what?

Have you ever been bereaved or in shock over something?

Yes, when my parents died.

Yes, me too. It's similar. You look around at the world, amazed about everything going on as it always

186

has, because inside you, something has broken off and your world is irrevocably changed. And you know it will never be the same again. And you look at people, envious their lives haven't been shattered.

But this time, we're the lucky ones. How amazing is this, Ellora?

Amazing but feels normal.

She turned her attention to the path, assiduously avoiding people. *I don't want to go through anyone— don't think it would feel right.*

Lee looked up and down the streets, wishing for a clear run. He wanted to stretch these limbs and feel the wind soaring past him.

Come on. He effortlessly spoke in her head, marveling at how quickly he had become used to this. They padded quickly through one side street, and picking up the pace as the side streets were near empty, they trotted down one avenue leading towards the Acropolis. It was to beyond there Lee wanted to go.

Wait.

Why?

You want to run and expend strength. I'm not sure we won't need the energy.

Are you comfortable in your body?

She purred as a reply, and he nodded.

Okay. But afterwards I want to run with you.

Agreed.

Together they went to the Acropolis, neatly avoiding all the tourists. His heart kept pace with their trot. What were they going to find? She looked serious as he posed the question.

Up the steps they went, scenting the air as they did. A strange, animal smell, of wind and air came to him and he stopped, paw raised as he looked up. There, atop one of the columns sat an eagle. Stony eyes met his and once a connection was made, wings spanning three meters spread and the eagle took to the skies, calling out as it did.

Do you think—

Yes. But it's not Zenon's power animal.

Why?

As they were communicating, the two cats prowled the periphery of the acropolis, looking for the entrance into the vault.

He didn't have any attributes of eagle in him.

He laughed, which emerged as a throaty purr. *And we have panther and tiger in us?*

Again, those eyes narrowed on him. *Now I'm here, it feels perfectly natural.*

Fair enough. *What can we expect then?*

I've been wondering about it. Zenon is sly and cunning, perhaps a fox or a coyote.

How about his cronies? And the eagle there? She was clearly warning someone.

I don't know.

They fell silent, and he stopped. He was sure the vault was below them. Shaking his head, he lowered his nose and smelled through the ruins. A waft of air, carrying with it the unmistakable smell of ancient artifacts, emerged from one corner. Ellora was right beside him, and she gave a low-throated purr.

It's below us.

How do we get there? I cannot see nor smell anything to allow us entrance.

They stood together, lightly panting. He thought back to what Marianne had said when Ellora asked about opening doors. She had just been amused, ergo, it must be something easy.

Perhaps we're being too human about all of this. Ellora listened with her entire body tensed beside him. He shook his head lightly and in his peripheral view, saw a slight shaking of a ruined column. Looking at it fully, he allowed his human vision to retreat and felt as though he was looking from the back of his eyes and his mind.

Ellora, clear your human vision, and allow your animal vision to take over.

The physical world shimmered and faded to an outline, and soon the appearance of the lower vault came into view. With one mind, they leaped from where they were through the ground and into the vault, landing lightly in one corner. He shook himself, instinct taking over, and turning to Ellora, saw her doing the same. She was strong, lithe, and sleek, and he had to drag his attention back to the here and now.

The vault wasn't as big as its name implied and was hewn from limestone with little corridors leading away. The temperature was cool, perfect for preservation. Long low wooden tables covered with dust were laid out with various items, some cracked, others in better state of repair. Gilt-edged religious pictures stared at them with a judgmental air, various crosses of all shapes and sizes, beads, and jewelry within cubby holes in the walls—probably containing the more valuable items—behind glass.

They prowled, looking for the chalice.

I wonder about everything under here. Are all of these accounted for, or have they too supposedly disappeared?

I don't know. Do you recognize anything?

The painting over there is by Titian, and it should be in a museum. Leads me to wonder if most of these shouldn't be here. He paused by some African artifacts, crazy looking masks. *It looks as though we're heading into shamanic realms.*

We can check after we find the chalice. I'm just conscious of the eagle having seen. The door at the end of the hallway shook as someone or something was coming through. She snarled, showing her white pointy teeth, hissing. His hackles rose—*now he knew what the phrase really meant*—and he circled her. Both cats planted their paws firmly on the ground and faced the door. Yet another shake, then nothing happened.

C'mon, Lee. They picked up their pace, checking out the tables together, tails swishing.

He shook his head as various smells came to him.

It's not here. But something is on its way. He hissed, enjoying the sensation of breath traveling from his lungs. He allowed the hiss to develop into a growl and started to shake, an adrenaline rush.

Don't, Lee.

What?

Invite danger. I can smell it from you.

Her eyes widened, and she padded to him, muscles bunching below her shoulders. She was incredible. But she joined him, and he felt the power of the pair, larger than the sum of their parts.

We need to be fast. Something or someone is coming.

The air thrummed lightly and they both looked up, waiting to see the bird. But nothing was there. However, he saw a faint depression in the wall in front.

There's another door somewhere.

Quietly, they walked over and she sniffed around the depression. *You're right.*

He joined her and picked up a faint less stale air current coming from one area. Pacing back, he scoured the wall and saw the depression was larger than originally assumed. There had to be a way to get through. Throwing all rationale to the wind, he butted against it, hoping against hope there was a lever somewhere. Something gave, and he redoubled his efforts. With a loud click, a square door the size of a large window opened out.

Good one, Lee.

A snarl rent the air, and Lee and Ellora looked at each other once before leaping through the gap in the wall. Quickly maneuvering their way through a narrow corridor, they emerged into a vast, long, and low room. It must've been dynamited. Candles glowed in sconces and the air seemed quieter, more hallowed. To the right was a series of indents and shelves in the wall, and they prowled beside it. Sparkling artifacts and jewelry greeted them—someone clearly looked after these items.

Quick.

They separated, he went down the far side whilst Ellora continued on the way they had come. As he rounded a faint corner, he growled almost inaudibly. For there in front of him was a tabernacle, the type used in churches to hold the Eucharist. His cat senses quickened—something was not quite right with it. Something dark clung to it, quickly dissipating as he watched. His eyes were drawn inexorably to it as his heat beat quickened. What was it? Narrowing his eyes to nearly closed, he espied a faint glimmer flickered through the blackness of the tabernacle. Or was he imagining it? Everything within him thought the chalice was there, in front of him. His belly churned, his heart cried *show yourself, for pity's sake!* Breath stalling, he couldn't believe his senses as a minuscule star blazed an outline, that of a large cup for sure, then all went dark once more. Was the chalice responding to him?

I've found it, Ellora.

Good, because they've found us.

Her last words rose high in warning, and he turned as she soundlessly landed on all four paws beside him.

We must learn the early warning systems that surely must come with being large cats was the last thought he picked up before red mist descended his brain. Adrenaline flooded his new adrenal system, and the power he felt pouring into all four limbs was intoxicating. He snarled, saliva dripping from his chin. He hoped this new foe was worthy of this strength.

A coyote stood in front of him. A large coyote, mangy. Snarling with small mean eyes. *Just the one?* Yet from behind him came another five, all snarling. *What they lack in strength, they make up in numbers.*

Don't, Lee. Ellora, beside him, turned to him. *We don't need to fight them. Let's just get out of here.*

But he was bursting out of his skin to try his new strength. The pack of coyotes smelled his fighting spirit, he was sure of it, the light in the leader's eyes turning a queer yellow. They advanced, and he stood his ground.

Lee. Ellora head-butted his shoulder, but he barely felt it, pumped up was he. He snarled. A long, low, drawn-out sound expanding to each extremity. She placed herself between him and the pack and his instinct was to lash out immediately. Goddamn woman. Yet her blue eyes shone back, and she didn't flinch an inch.

You're not just animal, Lee.

Advancing slowly, the coyotes snapped their teeth. It was clear by the way they moved they were communicating as they approached in a well-positioned V shape, looking to surround them. He backed up to Ellora in order to be side to side.

How many can you take?

Her reply was soft. *None. We need to leave. Speed and surprise are on our side. The chalice is here and safe so let's get to Imelda as soon as possible and have it validated.*

He wavered. She was right, but man, he wanted to get his claws into those damn coyotes. He could have them. He knew for sure. He growled, enjoying the resonance within his body, all his blood shaking and thrumming within him. The red mist thickened, and he let the growl turn to a full-on snarl, spitting and hissing from his jaws.

Lee. Don't do this. Don't forget they are people too. If you harm them in animal form, you're harming their bodies. And killing anyone won't help.

He didn't want to hear her, wanted instead to immerse himself in the intoxicating anger suffusing his body. But a part of him reached up. She was right. He shook his head to extricate himself from the red mist. What had he been thinking? Yet the coyotes advanced.

Which way out of here?

Her relief poured through him like rain on a dry day.

Straight ahead. Leap over and through the far door.

Can we do it?

I don't know—I hope so.

On the count of three.

They counted together—*one, two, three…*

He bunched all his strength into his shoulders and haunches, breathed power in, and flung himself through his forequarters. Then he was flying. He heard Ellora's inhale of surprise as they both soared over the coyotes to land lightly on their paws.

Amazing…

She sounded awestruck, and he had to agree. He couldn't wait to explore more of what he could do with this body, but not now. They both took off for the door and were through it before the coyotes could react. Once through the door, they followed the passage around, hearing the baying behind them. At a crossroads in the corridor, he paused. An odd smell, something quite out of the ordinary, emanated from the right. She stopped too, but they only had seconds to spare.

What's that?

I don't know. But I don't like it. It's making the hairs all over my body stand up.

Should we check it out?

We don't have the time right now, but we should come back.

Okay.

They headed to the right and felt the air clearing as the ground gently sloped upwards, moving quickly. The coyotes were no match for their speed and the noise of the pack gradually lessoned. He felt rather than saw the night air and they exploded out.

Stay as is or change back?

Let's get to Philippe's and then change back.

She smiled with her eyes and he warmed through.

Are we sure we can trust them?

We don't have any choice.

All is not what it seems.

As they were speaking, they were traversing the streets of Athens. Every now and then, they got an odd, unfocused look from someone as though they were seen but not.

How're you enjoying being Panther?

Not being Panther, rather welcoming Panther in. It feels right. How about you, Tiger? She gave a strange sound, and looking at her, he understood it was a laugh. He smiled with his eyes.

Tiger, I like that, Panther. This feels good.

They left the city and headed out to the coast, following their instincts.

Do we have an internal sat-nav? We seem to know exactly where to go.

Ellora, I don't want to question anything. I'm just going with it.

Before too long, they were outside Imelda and Philippe's house. Lights showed them they were in.

Maneuvering around the periphery, they came to the part Lee remembered seeing earlier, the lower-than-normal wall. From memory, the other side was clear.

Can you do this?

Of course.

They both backed up, then gathered strength and leaped onto the wall briefly before jumping into the garden below.

And yet, there was something not quite right with their view. *Something smelled off.*

I agree.

Together they prowled the grounds. A movement to the left of the front door caught their attention and they paused, crouching.

What is it?

The palm tree rustled once more and a shaft of moonlight fell squarely on a man's face. He was standing motionless, an air of bright attention about him.

They're being watched. Shall we back off?

We need to see them. Let's see if there's any way private we can get in. They must know they are under surveillance.

They continued up to the house, looking for lights. Around the third corner, they saw lights on in a ground floor room. Imelda was on the sofa, flicking through a glossy magazine. In repose, her face looked strained and she hadn't the attention for reading, judging by the constant turning of pages.

How do we get her attention? And once we do, how do we not scare her?

Transform back to human shape?

How?

Marieanne put us into a trance following the beat of the drum. But we can't do that here. I did think the journey was like meditation, so perhaps we journey inwards with our breath, thank our power animals, and they depart?

He stopped and breathed from his stomach, taking three deep lungfuls. Then he turned inward and looked into himself. There he saw the steady eyes of Tiger looking back. *Thank you, Tiger, for your shape, power, strength, and wisdom. I honor you.*

I am here. Always, just look for me.

He heard an echo of a drum somewhere, and he felt his limbs lengthen, a bit like a gentle version of pins and needles. He kept his eyes from Ellora, somehow feeling this was too intimate, watching her shape-shift.

It's okay.

Her voice faded, and he looked to her to see her once more as the woman he had first met. But more vibrant somehow, the light in her making her shine, almost fluorescent. And as he watched, he realized it emanated from her, and slowly, gently, it simmered around her and settled in, a warm glow. She was more beautiful than ever.

He stepped up to the window, and after casting a glance at Ellora to ensure she was ready, gently tapped. Imelda didn't react but, after a second or two, rose gracefully and came closer to the window. She peered through and saw them, and again, no surprise crossed her face, only relief. With a quick movement, she pressed something, the French doors swung open, and she ushered them in.

Inside, she pressed a finger to her lips, and both Lee and Ellora nodded. Imelda spoke into her watch. "They're here."

Lee watched her, still feeling something of the power of Tiger in him. Clearly, she had been expecting them, but there was nothing to suggest danger. He smelled nothing untoward. She gestured behind her, and all three walked through the door and into a small, square library, each wall lined with books. A bar jutted out halfway into the room, high glossy top adorned with shiny glasses. Looking around, Lee could see no sign of the outdoor world. There was a womb-like feeling in here, heightened by the long velvet red curtains, some pulled over the books, others not.

Once the door clicked shut and disappeared into the bookcase, Imelda spoke something softly into her watch. Walking over to the small bar, she looked at them both with a raised eyebrow. Both nodded.

She placed tumblers on the polished counter and poured a good measure of whiskey into all four, followed by a tall jug of iced water and glasses. Just as she finished, he heard a click and smiled to see a portion of the wall move in and over, allowing space for Philippe to come through. He heard Ellora gasp at the same time as he noticed his haggard appearance. Philippe looked half the man they had met before.

Imelda's face was soft as she walked over to Philippe. He limped to the leather couch and lowered himself into it with a sigh. He nodded to Imelda.

"We should be safe in here." Philippe's voice was low, and he spoke with a rasp. "This room is soundproof, and we have never allowed cameras in here."

Lee had never seen his old friend look as jaded, but somewhere within him there was a tinge of relief. His friend hadn't given up their whereabouts readily. After taking their drinks over and pouring water, he sat beside him carefully, trying not to displace him on the sofa.

****

Ellora stood by the closed door, swaying. Tiredness and more had caught up with her, and she didn't know how she would manage to get through the next couple of hours. And where then? Where would they sleep tonight?

"Is it safe?" Hell if she sounded rude. This man and his wife, whilst yes, they had come to them for help, had handed them over to whomsoever it was. She wasn't ready to relax—yet. If only she could speak in Lee's mind the way they had before.

Imelda walked over and caught hold of her hand. "Come and sit." She gently pulled her over and the two women sat on the sofa facing the men. "First we welcome you, but we need to know—how did you get in? We are aware we are being watched. Do they know you're here?"

Lee gestured to her to talk. Right. "Remember we spoke about shamanism and power animals?"

Imelda's eyes lit up.

"You were right—we have the ability to do it, and I guess strange times calls for strange measures. We managed to do it. So..." She stopped and looked at Lee, noticing his compassion upon looking at Philippe. It was time to hear his story. "We'll tell you more about it later, but first, please, what has happened to you?"

Philippe sighed.

"The afternoon after the ball, after you left here and escaped the hotel, Zenon set his dogs on us."

She wanted to clarify whether they were actually dogs, because really, who the heck knew anymore? But Imelda stopped her with a warning glance.

"They came in under false pretenses, all social and stopping by for a drink. We made small talk for a while and then they asked about you."

Imelda moved to the edge of the sofa allowing Ellora to see her face clearly. "The air changed when they asked about you—it became tense. Despite their relaxed stance, it was clear they thought you both were important. Go on, sweetheart."

"We said we had seen you the day before. And no more. They asked a couple more times. Then when I insisted I didn't know, they got insistent. Lee, pass me my drink." The eye Philippe turned on her was full of pain. Whether it was her recent time with Panther or tiredness or what, she read within the pained gaze a determination, and an absence of fear.

With a flash, she understood he had been in so much fear he could no longer withstand it. His body had gone through it and out the other side. Stronger. Determined. She acknowledged the new man in front of her and saw within his gaze an answering spark. For the first time, she felt safe in the house. Imelda felt her relax and gently squeezed her hand.

Philippe handed his glass back to Lee who watched with dark gold eyes. His body spoke of stress, all hard angles with elbows planted on his knees. She sensed a fury building—the one she had felt when Tiger was about to attack.

"When I insisted I knew nothing, they took me out, bundled me in a Jeep, and drove for about an hour. It was dark and I didn't recognize where we were." He stopped and gazed at his shaking hand. A vein on his forehead stood out, but he managed to bring his hand under control. As he did, he straightened his shoulders as though a small battle had been won.

"They led me somewhere underground—I know this because the air changed. Was musty. The ground below my feet was uneven, and there was barely room for one person guiding me. After about ten minutes of walking, the tunnel opened into something bigger, and I was led into the center of the room. There was muttering and whispering and then the blindfold was taken off.

"As my sight cleared, I saw I was surrounded by twelve people, all dressed in robes with hoods. I could not see anyone. Each person had their hands folded, one over the other and, as I'm sure you can imagine, was rather intimidating. But then I felt a prickle at the back of my neck."

He placed a hand there, rubbing hard as though trying to iron out a knot. He winced, putting his head on one side. Imelda reached into her handbag and took some pills out and handed them over to Philippe. He swallowed them gently with a grimace.

"I turned to look behind me. There was a rough shod altar, and on top was a chalice. It must be what you're looking for." He cleared his throat, almost as though he tasted something bitter. Taking a deep breath, he subsided against the back of the sofa.

"Now for the madness. The chalice looked much like you'd expect it to look. It was placed very much like in Christian Masses, where the body of Christ becomes bread, and I believe there was a tabernacle behind it. I didn't pay much attention because then the robed people, they started to chant. Some kind of plain song. It drew the hairs on my body to stand on end. I had turned to see them when they commenced chanting, but all their focus was behind me. On the chalice. A warm, stagnant air came from there, like someone or something was breathing down my neck. I froze. The chanting continued and my heart rate increased with it, as though it was joining in. At this point, I thought the hairs on the back of my neck were going to erupt, they were so painfully alert. Emerge like worms and wriggle away as fast as they could."

He had one hand massaging the back of his neck as he spoke, the blood drained from his face making him look cadaverous. Ellora melted and reached toward him, but he shook his head slightly.

"It's okay. I'm okay. It is good to talk and good for you both to know. I didn't want to turn around, God knows. But I had to know what it was. Slowly, I did. And the relief was instant. There was nothing there. There was no one there. But relief slid away under a new, more insidious realization. Just because I could not see anything did not mean there was nothing there. The warm stagnant breath hit me hard, a speeding car into a brick wall. I couldn't breathe. Like a wave, it receded. The chanting increased. I felt inside out, my skin on the wrong side and everything that I was, exposed. My blood raced around me screaming, 'What the fuck.' "

His breathing faltered, and he reached out for a glass of water. Holding it with shaky hands, he took one small sip, then another. He breathed, consciously, quietly counting ten breaths. When he finished, he took another sip with steady hands, then returned the glass to the table.

"This went on interminably. But then it dropped like a blanket from me. I felt exhausted, beaten up, a rag doll that had been pummeled. I stayed upright, though, as everything still worked and supported me despite my head saying 'fall,' I didn't. And the next moment, I didn't care. The chanting was very loud, the air almost was turned an orange shade, and I simply did. Not. Care. About. Anything. They could have stripped me naked and taken my heart out with a spoon and I wouldn't have cared. I heard someone come up and then stood in front of me. They asked me about you." He hung his head. "I told them everything I knew about you both. It made no difference to me whether I told them or not. I remembered the pain and told them. It was an easy decision, like whether to turn right or left. I cannot come to terms with it." He raised his head and looked at them once more and Ellora now totally understood the broken look.

"Everything. Who you are, why you are here, and either least or most importantly, that Imelda believes you, Ellora, are a powerful shaman. Who knows what kind of catalyst will occur when you hold the chalice," he whispered.

Lee reached across and grabbed his hand. "It doesn't matter. What does is the fact you are here and in one piece."

Ellora was looking at Imelda and only she saw the shadow passing over her face. She was deeply worried.

"What happened next?"

"Once they had what they wanted, they shut down the singing and led me back. And much like a local anesthetic wears off, slowly I started coming out of the numb state of not caring. So much so I couldn't recall what it was like. By the time I was home, all the feeling that I was deprived of—it returned twice-fold. I am furious."

"You had no choice, darling." Imelda's voice was a low caress. "We think this chalice, it robs you of free will."

"Did they try to control you since then? Have you felt or heard anything?"

"No. We believe it's a state of mind induced by the

chalice once it has been triggered by the chanting. It doesn't linger. At least not yet. But they had total control over me." He shivered and his face resumed its haunted expression.

"Do we think they could use it to control a group of people? A crowd, a…oh I don't know, an entire population?"

As she spoke, she could see Imelda and Philippe nodding worriedly.

"Bollocks."

She made to speak, but this time it was Philippe who stopped her. "What I want to know is why they want you badly. And not just you, Lee, but both of you. Together."

Lee stood up and paced around the room. "Who are 'they'?"

"Ah—the million-dollar question. Zenon runs the show—"

"Who *is* he?" She sat forward. "He gave me the creeps."

"Julian Zenon. Comes from old family here, ex-mayors and politicians, but if you dig a bit deeper, they also harbored their fair share of crooks. But only very deep. Zenon knows what I know about him, which is why I got off lightly. The family hobby was originally money laundering before ancient artifacts. They've also been known to sell fakes—superb fakes, but fakes, nonetheless.

"Again, I made it my business as insurance to know this. His grandfather ran the whole artifacts show in town, ran the folk out who used to run it." He stopped and looked over at his wife, who took up the dialogue.

"Those folk were my folk. We didn't stand a chance. Zenon bulldozed his way in, threw his weight and money around, and soon enough no one would work for us. We needed workers and we had no one. Then things went missing and we were no longer entrusted with artifacts. The Acropolis started to stink." Imelda chewed the words as though they were bees in her mouth.

"In comes Zenon and saves the day. I am only working there because this world of artifacts needs someone caring for it. And being on the inside helps—keep your friends close and your enemies closer." Her green eyes were unwavering. "I put up with a lot, but it's worth it. I can't disappoint generations of my family." She looked fondly at her husband. "And Philippe helps me to stay sane."

Philippe carried on. "Zenon is quietly running the show. At first, we thought he would be like a bull in a china shop, but unfortunately—quite how, we don't know—he has finesse, and so has a lot of support. He has the majority of the town's young blood working for him. Hence, he, more or less, runs the town. But the buck doesn't stop with him. He's someone else's puppet. Who, I don't know."

"What does he want?"

"What everyone seems to want in this business—power. And he was taken aback by you both. When I was under interrogation, I gathered he thinks the two of you, together, have some sort of power. My impression was that he didn't know what it was, and I'm surprised he didn't talk you around to his side. He's a wily one, Zenon, and I'm sure he would first want you to work for him."

"He did, at the table," she blurted out. "I thought he was just trying to talk me into bed, but the conversation could've had a wider meaning."

Lee looked sharply. "I thought he looked at you a bit like a wolf."

She straightened her back. "A wolf, I can handle." The words were true, even saying them brought Panther coursing through her. *Any day.*

Lee smiled in surprise. Could he hear her when she was with Panther? She smiled back shakily. What could he hear? She'd have to be careful. A blush rose through her. What if he could hear her body's reaction to him? Although tired now, her eyes felt bathed in coolness, as though looking at him was a holiday. Suddenly, she yearned to be just with him. Quiet with each other, just looking and touching gently.

"What does he want with us?"

Philippe took a drink, then left the glass on the sofa. Lee reached over and put it on the table. "He either wants the power you two share, or he wants to negate it."

Ellora snorted. "Honestly, sometimes I feel as though I left the world as I knew it behind the moment I stepped foot on our airplane." She stopped and thought. "Actually, that *is* what happened. So first question is, what power do we have, followed by what do you mean by negate it?"

Lee was back up and striding. "Let's look at the facts—Ellora and I have only known each other for a week, say. I know, when I'm with her, we can conquer the world. Yes, I've done dangerous things in the past—but that doesn't mean we are powerful. What the hell does powerful mean anyway?" He spat the word out as though it had offended him in his mouth.

Ellora stood and put her hand on his arm to stop him, mind still whirling. Should she lay claim to the emotions clamoring for voice?

Conquer the world? Yes! "Lee, what have we just done though?" She kept her gaze steady on him. "I think we have succeeded where others—all right, I'll say it—where angels fear to tread. And here"—she pressed on her abdomen—"I feel more in control, more knowing, more powerful."

His whiskey eyes flared, and her cat-like senses felt him stir beneath her words. *That's it, Tiger.*

He gave a brief nod, releasing her from their connection, and swung to Philippe. "What I want to know is what you mean by 'take us out.' Run us out of town, fine. But take us out?"

Philippe looked more uncomfortable. "I don't know the extent, but I do know Zenon takes no prisoners, if you'll excuse the pun."

"He'll try to kill us?"

"Perhaps. Although he's attracted to you both for some reason, and maybe the same reason will keep you safe."

"What do you recommend we do?"

"Do you have to find the chalice? Can you just leave and forget about it?"

No. Finding the chalice had changed something inside her, something integral, and she didn't yet know what it was. One thing was abundantly clear. It was in the wrong place at the wrong time. She looked at Lee, inwardly beseeching him to hear her, who rubbed his chin with his hand. Turning, he paced once more, stopped, looked at her, then slowly shook his head.

"It is really important, and I am worried about the extent of damage it could do—can you imagine that power in the hands of a megalomaniac? Or a president of a country." He stopped and laughed bitterly. "Or even both? But I need to get Ellora out of here and back home safe."

Ellora straightened her back and allowed cold clarity to flood her. "As Philippe has said, the two of us together have some sort of power. What if, and I think he is right, this is the power that protects us both? No, Lee, you go on and I go with you." She planted her hands on her hips and tilted her head sideways. No way was she letting this one go.

Philippe interjected, "Listen to her."

"I'll sleep on it." The words were a low growl, but Ellora's hopes leapt. Lee came back to the sofa and sat carefully. "What do I do next?"

Imelda leaned forward. "Get the chalice and then get out of here." Her nostrils flared.

Lee nodded. "We need to get back into the vaults."

Philippe put his glass back on the table with a clink. "There, we can help."

She couldn't help it, she felt a yawn starting up and it brought tears to her eyes. Imelda jumped up straightaway.

"Talk of this in the morning. Sleep—you both need rest. When was the last time you slept, and safely?" Her tone was slightly maternal and scolding, and Ellora loved her right then. In a deft movement, Imelda was by the bookshelves, opening a cupboard and pulling out luxurious blankets. "I'm afraid this is all we can offer, as getting anything more from outside this room might attract attention. But you should be comfortable enough here. Through the side door, there is a petite bathroom—I hope it will be sufficient." She gestured to the opposite side of the shelves, where a discreet door was inset.

Philippe moved to the edge of the sofa and leaned himself up using the arm.

"Lee, Ellora, we'll see you in the morning."

The two departed, and she made use of the bathroom, stripping to her tee shirt, conscious her lack of sleep had hit her like a ton of bricks. Exiting the bathroom, she saw Lee had set up both sofas and softened more lights. She chose one and dropped onto it, closing her eyes and feeling Lee come over. Without stirring, she held out a hand and he clasped it, bringing it to his lips.

"Are you okay?"

"Mmmm." Her bones were turning to liquid, and she stretched into her body, not wanting to disturb the oncoming sleep. "I'd love to stay up and whisper sweet nothings with you, but man…" She yawned. "I don't think I can."

Clasping her face between his two hands, Lee pressed his lips to hers before pulling away and whispering, "Sleep well."

Stretching out on the sofa, she put her head on a cool pillow and wrapped the comforting warmth of the blanket around her. "You too."

She heard Lee move around, preparing himself to sleep. Eventually everything went pitch black, and she welcomed the dark greedily. The thoughts spun, dishes on sticks. *Why she was here? Flicka, her parents, the dark woods, Lee, her feelings, flashes of running, dogs on her tail.* But even her tired mind couldn't support these thoughts, and one by one they fell in front of a comforting shadow presence. *Sleep.*

A time later, she became aware of a buzzing sound, like mosquitoes trapped in both ear canals. She couldn't move, couldn't dislodge them, and the volume steadily increased—the more she fought it the louder and more invasive it became.

Go with it. Try to relax. With a sigh, she realized she had not the energy to fight, tried to tell each and every muscle to stand down.

Had she entered another world? A shadowy, vague one. As her body further relaxed and deepened into the sofa planting itself, something, a vague and insubstantial shape sat up and got out of her body. She left her physical body through the door and drifted like a cloud. Her brain was still asleep, and so she no longer fought anything.

Shadows, nonthreatening ones, surrounded her. The places she had walked in and through were still there, providing structure to the environment but more in the background as though she were superimposed. The front door would stop her, but she found herself outside and drifting farther to the gate house. Two men were by the gate, smoking and looking out into the street beyond.

"…in there." A man, the one with the cigarette was speaking. "They might show up. They'd be fools. And from Zenon's reaction, they aren't stupid. He wouldn't worry about stupid people."

"What has he said?" The bald, stocky man built like the proverbial brick house had an incongruously high voice.

"The word has come from above to look out for a

couple like them."

A couple like them?

"And to recruit them. If that's not possible, they need to be captured. But high up wants them alive. Added bonuses for those who get them."

"What do they have?" Bald guy sounded confused.

Smoker exhaled, and a long jet of smoke tendriled around her vague shape. She felt a tug back to her physical body but overrode it.

"Zenon said to someone on the phone that he wasn't going to endanger everything they had built. Go figure."

"How? They are only two and we are Order. Nothing has stood in our way before."

"I don't know." Another long exhale. "But Boss must believe it."

"It's about time we knew what was going on. I thought we were going to be told after the ball."

"It was, but North and his woman showed up."

"Brings me right back to the start—what do they have?"

Smoker flicked his butt and ground it out under his heel. "Search me."

Cigarette finished, the two made their way back to the gate house.

She drifted back into the house and the library. She opened her eyes moments before she settled back into her body for an uncanny split second of time fragmenting and shattering. A deep sigh escaped her.

"Ellora? Are you alright?"

She stared up into the face she could've sketched with her eyes shut and reached out to cup his cheek. *I'm home at last.* A feeling like standing on a cliff with eons of history behind and oceans of futures ahead caught her and gently rocked her. She felt ancient and new, loving and loved, and a kernel seeded in her abdomen. *Remember who you are.*

Lee stared into her eyes, shock and knowledge deep in his glorious amber eyes. *I know you.*

He repeated his question. Struggling against both the depth of their realization and what had just happened, she sat up as though fighting her way through candy floss. Weariness flooded through her, and she wanted to shut her eyes and be enveloped in darkness and hold onto her glorious feeling. But first she must tell Lee, otherwise chances are she'd forget.

In a few words, she filled him in, watching him carefully. His face registered shock, then wonder.

"This is astral traveling, Ellora. Has this ever happened to you before?"

"Not quite as obviously. There were times when I felt as though I woke up as I was going back into my body—you know, coming through your bedroom window at night does that. Or the time when I put my head through the wall because I thought I heard intruders. But that was all when I was asleep—or I thought I was."

She wondered what else she had done without realizing it. Regardless, she felt as though a warm blanket had been placed around her shoulders. As though she were being loved and protected, by who or what she did not know. It felt glorious. But tired. Alert to her every mood, as ever, Lee gently pushed her back on the sofa.

"Sleep and sleep well, alanna."

She just had time to nod, smile, and enjoy the warm pressure of his lips before escaping into deep sleep.

Chapter Fifteen

Lee wondered if astral traveling too was a shamanic skill, the ability to move within this world without being detected. Although, it had sounded painful at the start. But again, with practice, it might ease. Without knowing whence it came, he intuited Ellora was powerful, far more so than he. Tiredness swamped him too in a wave, and kicking off his shoes, he stretched out on the sofa facing hers. How could he send her away? Gut instinct said in order to succeed—whatever success might entail—she was needed. But what if something should happen to her? At the first thought, his heart rose. At the second, it sank. *But you and she together can withstand anything.* Can we?

Ellora lay on her sofa looking as though she hadn't moved an inch in the night. A gentle click told him the door opened and he looked around to see Philippe holding the door open for Imelda, laden with a tray with a coffee pot and two cups on it, plus some small pastries.

Gently he reached out and touched Ellora's shoulders, smiling into her eyes upon her opening them. Awareness chased the softness of sleep away. She responded to his smile and reached for him before a gentle cough had her averting her eyes.

"Good morning. I'm sorry we don't have much for you to eat—this is all we think we can get away with without alerting Order to your presence."

The pair tactfully went to the end of the library and checked through some books, dropping down onto the low sofa and soon being engrossed in the words contained within. Ellora stood with a yawn and headed into the bathroom. Whilst he waited, he poured out coffee, eyeing up the pastries.

As Ellora came out and walked towards him, he was struck by how feline she was, padding towards him on the shaggy wool rug. She dropped down beside him and, turning to face him, rubbed her face against his and he sparkled into life. She drew back, smiling in those blessed forget-me-not eyes, and he felt as though she had wrapped him up in beauty.

"Coffee?" He reached over and handed her a cup. Quietly, side by side, they ate and drank and once they had finished, settled back to talk. Lee struggled not to stand and pace as coffee and adrenaline stirred him towards action. In a low voice, "Last night and what happened. Let's run through it again. I want to get an understanding of what went on before we talk to Imelda and Philippe."

Ellora responded in a similarly low voice, keeping their heads together as they murmured.

"Philippe and Imelda know."

"I'd say so, otherwise why are they being as careful?"

"Philippe seems very traumatized by what happened to him, and that has resulted in turning him completely against them."

She nipped at her lower lip, and he resisted the urge to stare.

"What is the Order, then?"

"It was Order, not The Order. Somehow it sounds more ominous without the 'the.' "

Lee watched her stare into space as she thought. He kept silent. Slowly, she brought her gaze back to him, thinking aloud. "Last night, when I came out of my body, there was a sense of purpose, as though something had to show me something. Why did I witness the conversation?"

"What else did you overhear?"

She shrugged, then massaged her forehead.

"Just what I told you—they wanted us. Not sure if they were scared of us, but that we might be endangering something or other. I wish, with all these odd things happening, a clear message would come through. Just something to direct us. Too much to ask for?"

"Well, looking at what you overheard, we've learned two, no three, important things. The existence of Order and whatever it is that we might harm, the chalice is hidden, and lastly, we are being hunted. Looking at your last fact—we are a force to be reckoned with."

She started to say something, then stopped, narrowing her eyes. "Are you saying that you and I together can make a difference?" There was no mistaking the inflection on "together."

He pulled back his head and smiled. "Yes. I am. I'll call Jonathon and cancel plans for you going home. Ellora, I don't know if this is the right thing, so you have to promise me to be careful."

An answering smile crossed Ellora's face, and happiness spilled from her eyes like silver mercury. "It is the right thing. You and I, Lee North, can save the world."

And there and then, he believed it.

"What's next?"

"Chase the chalice. Find out about Order. There's got to be some reason we scare a powerful man. Let's find out what it is."

He saw his words impact, each one igniting something within her until she was ablaze. "Let's do it."

In relief, they both looked outward as though anticipating their way was lying there, waiting to be found by them. Instead they met the eyes of Philippe.

"Ready to talk?"

He looked at them with new eyes. Whereas yesterday he had seen them full of purpose and intent, today they seemed weary and more wary perhaps.

"Please. We won't keep you long, but we would like some information."

"Yes, of course." The two sat gracefully, Philippe moving better than he had the previous evening.

"This may sound crazy to you, perhaps not."

Lee filled them in on the events of the night before, both how they had gotten into the vault and the subsequent results, and about what Ellora had overheard the night before. As they listened, their faces smoothed out and worry took a back seat in deference to wonder.

"I have heard shapeshifting is possible, but I have never met anyone who has managed to do it." Philippe could not keep the excitement from his voice. "This is great—this means we can actually do something against Order." Imelda nodded along but grasped his hand and squeezed it. He subsided back into the sofa.

"But what is deeply hidden in the vault? I'm sure there was something there, something calling to us. Do we just leave it?"

"That depends on your end goal. For me, I do not know what it is you are talking about, and I've been around the vault all my life." Imelda lifted her shoulders in a pretty shrug. "If all you want is to get the chalice, then do and leave. Unravelling any mysteries here in Athens will be tougher. You'll need to stay undercover, and from what I gather, shapeshifting into your power animal seems to attract attention, not vice versa."

"But we are here, and this Order don't know. Which brings me onto the question of whether Zenon is a shamanic worker as well? I thought all things shamanic were for the good of this world?"

"As it should be, but not how it is." Philippe shook his head. "Like with everything. We believe Zenon to be shamanic but have no proof. Perhaps it is you two who will confirm and overcome Zenon."

"Decide what to do." Imelda was firm and unwavering as she looked at Ellora. Lee followed her look to see Ellora with bags under her eyes, looking haunted. Her gaze softened. "Sorry, Ellora, I understand this is all new to you, and it must be mind blowing. My advice is to go with it and don't engage your rational brain. Logical understanding is not the point of shamanism, nor indeed any practice of faith. The road ahead will be tough. Zenon is aware of you, and he's like a dog with a bone—face it now or get out of Athens. You are strong together, and your choice will be the right one for you both. Know your truth, and trust in yourselves, especially the parts you don't understand. We will help wherever we can."

"Thank you, both. Although we should leave you now. We don't want to place you in any more danger." Lee wasn't sure, yet he thought he could detect relief in the answering look Philippe gave them.

"Don't worry about us." Philippe and Imelda exchanged glances, seemingly coming to a decision. "There is a passageway under the house—this used to be a smuggler's house—and it will take you into the heart of Athens. But how and where from there, I don't know, I'm afraid."

Lee looked at Ellora, seeing her thoughts in alignment with his. "We'll take our chances with the passageway. Is it only the one or is it a network?"

"We think just the one. Put it this way—the house has been in Imelda's family for generations and this one has only ever been used."

"Before we go, is there anything you can tell us about Order?"

Philippe frowned and cast a quick look at Imelda. She stared at Lee for a long breath. "We heard about Order a couple of years ago, when we were approached by Zenon's second-in-command, Oleander. This was about five years after he had taken over. Basically, it sounded as though it was a group of wealthy people who ran the antiques business worldwide.

"You had to be invited to join, and this was our invitation." She hesitated and looked at Philippe. "He gave us twenty-four hours to make up our minds but left us in no doubts of being wealthy beyond our dreams if we did join. For those twenty-four hours, we researched thoroughly, even calling you, Lee, do you remember?"

Vaguely, he could recollect a call from Philippe but nothing outstanding from it. He said as much and they both nodded.

"As we couldn't find anything, it roused our suspicions, along with the assurances we would be rich. We decided against joining."

"When Oleander called for our answer, he was shocked. Since then, we have been kept on the periphery, which believe you me, is the way we like it. We were told not to talk to anyone about it, more or less given a warning not to say anything. Which was easy, up until now.

"It seems they're gathering in power. They are also being more aggressive with us. Whereas before, our having been invited to join afforded us some kind of protection, Philippe was left in no doubt now they wanted us to join." Imelda looked troubled. "We're unsure what to do. We want to protect the vault and all my family have achieved over the years, but at what cost?"

"Would you leave the country?" Ellora sounded upset for them.

"Perhaps." They both fell quiet.

"Is there anything we can do for you?" He looked from Imelda to her husband, whose graying complexion spoke volumes about his peace of mind.

"You're doing it by leaving." Philippe's words were quiet.

Ellora was standing by the time Philippe had finished. "Thank you for everything you have done for us. We're very grateful."

Lee stood too and, as his friends rose to their feet, hugged them soundly. "I'm sorry if we've brought trouble to you both."

"No, it was happening anyway. Perhaps you two are the catalyst, but sooner or later it was going to happen. Don't worry."

Lee clapped him around the back. "Be safe and stay in touch if you can."

Philippe turned and rapidly spoke to Imelda. She frowned, then smiled. "Yes, of course. Lee, Ellora, you know I maintain the public vault's database? The catalogue is made from numbers and letters. You can see any recent activity on the website. Anything I make a change or add 317 to means we are leaving. Just in case there is any need for you both to know about us. Should we disappear, I will post it before we go."

"Good thinking. And what about if you need help?"

Imelda narrowed her eyes. "We will not need help."

"Just in case, please." He was not taking no for an answer.

"I will post 713 if we need you."

"Good, thank you. Now how do we go?"

After a hurried farewell, Imelda dropped to her knees beside the rug and lifted it out of the way. After pressing a couple of flagstones, the stone moved smoothly back to reveal steps leading away. At Ellora's gasp, she turned and smiled. "This was the old heating system and was made into an underground corridor leading away from the house. It will take you up in the middle of Athens. So be careful."

****

Imelda stood back and allowed access to the stone steps yawning downwards. Lee took out one of his phones and flicked the flashlight on, but the sharp beam of light couldn't stop the unease settling in Ellora's tummy. Swallowing dryly, she cast a glance at Lee, feeling somewhat comforted at his calm demeanor.

Lee went down the steps first, lighting the way, and she stayed close behind him. With a grating noise, the light from the gap they had come through narrowed and slowly faded to nothing.

"It's dark." Lee's voice rumbled in the empty space, his tone decidedly serious.

"No bother to us. There's only one way, right? The tunnel comes from their house and ends up in the center?"

The light cast by the phone was sufficient to make out the shadows on his face, and she took comfort in seeing it. He had to bend his head to fit in the surprisingly wide but low tunnel, whereas she only had to watch out for low-lying rock. They paused as they took stock of their surroundings. Walls made of stone were clearly man-made with little or no thought for ease of travel.

"Old smugglers tunnel, this. Makes sense, coming up from the sea the way the house does." His voice echoed through the corridor, and for some reason, she found herself holding her breath. Nothing was to be heard beyond the odd drip of water, somewhere far off.

"Let's go then." Dark tunnels with walls closing in on her didn't exactly thrill her. Not necessarily claustrophobic, she just didn't feel comfortable. "How long will it take?"

He grabbed her hand and squeezed hard as though picking up her emotions. "Not long. Come on, Cat Lady."

A laugh started in her. "Cat Lady? You make me sound as though I'm one of those women with a million cats."

"Ha, I didn't say Mad Cat Lady, did I?" His tone was amused.

"Who's to say having a lot of cats doesn't constitute you as normal? Maybe it's everyone else who's mad."

"You make a good point." Lee's eyes were shadowed in the artificial light as he looked, but nonetheless she felt a jolt through her.

Feeling a bit coy, she had to ask, "Why Cat Lady?"

"Panther is your power animal. And I know this because I saw you as Panther. But if I hadn't, I'd still have known there was something of the big cat about you."

"How do you mean?" *Man, I sound like a fascinated teenager.*

Amusement rent the air. "The way you walk, the way you look. All very feline."

"Hmm, feline?" *Work harder, man!*

This time there was no denying the amusement. "You prowl, rather than walk. I don't know quite how you do it, maybe it's something to do with the way you carry yourself—perfect as it is." The last made her smile inside and feel warm. *Watch it Ellora. You're going all squidgy.* "You balance your weight over your hips, you know, like the models do on a catwalk. Ha, get it, *catwalk*."

She laughed, enjoying the sheer delight with which he said the last word.

"And sometimes, the way you look. I don't know, maybe it's the focus or the determination or, hell, I don't know. But your eyes are mesmerizing. Sometimes…"

She absorbed his words, feeling a thrill unfurl in the base of her stomach. This man was nice. He was strong. He was clearly capable. *And don't get me started on his looks.*

"…sometimes, I feel the large cat in me respond to the large cat in you." His tone was totally back to teasing, and he placed an arm around her shoulder. "Grrrrr…" He gave a low rumble into her ear and nuzzled her earlobe, sending goose bumps chasing each other all around her body, culminating in her tummy to fizz quietly, waiting to see what would happen next.

She shivered dramatically and drew her nails over his hand on her shoulder, a hand that dropped until it cupped her bottom as she walked along. Much as she hated to bring his attention back to the here and now, she had noticed some kind of change in the air. "Lee, buddy, mind on business here."

He mock sighed and withdrew his hand to hers, holding it tightly. With the connection, she felt him tighten in awareness.

"The air is changing. Turn the light off." She kept her voice low, watching as Lee swung the torch around. Then all went dark, and she squeezed his hand. As she and Lee walked, the walls had changed from stone to chalk, no longer apparently man-made with sharp corners, but more rounded and clunky. The passage led farther on and slightly up, but there was something that halted her.

"How long have we been walking?"

Lee glanced at his watch and made a calculation. "About twenty minutes. And we walk fast enough, Cat

Lady. I reckon we've walked maybe a mile and a half, possibly two." He paused once more. "We should be in the center of town."

They both fell silent, listening. The silence was complete. Lee felt the walls, running his fingers over the grooves. She shut her eyes and watched the colors behind her eyelids. *Panther, what do I smell? What do I feel? Come with your glorious senses and show me.* She kept still, tracing the colors and allowing the action to relax her. Her shoulders slumped, and behind the colors, the contours of Panther outlined slowly until his entire face filled her inner vision. She smiled to see him at the same time as the scent of Lee filled her nostrils.

Warm, musky, and inviting, she had to turn her senses away from his intoxicating smell. Slowly, she walked around him, deliberately switching her senses to the air. To the right of him came a different smell, faint but discernible and calling to mind something else. Something she had smelled before when she was Panther. Still in human form but with the vision of her cat, she scanned the tunnel when she felt the change. It was almost as though the air turned yellow. Yellow for encroaching danger. A smell flickered through her, alerting her. *Coyote.* Farther ahead.

Danger, Lee. I smell coyote.

Cat time. Shutting her eyes, she began the process of entering trance by following the lights behind her eyes. Deeper and deeper went the whorls until she saw Panther's features once more. She greeted him and thanked him and now could hear his response. *I am you and you are me.* As though she were diving into a pool, she dived into his features, feeling his cat strength entering her limbs, feeling her face elongate and flatten into the now familiar features.

Languidly, she shook herself, glorying in the freedom and movement of the large cat, the strength and security she felt in being perfectly balanced on all fours. She stretched, luxuriating. Tiger growled beside her, and she swung her attention to the other large cat. Beautifully proportioned and graceful, the eyes staring back were Lee's, full of admiration and something deeper. Something she shied away from. The stripes on his back rippled as he moved his head back and forth, clearly, like her, acclimatizing to being in the cat's body.

She watched, admiring the bunch of muscles under the coat. What would it be like to be a woman around that cat? Something she would have to try out later, run her hand over the glossy coat. Feel the muscles as he walked.

There is another tunnel ahead. It's being guarded—if we are lucky, they are in human shape. If not, coyote.

What do we do if coyote?

Fight. I'll go first.

Be careful.

In one fluid movement, Lee was around the corner.

Good to go.

As she approached, Lee nuzzled her and together they turned to view the declining path, which veered around the corner.

The smell is stronger.

Yes. I don't like it. I'll go closer to the corner and see if I can hear anything.

Okay.

Lee padded onward, keeping low. He paused by

the crux of the corner, tail high and gently waving.

Two guards. Eating, so in human form.

Can we get past them?

As they are eating, perhaps they won't smell us. I think we have no choice here.

Except find a different way?

All ways will now be guarded.

Right. Let's do it.

Ellora silently joined Lee, who, lowering himself to his belly, crouched around the corner. Holding her breath, Ellora waited for the shouts to start. When none were forthcoming, she mimicked Lee and made her way around, endeavoring not to look at the guards. She always thought people knew if they were being watched. When she was a hair's breadth away from them, the smell of cured meats threatened to strangle her, and she held her human thoughts whilst Panther reached towards the smell. Closing her eyes did not help the smell lessen, and she stopped and gathered her thoughts.

A sharp bark from one of the guards threatened a visceral response, and she breathed deeply, trying not to betray herself by releasing her scared hormones. These men were too close to predators. The bark was followed by a crackle and then a burst of words. Seeing her moment, she sprang up and past them, scattering Lee who was watching from the corner.

Good work, Ellora.

Yeah, close one though, Lee.

Chapter Sixteen

The tunnel they were in was similar to the one they had come from, with one exception. There appeared to be carvings on the walls—crude, handmade carvings of animals and stick people. Ellora managed a snicker to herself; she would've liked a hand to run her fingers over the shapes and into the grooves. *Another time perhaps.* Panther smiled too. They descended the tunnel, which twisted out ahead, again different to whence they had come. The pair stealthily picked their way through, recognizing the air becoming increasingly stale the farther they went. At a hairpin corner, Lee stopped.

Caution. We're going up.

They slowed to single file, she lowered her head to get better air as claustrophobia encroached. Once they went up, the ascension became steep. She couldn't quite deaden the unease curled within her. She lowered her head and moved steadily forward, comforting herself with the thought that she could be back in her human form in minutes. *Fret not, sister.*

Sounds trickled through, and the walls of the tunnel became smoother and more formed. Carvings became few and far between and the air lightened. Another few paces brought them to a crossroads, with one path leading up, the other to the left leading down.

Which way?

Up, I say.

In agreement, Lee turned right. Sounds trickled through to them, of people and movement.

Caution.

Lee, do you think this could be the meeting those two men were talking about?

I do.

Will there be power animals there? Will another sense us?

Perhaps. Let's stay as circumspect as possible.

If before they had been quiet, now the two large cats were completely silent.

If it's dark, then no one will see you, Ellora. I can hardly detect you, and I know you're there.

Perhaps I should go first then. Your stripes might give us away.

Damn. You're right. With a reluctant air, he stopped and let her pass, but not without giving her a nuzzle first.

Be careful.

In response, she flicked her tail in his face, smiling as she heard him make a smothered approximation of a laugh from a cat's body. She liked this man, a lot.

A low tone, sounding rather nasty, floated on the air towards them. Her hackles rose. She paused to discern whether it was animal or human, hoping it was the latter. She sent a warning back to Lee, who responded by telling her once more to be cautious. Silently, she padded forward and slowed going around the next corner. The air spoke of many people, but few animals. A dim light appeared once she had rounded the corner, and she sent this too back to Lee.

Good going.

Where was the heart in a Panther anyway? *Your chest. Just like humans. But fret not, sister. They will not see you. We are good at being invisible.*

Panther's words warmed her and gave her the confidence to move on. The corridor narrowed further as she approached the gap where the light was. Putting her head to the ground, she dropped her belly to the ground and shuffled silently forward. Closer and closer she got, with Lee's voice cautioning her at all times.

Be quiet. She hissed it back to him. *I need to concentrate.*

The low murmur grew ever louder, and with her heart in her mouth, she pushed her nose through the break in the corridor wall. The path itself stretched out farther, but she felt they would see what they needed to see here. As her face went through the gap, her sight cleared, and she found herself looking down on a meeting. A covert meeting, for despite the steady incline, they were still underground.

A large round stone table had fourteen people around it, and as she counted, she noted eight women. No power animals appeared to be present, and she breathed more easily as she felt Lee quietly moving in order to shimmy up beside her. *No power animals present.* Yet she froze. A ripple in the conversation below threatened to turn to danger. Something said hadn't been received well.

As soon as Lee was ensconced, they both turned their attention to below. She strained to hear. *Go deeper, sister.* Following Panther's advice, she shut her eyes and recommenced tracing the colors, deeper and deeper. When her eyes flicked open, the changes in her body were palpable. She felt Lee look, aware on some level he was attempting to communicate with her. Her human side was prioritizing catlike senses whilst Panther became stronger. Looking at the meeting below, voices now drifted up easily to her.

"…sent them?" the young woman, hair the color of straw spoke.

"I do not know." Zenon's voice was a sneer in itself.

"Have you asked Boss?" She was persistent, straw woman.

"No. The less he knows about this, the better." But the air around Zenon was wrong.

"What do we do when we find them?" Smoker stood at the opposite end of the table to Zenon.

"He wants them alive." Zenon paused and from here, his eyes gleamed. "But not how alive."

A snicker ran around the table. Zenon stood and paced. "I, on the other hand, want their power." He cracked his fingers.

Rumbles of approval met his words. Saliva dropped from her jaws as Panther watched, images in her head of leaping down and eviscerating Zenon. Evil rolled and dropped from his words, much the way water boiled over. The air around him glowed a fluorescent green.

"When were they last seen?"

Bald guy stood up. "At the ball. They seem to have disappeared. We are watching Philippe Callas, and no one has passed through the doors."

"No one?" The very air stood still as the menacing tone in Zenon's voice became apparent. "How about any animals?"

"No, no one, sir." Nonetheless, it was clear he was

shaken but trying to put conviction into his voice. There was a pause.

"And did you shapeshift to make sure?"

This time the conviction was stronger. "Yes, Mr. Zenon, we did. Three times and each time checked the house. There were no signs of anything out of the ordinary."

The gleam in Zenon's eyes faded to disappointment. "We need to find them. Grayson, you take three men and question Callas. Laura, the hotel staff said Radley had gone to some local boutique—find out where and question the staff. Find out what Radley said to them."

Dismay flooded the human side of her, but she dammed it. She couldn't afford to allow her human back in yet. They would warn Marianne as soon as they were out of here.

"What are you waiting for? Go!" Zenon swept an arm to the door and they all hurriedly stepped towards it. "Johann. You stay."

Smoker took a step from the door and joined Zenon at the table.

"Pour me a whiskey."

Johann picked up the bottle from the table and poured a generous measure into it. Zenon threw it back, held it out for more. This one he sipped.

"What do you know about power extraction?"

She felt a low growl starting and beside her, she could feel Lee reacting similarly.

"What do you mean?"

"North and Radley are in possession of a dormant power, a power reaching back for centuries. When a man and woman have such a connection, they are capable of feats beyond normal thinking. Look at Pierre and Marie Curie, or in fact the very first twin souls ripped apart—Osiris and Isis. The power that comes from such a pairing is second to none, and this I want."

The oil in Zenon's voice was replaced with something deeper—something envious, something insidious, which gave her the crazy feeling he would suck her very soul out for himself. She shook herself. Yet a prickling sensation caught. Shivers ran over her back in the tiniest of waves. Twin souls? A wave beached but before she could examine it, Lee hissed *Listen*

and she pulled her attention back into the room.

"When we capture them, if they cannot be talked into joining us, then the next step is logical."

She held her breath.

"We take their power?" Johann finished Zenon's words for him. "How?"

Zenon walked around the table, eyes darting into each corner. "I have to find out. Perhaps the chalice might be able to help." Seemingly assured the pair were on their own, Zenon walked to the far wall, and she strained out so far, she felt Lee give an alarm. But what was Zenon doing?

"Ah, there you are." The tone in his voice dropped to an almost caressing level as he wandered back to the table, holding something as though it was a baby.

It's the chalice. Lee sounded excited beside her, and she couldn't blame him.

With reverence, Zenon unfolded the altar cloth, the look on his face akin to a priest unwrapping the covenant. She held her breath, only to have it escape in a *whoosh* as the chalice was revealed. Zenon placed it on the altar and stepped back. Dully the silver metal glowed, giving it an almost sulky look. From here, she could not see the various engravings over it. But there was something about it, something pulling her attention to it, a magnetism, and she wouldn't have been surprised to see everything in that dark place, animate and non, go towards it. Look into the very heart and hopefully fall.

Sister. The call within her was harsh. She pulled herself back and into safety, a slight trembling in her limbs. She had nearly gone over, without thinking, without caring.

A noise made her skin crawl, and she realized with a jolt it was the sound of Zenon laughing.

"Not taking long now, is it."

Johann muttered some reply.

She and Lee shrank back from the gap. Breathing became harder as the air seemed to get heavy, and the feeling of something heading towards them was inescapable. Her heart rate picked up, heating her blood, yet something within her wanted to stay and bear witness to what happened below. It was important.

We should go.

Slowly though.

The two inched their way back as the darkness encroached silently. The lights previously dancing happily were plucked from the air and sucked back.

"Can you control it yet?" From here, they could hear Johann sounded awestruck.

"Yes. Watch."

The pair held their breath as the feeling of approaching suffocation receded. Waiting for a few breaths as the air became more normal, she crept once more towards the gap. Nuzzling her nose out, no danger could be sensed and she slowly placed her entire face through the gap. She felt Lee watching as though through Panther's eyes too. What they saw below made them gasp.

Zenon was like a conductor, making the darkness flow and ebb with every movement of his hands. The chalice overflowed with darkness, and she could hear a faint hiss, almost like the hiss of waves upon gravelly shores as it undulated. But Zenon did not seem entirely in control as part of the darkness stretched away from the movements of his hands. Fascinating shifts of black seemed to hold voices within it, voices caressing her very ears, and she felt herself leaning out further, wanting to hear more. What did it matter if she was seen?

"Back." Zenon's face changed in color from pale to pink to puce as he gesticulated wildly to get the darkness back. With what appeared to be an immense struggle, he yanked it back and into the chalice, quickly covering it over with the cloth. Zenon struggled for breath, placing both hands on the table. She jerked back into the corridor, shaking, sweating.

"It has changed." Johann sounded stronger.

After a few moments, Zenon straightened. "Yes, the darkness is quicker to come but also getting stronger." His voice cracked on his words. "Come, let us place it back and allow it to carry on recharging."

"But if you can't control it?"

There was no answer, Zenon's face back to pale and implacable.

Without further conversation, the room was plunged back into darkness. She looked at Lee.

Can we get it?

Not like this.

Both looked below. There was no way they could climb down as humans either.

What did Constantin want with it?

He said to return it to its rightful owners, which I assumed to be the Vatican. But now I wonder…

What?

If it was used by pagans before, then perhaps it should go back to them.

It overflowed with power, but here's the thing, Lee, that wasn't good power.

Both looked once more into the cavity.

And Zenon—what was he doing?

Trying to control it.

He did, eventually.

But it cost him.

Thoughts were lightning fast between them, and she didn't stop to question the speed at which they were processing things.

Time to go.

She acknowledged the final expression from Lee by turning and following him back. Within half an hour, they were back at the start point. She recognized a sense of cool relief as she slowly re-inhabited her body. She looked at Lee to see if he felt the same and met only clouds where before there had been bright thoughts. *Of course, they were back in human form once more.*

Once their bodies were fully occupied, the sense of urgency she had carried with her asserted herself. "Marianne. We must warn her."

Lee nodded. "Philippe said this way brought us

into the city, let's keep going."

She no longer felt any claustrophobia as they strode along the passageway. "What about the chalice—what should we do?"

"Tell the Vatican where it is."

"Good thinking. How?"

"I know a few good men. I'll pass the message on."

"Really? Are you sure it's safe?"

He paused. She went a good few paces before she realized he'd stopped. "What is it?"

"I've finally got it. It's been bugging me, and as Tiger I couldn't quite access the information. One of the men I had commissioned to help me find the cross was there. Third from the right from Zenon. T-rex they called him, because he's a bit of a dinosaur. But superb at tracking."

"He might have taken the cross to Zenon?"

"I'd stake my life on it. Also, before I saw him there, I'd have put my life on him being an honest and good guy. Who can we trust?" His voice meandered away into his thoughts.

"What did you think of down there?"

She thought back. "I do wish we could have seen what was in the wall when he took the chalice out. My cat senses smelled danger, something with a gold vein of strength running through it. Power. The place itself stank of power, a warped power. A power bent to something else."

"I agree. And the chalice was soaking it up, rather than emanating it. Zenon did say something about charging it. What was the darkness?"

"I don't know."

"Might there have been other artifacts in there?

Have there have been many missing? And how can a room be so evil it'll charge things? I felt on the way there, with all the carvings on the wall, we were headed toward a place filled with shamanic power."

"Maybe we were, but the other side of shamanic power."

A chill ran through her, like an electric current, leaving her uneasy. "What is that? The devil?"

He was silent for a minute, his answer when it came, subdued. "Only if you could call what we're doing Godlike."

"Good point. I don't feel as though this is anything to do with one singular god. To me, it feels like the energy of the universe is manifesting itself in different ways."

"We're nearly there." The tunnel had again been leading them gradually upward, the walls becoming more man-made than previous. Soon they came to a perfectly round opening, too round to be anything but man-made. The tunnel narrowed and stopped once more. Looking through it, Lee called back there was a ladder stretching both upward and downward.

He pulled his head back. "Looks like it serves a waterway. I vote for up."

The sense of unease she had felt for Marianne mushroomed into panic. "Quick, she's in danger."

Without a word, he disappeared, only for his ghostly face to reappear. "It's safe enough. I'll go first to check out where we emerge." His boots rang dully on the ladder before he stopped. *Hot dang, but it's dark there.* A constant tapping echoing noise emanated as though someone were consistently throwing pebbles into still, deep water. Ignoring the shudders running through her, she swung out, clutching the iron bars. Once she was stable, she called "okay" to Lee and they started climbing.

It seemed to go on forever, the bars they trod upon quite rusty. Once or twice, her foot slipped, and her heart jumped into her throat, but she maintained a steady pace. So much so she felt herself slipping into a trance.

"Lee? How are you doing?"

His voice dropped down. "Okay, we're nearly there. How are you?"

"Need some distraction."

There was a pause, before she heard him take a deep breath and suddenly just launched into singing. She nearly fell off her ladder in surprise but smiled. That was one way of doing things.

And it was a song she knew. Raising her voice, she sang along with him, repeating the chorus with gusto. Until he broke off. "Okay, I see a circle of light ahead."

"Hmm, circle of light, isn't there a song there somewhere?"

"Time to focus, girl. There is no other way of getting out of here without lifting the lid and going straight through. Let's hope it's not in the middle of a busy street."

"Or that anyone will see us climbing out of the gutter. Anyone normal, not just any of Zenon's men."

He came to a halt above her. With one hand holding the ladder, he reached with his right hand.

"It's a manhole. Just a bit heavy."

"Is there anything I can do?"

"Hang tight."

He went up another rung of the ladder until his

head was pressed against the top of the tunnel. "Umph."

There was a slight screeching noise and an extra shaft of light entered before he shut it again.

"I couldn't hear nor see any sign of traffic. We could be in luck. Come up as far as you can and let's see if I can lean against you whilst I use both hands to raise it slightly."

She did as he asked and positioned herself around him, bracing her hands on the ladder. He shifted as close to the ladder as he could. "Just trying to center my base of gravity. The closer I am to the ladder, the less weight you should have to bear."

As he settled, she steadied herself. "Okay, you're good to go." She spoke into his jacket, muffling her voice as she did. He loosened one hand.

"Still all right?"

"Yup. Go for it."

He let the second go, and she could feel him leaning as much as he could into the ladder. Then he placed his hands under the cover and pushed. Slowly the top rose. She held her breath, waiting, as he held the cover in place. Nothing happened. No car drove over them, there was no sound of anyone rushing over.

The muscles bunching in his back told her he was about to push it, and she steadied and braced herself. With a low *umph*, he pushed the cover further and she blinked in the sudden sunlight. *Damn.* Lee paused before decisively pushing the cover over and exposing the entire hole.

"Okay?" he whispered.

He rose up a rung and slowly pushed his head through, then in one smooth movement was up and out of the cover.

"Quickly."

She went up the remaining rungs and emerged, blinking hard, and pulling her backpack through. Lee put the cover back in place while her eyes acclimatized. They were standing in a back street of town. To their right crisscrossed a stream of traffic, hopefully too far away for anyone to clock what was happening. To their left, their street opened out onto what appeared to be a wasteland car park.

"Come." Manhole cover in place, he grabbed her hand, and they both ran over to the cover of the buildings, tall, high, industrial buildings with windows only up high. There was an alleyway between two such buildings, and it was to there they ran.

"Not a bad place to exit." Both were breathing hard after their exertion and no small amount of panic.

"Where are we in relation to the shop?"

He checked his phone. "About five minutes. We can get there through the back streets except for the last three hundred yards. We should split up—they won't be looking for us on our own."

She had to acknowledge the truth of it.

He stared at his phone, chewing on his lip. "Right, this is the way I shall go, and this yours. Here, look."

With a sinking heart, she followed their tracks. They stayed together for about half of the way, then he looped around and back over to the shop.

"If the shop is closed, come back here." He pinned a point on the map, easily remembered and recognized.

"Any problems in fact, and we'll meet here." She nodded.

"What happens if Zenon's men are there?" They made their way cautiously up the street.

"Come back to the meeting point. Don't get involved. Promise me, Ellora."

He stopped her by putting his hand on her arm. "Please?"

She stared. "But it will be our fault."

"Well, we can do her no good by being captured."

He had a point. "Okay."

"Time to split up." They had reached the turning point. He pressed the phone into her hand. "I want you to have this. If anything happens, I have the number. Hang on." He scrabbled in his backpack and pulled out the mobile charging unit. "Take this too in case we are split up."

She grabbed it and put it in her bag. The sounds of traffic encroached, and she took a deep breath. "Good luck. See you at the shop." Try as she might, she couldn't take her gaze from his face, drinking in the sight of him. He softened and reaching out a hand, cupped her face. Stretching into the warmth of his palm, she kissed it, wishing with all her might they didn't have to split up. *You'll be okay,* Panther purred.

"Okay, let's do it." Shouldering her pack once more, she turned.

Chapter Seventeen

Lee watched her go, heart in his mouth. He gave her thirty seconds before retracing his steps to loop around the back. More and more people appeared, each intent on their own business. It was lunchtime, a particularly busy time as office workers were on their way for lunch. Hopefully, Marianne didn't close for lunch. The thought quickened his steps, and he hit the main street. Farther on, he could see the flags raised outside the hotel they had stayed in, and everything seemed normal. No flashing lights. Folk passing him were clad in suits, and beyond an air of purpose, everything seemed normal and calm.

Until the shop front of Marianne's came into view. From his angle, it looked as though the door was off its hinges—all he saw before the press of people around it blocked his view. An ambulance was outside, and three people were pushing and protecting a covered-over body on a stretcher. Ellora approached it from the other side and walked straight past it without glancing in. Pride filled his veins at the same time as worry. He crossed the street and headed up to the left and doubled back to their meeting place.

He stood at the corner, forcing himself not to pace. Time ticked by slowly as he waited her reemergence. With a glad heart, he saw her rounding the corner. She saw him, and her hand flew to her mouth. She flung herself into his arms.

"Oh my God, Lee. Oh my God." Her body shook in his arms, and he stroked her hair gently. They should move, but first his woman needed comfort. She shook and shuddered in his arms. Tenderly, he eased the hair from her face and dropped a kiss on the corner of her mouth.

"Come on." He placed his arm around her for support and gently led her away into the more deserted back streets. She hiccuped but went with him. When he felt they were safe from prying eyes, he stopped and pulled her closer to him, feeling her breath catch.

"She's dead. I didn't look inside, but I know she is. The store was broken into." Her voice collapsed into keening. "And it's all my fault. All my fault. If I had never gone in there, she'd still be alive."

He grasped her by the shoulders and looked clear in her ravaged face. "It is not your fault. Marianne was all too aware of what was going on, you said it yourself. She was ready."

She quietened and became all eyes, looking searchingly. "You are right, I know you are. But…"

"But nothing. Come here." He pulled her into a bear hug, prepared to stay here as long as she needed him.

She cried, but they were cleansing tears, good tears. But they switched again, and as he held her close, he felt hot blood swirl though her.

"By God, they'll pay." The words were so strangled, he wasn't sure they had come from her, and he looked in surprise. Her beautiful face was screwed up against the flood of emotions. She pulled herself out of his hold and straightened.

"Let's get them, Lee. They can't do this. First, see what they did to Philippe? Now Marianne. We can't let them away with it."

She was right.

"What do you suggest we do?"

"Go to the police?" As she said it, he could see the hopelessness of her comment strike her. She ran a hand through her hair, mussing it up more. "Well, look, everyone says we have power so why not do it ourselves?" A gleam had entered her eyes.

"Do what? Payback? A life for a life? What kind of battle are we entering?" He was playing devil's advocate, he knew that. For the thought of running this pack of coyotes to the ground filled him with fiery resolve.

Steady, brother. All in due course.

Judging by the determined tilt of her chin, her thoughts were taking her someplace similar to him.

"We can do something good together. But not until we're forced to do it will we know what our power holds. Don't you see? We need to trust what we have and put ourselves out there. I'm not saying let's walk straight into the lion's den without being prepared."

He paced, head spinning. "I'm with you. At some stage, we need to return to Marianne's. Find some disguises. We need to look different. Being our power animals won't help. We go get the chalice. Bring it back to the Vatican if needed. It's dangerous in the wrong hands."

Resolve glowed from her. "Yes! What Zenon is doing under there, it's a big threat. The chalice has some great power, and if its power is misused, then it will be to everyone's detriment."

She paused and placed a hand on his forearm. "The world as we know it will change. And not for the better."

"Marianne. Philippe. Panther. Everything. The way we feel around each other. Don't you see, Lee? You already said you feel like you can conquer the world with me by your side. That's not normal. Unless we were meant to do something great together." She reached and picked up his hand and pressed her lips into the palm of his hand. "Perhaps this is it."

Everything she said was right and true. But—and here his heart hit his boots and he winced, sure he could hear a clank—it was too dangerous. Oh, not for him, he didn't care about himself. But for her, for Ellora. Now he had found her, he couldn't lose her. It was too damn dangerous for her. He dragged his gaze up to meet her unflinching one.

"Don't think it, North." Slate gray eyes glinted. "If it weren't for me, we wouldn't be in this."

"How do you make that out?"

"This situation wouldn't have arisen unless we were together to fight it. Like it or lump it, this is something we *both* have to do. Let's take it to the worst-case scenario, shall we? Let's just say Zenon has found a way to corrupt the chalice. Much the same way as Christianity spread like wildfire, this too, whatever he is doing, will. It looks as though he already has his disciples. And, Lee, we felt the evil. It was strong, and I don't know about you, but it sucked at me, trying to pull me in. Panther, not me as a human. Perhaps humans are weaker to refuse it. And worst-case scenario, darkness takes over the world."

As she spoke, there was a vague memory tugging.

Of her and him doing something, but what it was, he couldn't recall. *She's strong. You're strong. Together you are stronger.* But she was side by side with him. He stared. When had her features become so dear to him, imprinted in his mind? With his eyes closed, he could trace the outline of her. And one thing became abundantly clear to him; they were together for a purpose, and if they didn't fulfill it, then they would come apart. He said as much to her and saw gratitude fill her face.

"Exactly. Ergo, we have no choice."

"No free will?"

The look she cast him was laughing.

"Don't distract me, Lee North. We need to make plans."

She was right. "Going back to Marianne's could be dangerous."

"True but if her murder was all over the news, they would never suspect we would return there.

"And if it wasn't?"

"We find a different way to disguise ourselves." She stared off into space, clearly thinking hard. "Like they do in the movies. Bleach and cut our hair?"

Clouds were rolling in overhead, and the sound of the traffic on the high street muted. Tiger stretched in him, sending a sharp alert through him.

Without thinking, he grabbed her and pushed her farther down the road looking for someplace undercover. There was nothing. A large skip was filled to the brim with house debris, and he stopped by it.

"In." He gave her a leg up and scrambled up beside her quickly. Pulling an old heavy door over them, they lay as motionless as they could with heaving hearts.

The bright sunlight dimmed and they both turned cold, but the sound of wings took the shadow away. They lay there for a couple of minutes.

"Hope that wasn't Eagle."

"I have no idea. But one thing I do know. You are right. We need to battle this." Pulling his phone out, he cursed as he saw the low battery light but nonetheless flicked on the torch. A skip was too good a place not to check out. There weren't many useful items, but tucked away in a corner, he saw a crowbar. Hefting it, he nodded to himself and put it in his bag, sitting back by Ellora.

She grabbed his hand and held on tight. "We can do this." But he could hear fear in her voice. He squeezed back, " 'Course we can. It's the only reason we're together, right?"

"One thing's for sure." She stopped and forced a laugh. "I'm glad I don't have children. It's one thing going into something dangerous, knowing no one would really miss you. It'd be another thing going into it wondering if you were going to get to watch your children growing up. Not doing so would be heartbreaking."

In the yellow skip, under someone's old door, his heart had never been fuller. Shifting awkwardly to face her, "Ellora Radley, we will do this. And you know what? Someday, you and I will sit watching our grandchildren playing in cotton candy fields and all will be right with the world."

"You think so? You think you and I will have children together?"

"Sweetheart, if you want them, then I know it." He pulled her to him, and they lay together, entwined, listening to each other's heartbeat.

****

"Man, I'm starving," Lee whispered to Ellora as they made their way toward Marianne's back door. They had been watching for an hour, and he had remarked how efficient the police were, as they seemed to have cleared out early.

"Me too." She couldn't quite put her finger on it, but there seemed to be a lightening between them, almost an agreement to make light of the moments they could. It was incongruous to be tiptoeing through the dark, and she would laugh if she could. Maybe it was due to their conversation earlier, the fact they had confronted the worst and decided to do something about it, but there was a certain devil-may-care attitude in her. Lee was by her side, all else was immaterial. Saving the world, *pshaw*. But saving it with Lee? That was a good thing.

As they neared the door, they quieted, and Lee took a wire from his pocket to pick the lock. Bending, he jiggled the lock for a couple of moments before she heard a click and the door swung open to darkness. He nodded in satisfaction and stepped through—a warning hand splayed to Ellora. Ignoring it, she came through with him and shut the door behind them, placing it on the latch.

In the poor light of the phone, she saw the scowl on his face. A strange smell saturated the air, and her feline senses came on alert. They had come through the storeroom at the back, complete with half full cardboard boxes spilling clothes. Sidling to the door, they peered through to the dressing rooms. There was no outward sign of anything untoward having happened there. With the door open, they ventured in as one, back-to-back. Nothing.

"I don't like the smell. Let's get some clothes and go."

She looked inside her for Panther and closed her eyes, feeling her senses open. She inhaled deeply, now with her enhanced sense of smell, there was something metallic somewhere. The air was uneasy and shifted about. From the entrance to the upstairs came a stronger stench, and she shrank back from its flow and direction, not wanting to be caught up in it.

Without further ado, they went into the wig room and got busy.

"Blonde?" Ellora pulled a shoulder-length wig with a fringe over her black locks and pirouetted for Lee's inspection.

"Looks great, but blondes get a lot of attention. You would be better going dark chocolate brown, would fit in better with Athens too."

"Good thinking." In other circumstances, this could be fun, but the ever presence of danger leant them both an edge. Before too much time had passed, they stood looking at each other, scarcely recognizing the other. Lee had selected a longish, rather foppish wig, and both had changed clothes into smart but comfortable suits. Placing his hands in his pockets, Lee struck a pose.

"What do you think?" He lounged against the doorframe.

"Perfect. You just need sunglasses on the head to complete the look." She was joking, but he picked up a pair from the accessories table and perched them on his head.

"We should take more wigs." She spoke over her

shoulder as she fixed the brunette wig on her hair.

"Good thinking." He moved over and took another three wigs, black, grey, and brown.

"Great. Now, how about me?" She swung to face him, feeling odd in the borrowed clothes.

Starting at her toes, he scrutinized her, and she could've sworn she felt the weight of his look as strongly as though he had reached out and touched her. As a result, her blood heated to course through her, opening her arteries, the added oxygen causing a slight head spin. Slowly her calves warmed to his touch, up over her knees and into her soft inner thighs. With a desperate edge, she tried to focus on something else, anything to distract her from his eyes' caress. He had woken Panther, and she stretched within Ellora, a primal instinct to mate woken.

Flustered, she could not move as heat swept through her lower belly, pooling between her legs, rendering her legs a mass of jelly. Upward went his gaze, and she shivered as the hollows on either side of her stomach felt as though kisses were pressed into them. Upward over her stomach and ribcage, her nipples hardening in anticipation of the heat that the molten gold gaze induced.

A blush started, and like a tidal wave it spread out to her face and she bit her lip in an attempt to hold it back. Without being fully aware of her actions she arched her back as though to accept more of his gaze. Her sense of smell flared and picked up the musky undertones of his skin, the smell under her own. She employed more of her catlike senses, her eyes narrowing in on him, her ears picking up his breath, his shallow in and out breath matching hers.

But somewhere outside, she heard a sound like someone opening the door. They both froze, Lee's dilated pupils thinning to pinpricks. She listened harder to the sound of the door handle jiggling but couldn't pick up anything else. A questioning glance at Lee told her he hadn't heard anything more either.

Walking through the shop, they got to the back door and stopped.

"Damn. This doesn't feel right. Let's do the front door."

She was glad he had said so, for she had felt a prickle of awareness, heralding danger. They retraced their steps to stand by the front door. Not a moment too soon either for they heard the door open around the back. They stared at each other. Walking out the front door was a risk, but they had no choice. Taking a deep breath, she reached for the handle. *Invisible. Think transparency, let your mind see nothing but opaque mist.* At Lee's nod, she unlatched the top and bottom bolts, slipped the nib, and they slipped out silently into the busy streets turning to their left and falling quickly into step together. Speed walking helped keep the sense of danger at bay, and she relaxed the further they got from the shop. Her stomach rumbled reminding her she hadn't had something decent to eat for a long time.

"What do you fancy eating?"

"Lots. But we should go quick and easy. I don't want to be so full I want to sleep. We have work to do after all."

He stopped outside a French café, gesturing inside and raised an eyebrow. She nodded and he pushed the door open for her. "After you."

The smell greeting them made her mouth water. A

waiter bustled over and showed them to a table in the window. She shivered.

"It's too cold to be by the window. Have you a table in the back somewhere?"

Good call. But she hadn't heard it in her mind, rather she had read the look on his face. Being human. She smiled.

They were shown to a quiet table and given menus. For a brief moment, she felt she could forget all about the craziness her life seemed to have become. She relaxed into her dark red high-backed chair and placed her arms on the rests. To her right were a set of electricity sockets and without hesitation, she pulled out her charger and plugged her phone in, holding her hand out to Lee in order for him to give her his to do the same with.

"Phew."

Lee smiled over the menu. "Better?"

She took a double look when he moved the menu away. "There's no mistaking those eyes of yours, but the hair and the suit, well, you could easily be a gentleman of the city. It's a good disguise. Thank God for Marianne and your lock-picking ability."

"You look very different too. She has, sorry, had good quality items." He fingered his hair. "This does feel very natural."

She shivered. "I don't think it is. At least I hope not." She scoured the menu, absentmindedly choosing hummus and olives, breadsticks for a starter, followed by a smoked trout with horseradish salad and chips. Her stomach growled appreciatively.

"Drink? Wine?" Lee asked as their waiter materialized beside them. Wine would be lovely, but she wanted to keep her wits about her.

"Thanks, but I'll have a fresh lemonade."

"Two of those, please. Are you ready to order food?"

She nodded and they both placed their orders, sitting back in their chairs as the waiter took his leave.

"Let's do our plan of action and then relax and enjoy our food."

"Good thinking." She sat up straight. "What's next?"

"I vote for going to get the chalice tonight whilst we're still fresh in our disguises."

"How?"

He played with his fork, testing the tines against the soft ball of his finger. "You remember where we felt the air change, when we were coming back out of the vault? I think the tunnel we were in leads to the big room."

She nodded. "How do we get there? The doors are going to be locked."

She waited. The waiter reappeared and placed their drinks and starters on the table. As one, they both tucked into the breads and hummus. Lee waited until they had both eaten enough before continuing on.

"The tunnels—we go back in the way we just came out."

Their waiter arrived to clear away the starters before placing their main course on the table. Picking up her fork, she first devoured the dish with her eyes. Pink and perfectly cooked, she could trace the trout's fins along the back, the rocket salad being embellished nicely with horseradish.

A bowl of french fries was placed in front of them,

and she leaned over to check out what he had ordered. It looked almost as good as hers.

"Dig in."

A comfortable silence fell as they both appreciated their food. Over too quickly, she wiped her mouth with her serviette and pushed her chair back.

"Delicious and just right. Coffee now would be perfect."

Clearly the serving staff had been keeping an eye on them, for their table was soon cleared with coffee steaming in front.

"Okay, where were we?"

"In the tunnels. And what do we do, shapeshift or not?"

"Both."

Ellora drew her chin back in as she considered. "Shift, explore, come back into our bodies and off we go? Bit time consuming, isn't it?"

"No. One of us shapeshifts, and the other doesn't."

Something inside her squirmed at the thought of the separation. Which didn't make sense as they wouldn't be apart. But she was used to having Lee by her side, whatever form they both took. She wasn't sure she wanted to be in a different form.

But what choice had she? "Okay. Who does what?"

"I'll shift."

Okay, the image of her striding out with Tiger by her side was somewhat appealing. "Will we be able to communicate?"

"I don't know."

"I need more coffee." She raised her hand to the waiter, and as if by magic, another pot of coffee appeared. "Tonight?"

"Yes. We go into the tunnels, find the crossroads. I'll shift and then we'll, or rather I, will explore farther."

She swallowed hard against a sudden dry throat as the reality of the situation encroached. "Okay. Let's do it." She pushed her cup away, replete and sure she couldn't eat nor drink another thing. "How are we going to get to Rome, by the way?"

"Train out of Athens. We'll just have to meander our way across, taking one step at a time. With a bit of luck, no one will know where we're going. Let's trust our disguises."

"If we get attacked, what are we going to do? Stay and fight—although how I'll fight in human form is beyond me—or turn and run?"

"Run." There was an implacable expression on his face.

****

Lee called for the bill, mind whirling. Outside night was thick and dark with lots of cloud coverage. He glanced at his watch, 9 p.m.. How would they feel in twelve hours' time? The streets weren't as busy, most folk were safely ensconced in their pub or eatery of choice, and there would be a lull in the traffic for now. It was a good time to head for the manhole cover.

Chapter Eighteen

As they wove their way through, Lee kept a sharp eye out, trying not to make it too obvious. Colorful tourists passed by, and it was only because they were dressed in black that he noticed them. Two men stood at the street junction ahead, trying to act nonchalant. Ellora grabbed his arm at the same time and they both ducked into a side street.

"It may not be us they are looking for, but let's not draw attention to ourselves."

They carried on, picking their way carefully through the streets. Upon reaching the street, they checked before crossing over to the manhole. Blank windows gazed inscrutably, the only lights coming from the traffic at the main street. An image of this street full of light and people flashed up in his mind, but he banished it quickly before it would be conveyed to Ellora, there being nothing to say—it was a flash of perspicacity, after all. With a grunt, he got his crowbar in the groove and heaved it up. Quicker than expected it came free and he sat hard, his breath escaping his lungs. Ellora giggled, a long low sound turning his heart over. He smiled back, appreciating the ability to laugh in such situations.

They both gazed into the black hole yawning open. He looked at Ellora who returned the look with a smile.

"I'll go first, shall I? Then you can replace the

cover." With a decisive nod, she swung her legs over onto the ladder and disappeared before he could reply. Switching on his phone torch, he held it between his teeth as he maneuvered himself, careful not to go too fast.

Her disembodied voice floated back to him. "I'm down."

After a couple more rungs of the ladder, he too felt the reassuring security of the ground below his feet. As he stopped, he felt the thick darkness surround him. Whether it was because of what they were about to do or what, he smelled danger in the air.

"How're you doing?" He reached out with more than his voice to her, sensing her uncertainty.

"Fine, thanks. Can you remember which way we came?"

"Offhand, nope. But the compass on the phone will tell us. We came southeast last time. Let's head northwest."

Taking his phone out, he balanced the compass. Once it pointed consistently in the direction they needed, he nodded to her. After shouldering their backpacks, they picked their way through the dark to the opening. He had forgotten how oppressive this darkness was, compounded by the dripping of water somewhere in the distance.

"How're you feeling?"

"All right, thanks. Wondering how I managed to place my feet on a path that led me to becoming a burglar, but you know, wonderment is the beauty of life, right?"

"We're not burglars, Lorrie." For some reason, shortening her name gave him a little frisson of happiness.

Her voice too held a smile in it when she replied. "Oh, aren't we, L?" She gave the letter its phonetic sound. "What? Well, you can't shorten Lee to anything else, can you?"

"Seriously though, we are rescuing something, not stealing it."

"Yes, I do know. Tell me as we have about half an hour wandering here, what you think would happen if we get caught?"

"We won't get caught."

"Hopefully not. But say we do? What's our backup plan? If we become separated?" Her voice had risen a notch, and he reached out and squeezed her hand.

"We have a pretty good connection, perhaps we would be able to communicate when not in each other's company?"

"Not good enough for me. Say you get captured and I don't, what happens next?"

"You go to Philippe's and ask him to get you out of the country as fast as possible."

He heard her mutter.

"What?"

"Nothing. Your mobile number and anonymous email I have by heart. Any other way I can contact you?"

"It's all you need. Likewise me with you. Should you get away with the chalice, what will you do?"

"I'm not going to leave you, Lee." It wasn't just bravado either. She couldn't imagine leaving without him. Ever.

"But you'd have to. The chalice needs to be returned. It might help me become free."

"Hmm. Hopefully we won't have to put it to the test. Same goes with you, by the way. If we get split up, where shall we meet?"

Good question. If they became split up, then no doubt there would be an alert out for them. Any places he could think of would be busy. Except for…

"You remember the beach hut out by Philippe's house? There. Walking should take about an hour, but once you get out of the main streets, there's a lot of cover and you should be fine."

"Good thinking." He could almost hear her thinking. "And Lee?"

"Mmm?"

"It's been awesome getting to know you." There was a catch in her throat. He stopped and pulled her into his arms.

"We're going to get through this, you and I. Don't worry. Who could beat a big cat and you side by side?"

"Um, a pack of coyotes and some men with machine guns?"

She tried to make it sound as though she were joking, but the catch in her throat belied her words.

"We're too clever. I don't think the coyotes will go for you. You need to dodge the men. Also I doubt there'll be anything as obvious as machine guns. Remember we have a power they want, let's use that knowledge to our advantage. If we get captured, we promise anything to get out. Deal?"

"Will they know if we communicate?"

"They may notice, but they shouldn't hear us."

Reluctantly, he released her, and they resumed their steps. Ellora remained quiet all the way up to the opening where previously there were guards. Straining her ears, she could hear nothing. A deadening nothing.

"Lee, I think this way has been blocked up." She shone the torch around and sure enough, where they had turned into was full of newly concreted bricks.

"What do we do now?"

"Keep going. Remember the other disused tunnel?"

"You mean the one we chose not to go down? Um, yes."

"No choice now. But I'll shapeshift here."

"Okay."

He took off his backpack and checked it to see if there was anything she might need from it besides his phone and spare batteries. Wrenches and tools could all remain here, unless…

"Take this." He thrust the crowbar at her, and she paled at the same time as she reached out for it. A glint entered her eyes as she hefted it into her palm. Looking, he had no doubt she would use it and for some reason, his heart expanded further with admiration for this beautiful woman—no, *creature*—walking by his side.

"Okay, let's do it."

"Just be careful, you great big oaf."

Much as she teased, he knew she could feel this separation. He closed his eyes for the shifting process. Ellora found it easy, but he didn't. But he followed Marianne's instructions to the letter and soon felt Tiger stretching and saw his beautiful face staring intently at him. *Time to go in.*

****

Whilst Ellora waited, she examined her feelings. Curiously, the predominant feeling was one of an overwhelming numbness. She knew she ought to feel trepidation and more, but something in her seemed to rein it in. Almost as though there was a dam in her, strong and unmoving.

Probing deeper and with a flash of something, inspiration perhaps, she understood. It was because she and Lee were doing the right thing. Not a shadow of doubt in her mind. And that provided her strength. The knowledge of right being on their side. Their gifts were out of this world, and they wouldn't have been bestowed on them unless they were going to do something useful. For once, she could fully buy into the fact of Lee and her meant to do something awesome together. This was it. *They weren't going to fail.*

She repeated her phrases over and over until a low growl alerted her to the fact Lee had changed. A slight scrabbling noise and his head appeared, a beautiful proud face, yet with Lee's eyes. She stared, mesmerized as he gracefully clambered over to stand by her side. Taller than she had expected, he reached up to her ribcage. Hesitantly, she placed her hand on his head, searching her head for his voice. Contact made, she heard him.

This still takes some getting used to.

What do you think it's like for me? Everything else is odd, but this? You as Tiger and me, well as me. Madness personified.

Tiger purred, and she stroked his ears automatically. The feel of his soft yet strong fur was thick under her fingers.

Mmm, good. Hey, I wonder what you scratching my belly would be like?

He bumped his head into her waist as though to tumble over, but she lost her balance and landed on her ass with a whoosh.

Sorry, Ellora, are you okay?

She was winded, but comforted. *Hey how come I felt you?*

Maybe because we're connected.

When we're out of this, we should see just how connected we are. It'd be interesting.

And fun. There was no mistaking the salacious note in his voice and she laughed.

They were nearing a corner, and Tiger halted.

Let me go first.

Okay, but don't go far, please.

They were doing the right thing, but who was to say they were doing it in the right way? Her stomach twisted, and she sternly told it to stop. Feeling like this wouldn't help anyone. Noiselessly, he padded off and disappeared from sight. Adrenaline picked up a pace, and she alternately felt hot and cold. Bright flashes appeared in her peripheral and in her head. Just as she felt his absence, Tiger came back.

All clear ahead. No guards, which makes me nervous.

She fell into step beside him, enjoying having him back.

The corridor became increasingly winding, with the walls appearing bumpier with rising damp. Soon they had to walk in single file, Tiger leading the way. She listened to the sound of her heart filling her ears and had to admit to herself it just wasn't possible to hear anything else. Still with Tiger at her side, she was fine.

When they came to a crossroads, the way to go involved her crouching as the passageway was increasingly narrower. Butterflies scrambled in her stomach, but she breathed deeply in an effort to quell her nerves. *It was just another corridor, right, just slightly smaller than the last.* As long as it didn't get any smaller.

The good thing is we're coming into increasingly less-used places. If it was more accessible, it would've been used more.

True.

She could manage no more, instead she gestured to the opening, admiring the gait of the tiger as Lee leaped into the gap. He craned his neck back.

It all looks fine ahead. Smelling the air makes me think we're coming out soon, the current seems much stronger.

What a relief. I hope we don't have to run back through this corridor. It might prove hard.

Whatever happens, we'll deal with it.

The tone in his voice broached no arguing, and taking refuge in it, she clambered into the opening and nodded to him. He swung his great head back and stalked ahead of her.

Hope you've got a nice view back there.

She smothered a laugh. Seeing the haunches and rear end of a tiger wasn't exactly her idea of a good view, but it certainly distracted her, seeing the bunch of muscles, and admiring the smooth movements.

Just don't stop suddenly. What were these tunnels built for?

I can't see it was anything legal, otherwise they'd be finished properly. The sides are too rocky, too clunky, lacking the finesse of an organization.

Escape route?

Perhaps. Lee took a deep breath. *The overriding*

air is one of disuse though. I can't sense any human activity here at all.

Ellora nodded. The air was becoming closer, and she had to breathe deeply, not an easy thing to do when practically bent double. She tried to concentrate on her breath, all the time conscious of panic a mere millisecond away.

Don't let it in, don't think about it. Think about…what? What had she, Ellora Radley, to distract her. Her job? Heck no!

Lee, will we be able to turn around if the tunnel is a dead end?

If we had to, yes. But we won't. I can smell it.

More deep breaths. All was okay. Yet childhood memories crowded in. Images of the plane crash, as though they were waiting for when her defenses were weak, crowded in. Masks falling from the ceiling in a flurry of *panic, it's time to panic.* Sudden sharp shock on fellow passenger's faces. Bright sunlight laughing through the windows as the wing of the plane turned at an unnatural angle to the earth. And the noise. Her ears roared with the memory—a memory she had no business remembering.

It seemed as though all 365 passengers had held their breath at the same time, as collectively, the unswerving reality of what was happening hit them all. Hard. Roaring of engines filled her ears like blood. Then suddenly, silence. Everything stopped. The plane, the passengers. Even the babies stopped crying. Suspended. In the aisle, a bright light. A light too bright to look into.

But she did. There in the center of the light, was her. An older, ancient, and young her. And by her side was another light, encircling her. Features developed the longer she looked. With a feeling akin to being inside a star shower, she recognized Lee. Compassion and sadness emanated from them, and she stared into her own eyes, thinking if she could maintain contact, she would be safe.

Screeching noise returned, screams, the deep booming voice of some pastor chanting. The acrid smell of fear, something that should never be smelt keenly. Her mother, her father, all three linked, she could see her parents' thoughts, the horror and the fear, and she squeezed their hands tightly, feeling the love from her higher self flow through her and into them. Calm. *At least we're here, together* was the last thought she sent, wrapped up in velvety love and age-old acceptance.

Sharp shiny metal, crumpling like tinfoil. Her parents, wrenched from her side upon impact, both remained upright, belted into their seats. But the seats themselves were wrenched and flung apart. Acceptance fled in the face of horror.

She only then became aware the repeating sound in her head was Lee.

Ellora, Ellora. You're okay. I've got you. You're safe. Let go.

Her awareness of the current situation returned to her. She felt weak as a kitten.

I don't know if you know, but you transmitted those memories to me, clear as day. Horrible for you.

Lee had maneuvered himself to face her, the beautiful tiger face staring at her with such a depth of compassion she thought it would be her undoing. *Let go.* Right now, she wasn't sure who the voices in her head belonged to.

Lee, the thing is...I wasn't actually there.

Yes. It was hard.

It was. But there was a beautiful sense of acceptance at the end. My parents didn't die in shock and horror. They were comforted by us all being together.

You made it easier for them.

She sniffed in response. At least she had.

But why now? Why did this happen now?

Maybe you needed to feel your ability in order to be stronger. The knowledge of being on the right path brings strength, no?

I guess. Did you see it all?

There was a pause, and she knew he was just looking for the diplomatic answer.

S'okay. I know you did. And she felt no small measure of comfort she had helped her parents right at the end. Her age-old grief of not being with them in their final moments now escaped her, unlocking the vice around her heart. She shut her eyes, exhausted but exhilarated, and felt it.

The love and support rolling from Lee, made her heart unfurl and sent sparkles of pure gold through her. Her veins sang in response, and she told herself this was the moment. This was all there was. Ever.

Ellora, you're glowing.

She smiled. She wasn't surprised. She could feel the glow inside her, and she embraced it.

But I guess we must move.

Yes, let's get the bastards.

Or rather, the chalice.

She unfurled herself from Tiger and stretched out

in the tunnel.

Lead on.

As she came behind him, she realized she didn't care what was going to happen to them, as long as they got the chalice out. Somewhere within her, knowledge, pure and right, told her the chalice needed rescuing. It was far too important an item to be in the wrong hands and had the ability to wreak havoc on a large scale. *Get it out.*

Lee? What would the chalice be like in the right hands?

Like us, you mean?

Well, yeah.

We don't know enough to wield it properly.

But we trust the Vatican?

Have you a better idea?

She bit her tongue. For she had her doubts. After all, how had it ended up here?

In silence, they carried on. The walls remained the same thickness for the large part but gradually widened out. Lee stopped.

Nearly there. The air is changing. He raised his head and inhaled deeply.

She copied him, employing Panther. Along with the lighter air came awareness of people, emotions, and warm bodies. Amidst the cooler, almost implacable nature of the vault came a sense, a feeling—*I have stood here for centuries and centuries. After you are gone, I will stand. Above or below the earth. Nothing can impact me. And when the time is right, I shall be known.*

Lee, did you hear that?

The sound of life ahead? Yes.

But no. Was she going mad? Buildings and places talking to her. But she remembered Marianne telling them everything has spirit. *Hello?* Nothing came back, and putting a hand on the wall, she tried again. There was a slight shifting in the air, but nothing more. She shook her head slightly. She must've imagined it.

Easy goes it, now Ellora, we're getting there.

As if on cue, the tunnel stopped, opening into a larger corridor. With a graceful bunch of muscles, Lee checked it out and then bounded down. Ellora turned around and shimmied the same way, leaving a drop of about a foot.

How the hell are we going to get back? It was a real and valid fear.

Let's see how we go.

As one, they turned to look at the gap as though to memorize it.

Will we remember the way?

I'll be able to smell it.

Yeah, I just hope we're together.

They both stood, sniffing the air.

I reckon to the right.

I concur.

They turned and walked, Ellora luxuriating in being able to stand upright. Hearing voices faintly on the air, they flattened themselves against the wall to wait.

Can you make out how many there are?

No, nor what they are saying.

But the more they listened, the more the sounds turned from a dialogue to a flat monotonous tone.

What's going on?

It sounds like Gregorian chant to me.

I don't know. It makes a strange kind of sense. Chanting puts you into trance. Maybe we're coming across a ceremony.

She thought for a moment.

By Jove, I've got it. We have actually stumbled into a film set. We're being filmed, and we're going to round a corner to see thousands of Zenon's disciples chanting whilst over a hot pit of lava, there is a small child roped to a spit. I'm glad I've managed to figure it out.

Ha. Indiana Jones was great. I watched all the movies at a young age.

And an impressionable age too, by the looks of your life. Her tone was dry, and she smiled to herself. For it did explain a lot. *What am I then? Just one of the women who come in and out of your life? Should I have a pet monkey or something?*

And I a whip?

She looked at Tiger by her side. *How had she gotten this lucky?*

I heard.

The corridor went into a sharp corner, with the chanting becoming slightly louder. Intuitively, they both knew around this corner was what they were looking for. They stopped.

Wait here. I'll check out what's ahead.

She opened her mouth to argue.

Whoever's there might be just in human form and won't see me unless they are looking properly. And from what we can hear, no one is on the alert.

Mutinously, she nodded and watched as Tiger padded slowly around the corner. Holding her breath, she listened with all her might. No change in the chanting was heard and bit by bit, she expelled air, forcing her limbs to be calm. To breathe deeply and to be in tune with the moment, all the better to react quicker. She sent out a seeking breath to Lee and felt him to be safe. Could she move in too? What did he see? Not able to withstand the suspense any longer, she slid to the corner and craned her neck to look around.

Nothing but more darkness greeted her. Taking a moment to discard her backpack and leave it around the corner, she sidled around. The chanting was louder, but it sounded only like one person. Further around the hairpin corner she went, smelling the air growing lighter and thicker at the same time. Lighter because there was more air, thicker because something was happening.

She stopped and breathed in with her belly, opening all her senses. Syrup-like wrongness clung to all her senses. *Wrong.* Again, a voice. But not imagined this time. And her entire being agreed. Wrong on a whole raft of levels. The air stank, and she shrank back. Something inside her wanted to run as far away as she could, and in fact, her feet turned her around and she was heading back through the corridor before she got a grip on herself.

Lee was there and they had come for the chalice. What was she doing? Giving herself a stern talking to didn't soothe the butterflies in her stomach, and she paused, feeling the perspiration break out on her forehead. What was going on? She felt inside her for Panther, only to discover he lay sleeping. What? Her reason kicked in big time, and she sent out seekers for Lee.

No answer, just a blank space where he should

reside. Panic swooped towards her, a big black bird in a low tunnel, claws outstretched and reaching for her. With a gasp, she flung her arms over her head and felt the whoosh of the wings as it passed her by. She had to get a grip. Her fingers felt thick and clumsy as she fumbled in her backpack for the torch. She couldn't stand the thick darkness anymore, felt as though the air had morphed to bats flapping and flying at her, getting stuck in her hair and urging her back to whence she had come.

Breathe. She could do this. Deep breaths, one at a time.

Cold realization showered over her. There was no way she was going to leave Lee. And if she did, she would have no way through the corridor herself. Panther was sleeping, and she wouldn't be able to get up to the gap.

Brutally, she shoved away the panic, ignored the sense of swallowing bats and inched forward again. As the corner straightened out, the darkness lessened. Vague shapes emerged and she paused, focusing on one thing at a time. Sight was what was needed right now.

Bit by bit, she saw she was at the end of a long room. It appeared empty but had archways to the right and to the left. She smelled, at the same time she realized she didn't have Panther's senses to tap into. Why did he sleep? She was alone. More alone than she had ever been. Just a human, a weak human with nothing special about her at all. She couldn't move.

Chapter Nineteen

Going around the corner, a weird, heavy dragging-to-the-earth sensation made him want to lower his belly to the ground. Lee shook his head and carried onwards. Wordless chanting entered his blood stream, and he could feel it going around and around his body. *Focus, North.* He shook his head and tried a long, low growl to clear his mind. *Combat sound with sound.*

Plain archways at the end of the corridor opened into a large, dark room. Rumbling low in his throat, he padded soundlessly towards the increased chanting. Yet the closer he went, the more akin it was to wading through setting concrete, and he had to use all his strength for each step. *What the hell?* Crossing into the next room, he saw it was the one they had seen from above.

The chalice, uncovered, was on an altar beside a statue, the details of which he couldn't see. Sitting cross-legged in front was the source of the chanting—a hooded monk dressed in a cloak, arms outspread to the chalice in worship. With his rapidly dwindling human senses, Lee understood he was chanting to the chalice. To the right of the altar, darkness shifted, and he shrank back into the shadows to watch a new figure approach the chalice.

Dressed similarly in black robes, his hood was not yet up and the features of Johann were apparent. He placed a hand on the other person's shoulder, who rose as he did, still chanting. As one, Johann lifted his hood and the other dropped his; Johann took up the chant as the other stopped. It was the aggressive man from the table, but now his eyes drooped, and moving as though in a trance himself, he left the room.

Johann bowed to the chalice and the chant switched slightly, swirling through the air, bringing a new awareness. With a flash, Lee understood this treacle-like air was the result of the chant and the effects on the chalice. But the flash of perspicacity winked out and he floundered. What could he do, after all? He contemplated stretching out on the floor and catching a nap. He hadn't slept in a while, after all.

An image came to him, and he idly wondered where he had seen it before. A beautiful woman, long black hair, piercing blue eyes.

You're pretty.

Lee, come back to me.

Urgency tapped on his bones. Somewhere, deep inside him, was a river. But the sound kept tempting him towards slumber.

Lee. Ah, the river. But it was dammed. Why? Did it matter? *Yes.* With a sigh, he reached in and plucked a bough from the dam, watching in amusement as it all came tumbling down. Awareness flooded him, and he gasped and couldn't breathe as his chest fought. A brief moment of panic subsided until he got it under control, breathing normally. Cautiously he explored himself.

His sight worked, but it wasn't with the keen edge of Tiger, same with hearing and smell. He looked at his feet and saw, to his distress, his shape twitching. In his massive paw, his hand appeared and flashed back again.

Same with his chest. He was shifting back into human form. *No dammit.*

The chanting continued, and glue returned once more to his limbs. With a massive heave, he flung it from him, visualizing dispersing it like a cloud. It worked but required all of his concentration to shut out the undermining, insidious sound. A change in tone, very subtle, alerted him to the fact something was changing. He needed strength. He needed Tiger in full force. But access was denied.

He felt as though he were flinging himself against a heavy wooden door with no give whatsoever. No. This could not be happening. He was still Tiger after all. Closing his eyes, he threw himself into the animal. Sounds, visions, smells all warped in him, like a television channel struggling to tune. Pure adrenaline set him alight and he burned inside Tiger, exploding into this body. A sense of wrongness lingered until, like a light, all human senses zoned out.

The chalice. The person in front of it. *Rip to shreds.* A snarl exploded, and he leapt from the shadows and onto the table. The chalice burned with a blinding light, and he turned his attention to the monk. Sounds and vibrations echoed and changed, providing a barrier that shocked when touched. But nothing would stop him.

The monk, the wrongness around him, he had to be stopped. Jaws held wide, he sprang for him. A coyote sprang back, and they locked jaws, Tiger feeling the satisfying crunch as the coyote succumbed. Jubilation spread in a haze throughout. He was supreme, invincible. He dropped his head to deal the final blow when a movement at the back of the room caught his attention.

A woman stood there, hand to her mouth. She ran to him, strange noises coming from her. *Finish the coyote.* He went for the jugular, mouth watering with the anticipation of bursting the strong vein in his neck and feeling his blood bubble into his mouth. But he didn't get there. The coyote was flung away and once more, he saw the woman. Growls rippled through his body, perhaps this woman was worth eating. He advanced slowly, the low growls in perfect synchrony with his steps, glorying in his strength. Knowing this life was his, he prowled, watching her. The coyote was motionless.

Somewhere, deep inside him, was recognition. He shook his head. He wanted the glory of taking her life. Bunching his muscles, he sprang. But she, this woman, leapt to meet him. Large cat met large cat, and he rebounded, winded. Confused. In front of him was a panther. Again, his spark of recognition had to be quashed in favor of the kill, and he launched himself once more. Once more, muscles met muscles. The panther wasn't fighting him, merely protecting herself. Again, he launched. And again. Each time, a wall of muscles. He tired, the thrill of the kill fading under heavier acceptance.

Lee.

He shook his head. But didn't spring. He snarled instead, feeling froth bubble from his teeth. Panting. The panther was not as easy as the coyote. Turning his attention to the dog, he ignored her. Until she yanked the dog from under his nose. He could only watch as the coyote, as though in slow motion, bit down hard on her haunch. She doubled up as the coyote slowly loosened his death grip and slid to the ground. Again, a strange noise and a strange feeling. Raising his head, he looked around expecting his home terrain of the plains. He smelled, expecting the fresh smells of home. *Wrong, all wrong.* He was in a cage. Swinging his head from side to side, he felt the wrongness all the way through him. Looking back in the direction of the panther, it was the woman he saw.

She limped to the table without turning her back on him. Moving quickly, she covered an item, an item stinking of wrongness, with a hessian sack and the wrongness diminished—not gone but lightened. Now his adrenaline had receded, he knew her. Without questioning, he would follow her to the ends of the Earth—why he knew not. When she left, he did too. She stopped around the corner and picked up a bag, into which she put the instrument of wrongness and then hurried away, away, away. He followed at a trot. When she stopped suddenly, he knocked her over.

Again, she made some noise. Then she placed a leg on him. He shied away. What was she doing? Noise. Hands stroking his head and his back. It was nice. She was nice. She smelled good, like something he used to know. He could trust her. She tried again, and he stood firm. Clutching the hair at the back of his head, she sat on him, the smell of fresh blood assailing him. But he shook his head, there was something somewhere warning him to care for this human. He heard her breathe deeply, once, twice, three times, and a foot stood on the flat of his back. She wobbled but stood straight, and he heard a whoosh of air as she left him. To go where?

He backed off and looked up to see an opening.

There, he must go too. Her head appeared, and he knew she made some noise. Backing farther off, he gathered speed and movement and sprang upwards, scrabbling but managing to get inside the gap. The woman put her hands on him. Forwards they moved, the woman's fast breath telling him she was panicked. He banged his head into her legs and whined, wanting her to climb on his back. She stopped, stared, and nodded. In a flash, she was on his back and they flew through the corridor, her bouncing on his back but slowly gaining her balance, her arms loosely around his neck. They arrived at another gap, and they went through.

A strange smell greeted him, and the woman slipped off his back.

****

Think, Ellora, think. Her mind was shifting in and out of reality, both ordinary and non. The pain coming from the gash in her thigh, she thrust firmly from her. *There was no time for pain.* The plan had been for Lee to shapeshift, but there seemed little awareness there. Her senses jangled. *Move!* No doubt once the chanting had stopped, the alarm had been raised.

Leaving Lee here was out of the question. Could she ride on Tiger? It had been exhilarating, yet she doubted it. How could she get Tiger to understand? She tried communicating once more with Tiger and felt nothing but the small spark, like a car catching ignition and then dying away into nothing. What the hell was she supposed to do? She was here, in a tunnel with Tiger and nothing else. Pursuit would be close.

The chalice.

Could it help? All she knew for sure was that it had appeared in a mid-seventeenth-century painting where two witches were being burned.

Those monks had clearly been chanting to it—why? Clarity returned to her as quickly as the lethargy which had assaulted her before she had gotten a grip and headed to Lee's aid. The chanting must've been recharging or recalibrating the chalice to their uses. Perhaps where once before it had been an instrument of peace—although this she doubted if used in converting reluctant subjects—now it was going to be an instrument of evil. Certainly, Lee had been affected by the chanting and the chalice more deeply than her because he had been in animal form.

Yet how on Earth could it help?

But she had nothing else. She drew the chalice in its sack from her backpack. With trembling fingers, she undid the string. Below her touch, there was the slightest of slight vibrations as though electricity hummed through it. She snatched her fingers away and let her eyes examine the chalice instead. Beautifully simple, it lay quiescent. A dull glimmer showed the triskele, the cross, and the eagle, and for all their crudeness, a prickle at the back of her neck told her of its immense power.

Her finely tuned ears picked up sounds of pursuit, far away but still pursuit. She had to try something. But what if the chalice now affected her like it had when the chanting was going on?

Panther, Spirits mine. Give me strength to do what's right.

Perhaps it was her imagination, but she did feel stronger. Glancing at Tiger, a shiver ran through her. The part that was Lee in those magnificent whiskey-colored eyes was fading. What if the longer you were in your power animal, the less likely you were to come out unscathed?

Fret not. You will do what you need to. With a deep breath, she grasped the chalice under the cup and pulled it out. Once free of the sack, the weight increased. Currents ran up her arms, grasping, seeking things. *Barriers.* Remembering what she had been told about how to protect herself, she ran for her inner tree, barricading herself in the thick bark, metaphorically slamming the door. Not panicking. No. *Safe.*

Wrapping herself in her safety, she picked up the chalice once more. The chalice itself was a generous cup, fitting at least five hundred milliliters. Entranced, she examined further, admiring the eagle on the curve and the stem, although it had clearly been added later.

A low rumble dragged her attention away. Tiger paced and awareness rippled through her. If the chalice had some effect before, it might once more. And Tiger was no pussycat. She swallowed deeply and wondered what to do. Could she wave the chalice around? Rub it over his body? Holy moly. Chant? It kept looking for her attention, this thing, and it was like wading in syrup, trying to drag herself away from it. *Remember who you are. Remember your strength. Your protection.*

With that came an idea. Noise, she had to make it make a noise. Give it a voice. *Hurry.* But how? An image came to her of her dad making a glass sing by rubbing a wet finger around the rim. She looked at her ripped jeans, with blood oozing from the cut. With a sinking heart, she dipped a finger in it, then ran her finger over the rim of the chalice. Nothing. Her heart sank. *Again.* She wet her finger this time, wincing as first she felt it renew the pain of the wound, then the metal of the chalice's rim felt like it sliced through her finger. A faint sound echoed, enough to give her hope. Once more, ignoring the pain, she wet her finger and did the same. Deeper sounds. Looking at Tiger, a smidgen of hope blossomed. His head was low, ears pointed forward, but the eyes had it—a spark of something.

Holding her breath, she used two fingers over the top, hearing the chalice come alive, the harder she pressed. Giving in to something compelling, she pushed ever harder. The chalice responded by the vibration increasing as the sound increased, yet as she pressed, it seemed to dull, then vibrate more when she lessened the pressure. *Ouch*! Her index finger split open and she snatched it back only to see a deep red drop swell and emerge and drop into the water pooling in the curve. Frozen, she watched the ripples as the ruby red blood sank to the bottom, only to flower out in a parody of roses.

Automaton like, she ran her middle finger lightly over the rim for the chalice to emit a beautiful, low tone, a tone caressing her senses. The chalice, this sound would forever provide for her, it was all she ever needed.

Enough, Ellora. Return to who you are. The voice broached no arguments, and it was with a sense of relief that she shook the lethargy from her. But it was Tiger with the biggest change. Looking deep into his eyes, she sensed Lee.

Hurry.

She sent the thought and heard an acknowledgment somewhere. Excellent. Feeling as though she were about to witness something private, she averted her eyes to the chalice. After a couple of moments, she felt Lee and turned to see him sitting up, head in his hands, groaning.

She had never been as glad to hear anything in her life. All of a sudden, she was not alone anymore. Her big strong man was back and by her side. Breath released from her in a whoosh, breath she had not realized she had been holding. She hurried over to him, cupping his face in her hands, and raising it to see him clearly.

Lee was back. She hugged him and enjoyed feeling his arms around her, gradually tightening as his strength returned. "What happened to your leg?"

"Later."

"Are you okay to walk?"

"Sure I am, as long as you help."

"Okay. Let's get out of here." His voice rasped as he wrapped an arm around her, and they moved as fast as they could.

After what seemed like hours, they were at the ladder. Lee went first to open the manhole cover, moving fluidly and quietly. Reaching the open, Ellora gasped in the cool night air and weakness swarmed her body.

Galvanizing her last remaining strength, she crouched as they ran for cover, moving as quickly as her injured leg allowed. Along the route they had planned earlier, they silently wove through the streets, doubling back and at all times avoiding streetlights if possible. It was past nightclub kicking-out time, and besides for the odd tramp sleeping in the doorways, nobody was about.

When they were far enough away, Ellora stopped

to grab a tee shirt and wrap it around her leg. They had to keep going. Reaching the suburbs with sprawling houses, they looked for a suitable car to hot-wire. Seeing a nondescript old gray Honda outside a house and on the street, they ran over.

She knew this age car wouldn't have a built-in alarm, it was just anyone's guess as to whether the owners would've installed one. Holding her breath, she jiggled the lock, smiling as the door opened with a quiet click. Lee ran around to the passenger's seat, and she reached over and opened it, then took the hand brake off, checking to make sure the car was in neutral. She nodded to Lee, who pushed hard and got the car a hundred yards down the road before jumping in. Reaching under the steering wheel, she got the necessary wires together, keeping her fingers crossed. The sound of the engine sparking and finally firing was bliss, and they both belted up as Lee opened Google maps on his phone.

"Let's get to the outskirts and pick up the train there. Let's see…" He glanced at the clock on the dashboard. "We should make the next one out in about an hour." She pressed the accelerator, and they were soon eating up the miles. Exhilaration thrilled through her blood.

"What are the chances they're behind us?" She kept glancing in the rearview mirror, reassured when nothing was to be seen.

"Well, I don't see how they'd track us. If they could follow us to the car, they'd not know in which direction we went."

"How long do we have before an alert is out for the car?"

"Let's say the owners wake up at 7 a.m., call the cops, they arrive an hour later, put out an APB." Lee dashed back his cuff to look at his watch. "Which all would mean we've got just over four hours."

"Do we keep driving, get the train, or ferry, or fly?" Privately, she wanted to stay in the car forever, cocooned from the rest of the world and danger.

"We have all the options we could wish for. I'd prefer the ferry. At least this way, we have space should they happen to catch up with us."

"But it takes much longer." Although she did agree with him. She couldn't imagine what it would be like trying to board a plane with the thought of Zenon and his men on their tail. This way might provide more cover.

"Will they know where we're heading?"

"They could so it's not worth taking the risk. We should plan with the thought they know exactly what we're going to do."

"Okay. If they know we're going to the Vatican City, they'll search the routes." She worried at her bottom lip.

"Exactly. According to Philippe, Order is widespread though, and time is the only thing on our side. Let's dump the car somewhere, perhaps torch it, and head to the station to get the train." Lee sounded sober.

"Where would we go from there?"

"Train to Patras, which is a port on the southeastern side of Greece. From there we have a choice of ferries over to Italy."

"I'm not sure, Lee."

"It's the least obvious route."

"Right, let's do it."

With Lee directing her, they fell silent, each one lost in their own thoughts.

"Lee—"

"Ellora—"

They both broke off.

"Ellora. I'm struggling to put words on what's going on inside. My whole world has turned upside down since the moment I saw you with your MG."

Her heart pounded—these words, were they the precursor to him telling her he didn't want to be with her? Blood flooded her ears and she pushed it back, desperate not to miss a word.

"I no longer am sure of who I am. I remember everything that happened under the vault." He ground to a halt, running a hand through his hair. "Man, I need a coffee. And I know you remember everything too. Ellora, I attacked you."

Enough. Time to get off the road. She saw a lay-by and pulled over.

Tenderness swamped her, and she reached out a hand to him. After a couple of seconds' hesitation, he took it.

"No, Lee, you didn't attack me. At the time, you were so deeply in Tiger you had no part of you in existence. I looked into your eyes, and there was a complete absence of you. It was purely primal. However you had entered the room, that part of you had become submerged under the heavy weight." She broke off and suppressed a shudder at the memory of how heavy and soupy it had been, how alone she had felt.

When she had seen Lee lost in Tiger, something had switched in her—also something primal, a mate-like protection where she knew she had to be cruel to be kind. Seeing him, the way he was, had saved her. She told him as much.

"But you, the animal part of you ended up doing the right thing. The connection we share reached you somehow. And hey, every couple has fights, right?" She injected as much teasing into her voice as possible. She just wanted him to lighten up.

"But it could happen again."

"Yes, it could—to me this time, who knows? It's not a problem, Lee. We can both look after ourselves, after all. Much as I love you, I am strong enough on my own. As you are. Together, we are invincible though." This time she kept her tone serious—for it was true what she said.

"Love, hey?"

Inwardly, her blood slowly fizzed—fireworks waiting to be set off. He reached out and raised her chin so her eyes darted to his.

"Love, you say?"

Her face heated, but she maintained the look, felt inside her heart, and unlocked the love, allowing it to light those fireworks. "Yes, Lee, I love you."

Those whiskey-colored eyes deepened to a dark amber as love flooded them. "And I love you, Ellora. I think I have from the moment I saw you bang your head under the bonnet of your MG."

He dropped his gaze to her lips and slowly lowered his head until his warm and tender lips met hers in a kiss of love, promise, and hope. He pulled back.

"Think we can get this chalice to the Vatican and then head home and take some much needed time for ourselves? Head to the Rockies and just be you and me for a while?"

    "Sure do."

    "Let's do it then, Ellora Radley."